More praise for

The stories in *The Ill-Fitting Skin* are funny, unflinching, and strange. The mundane and the magical rub together until they're transformed into pearls in Shannon Robinson's sharp and lucid prose. Mordant and morbid, these stories will stay with you and take up residence in a dark chamber of your heart.

—Katya Apekina, author of *The Deeper the Water the Uglier the Fish* and *Mother Doll*

Shannon Robinson is a writer so stylistically nimble, so protean, she can move with blithe grace from the fabulist to the brightly lit realist, from werewolves to a dead pet portrait artist, from Choose Your Own Adventure to a zombie parade, and all of it keen-eyed and psychologically astute. Like Angela Carter, she enstranges the world so that you can glimpse fresh and essential truths about the competing impulses at the heart of human behavior. Robinson's sensibility is characterized by a wild wryness, a knowing side-long glance at the world, that cannot help but eventually yield to grudging tenderness. And all the while her characters are just trying to lay claim to some tiny scrap of agency to anchor them, however provisionally, amidst the everyday squall that is living. A brilliant debut.

—Kellie Wells, author of *Skin, Compression Scars*, and *Fat Girl, Terrestrial*

Clever, harrowing, bitingly funny, imaginative, absurd, anatomical, and wise, these stories expertly shift from the magical realms of werewolves and zombies to the stark realities of trying to claw out a semblance of existence one can live with. Robinson's inventive tales are sure to delight admirers of Kelly Link and Aimee Bender.

—Melinda Moustakis, author of *Homestead* and *Bear Down, Bear North: Alaska Stories*

the ill-fitting skin

SHANNON ROBINSON

Winner of the Press 53 Award for Short Fiction

Press 53

Winston-Salem

Press 53, LLC
PO Box 30314
Winston-Salem, NC 27301

First Edition

Cover design by Claire V. Foxx

Cover art: "Part of woman face in black shadow background
halftone pattern illustration stock photo" by Rytis Bernotas,
licensed with permission through iStock.

Library of Congress Control Number
2024935483

ISBN 978-19-50413-75-1

for James

CONTENTS

ORIGIN STORY

Never bite back. That's what all the parenting websites tell you. None of this tit-for-tat nonsense, however tempted you may be. Giving a mixed message is not the danger. The danger is that you will be making yourself all too clear.

Genna had done enough scrolling and clicking to make her wrists burn and her contacts bake to her eyes in the blue light. But the next time her son bit her during one of his tantrums, she crouched, grabbed his flailing arm, and bit him halfway between wrist and elbow, just as he'd bitten her. "Wystan, if you bite Mommy, Mommy will bite *you*," she said. "Do you understand?"

He bit her again.

She bit him back.

They had about three more rounds of this, leaving marks on each other's arms like parentheses rendered in little red stitches, before he gave up.

Wystan had already been expelled from one preschool for biting, and he'd been stamping on thin ice at his current one, with several parents having already complained about teeth imprints left in their children. "If he ever pierces the skin," the preschool director had said, "my hands are tied."

In the hours and days that followed Genna's skirmish with Wystan, he did not bite her or anyone else, and she allowed herself, by degrees, to feel relieved. Roy, her husband, said they should wait and see.

Wystan remained prone to screeching and crying, apt to smack, to throw toys, or to assume what Genna and Roy had come to call the "hell no I won't go" weighted floppiness only to suddenly revive and pull hair and kick, but there were no further incidents of biting. Once, after Genna wrested a Sharpie from Wystan that he'd been using to plow black furrows through the beige plush of the couch, he paused mid-scream to pull forward Genna's dress and sink his teeth into the fabric. In that moment, she felt a surge of affection for her son: he was obviously trying to control himself. She placed her hand softly on the boy's blonde head, and the folds of cloth dropped out of his mouth as he smiled at her.

Genna awoke to a crashing sound, and her first thought was that someone had broken into the house and was ransacking it. Furniture thudding against walls, something smashing, a percussive cascade of objects hitting the floor . . . all coming not from downstairs but from down the hall. She didn't stop to wake Roy, still tethered to the depths of sleep by exhaustion. She ran to her son's bedroom and flung open the door.

Wystan's bookshelf had been tipped over, and his lighthouse lamp lay shattered on the floor as if broken by some tremendous wave. His bed was empty. In the glow of the night-light, in the midst of the fallen books and toys near the closet, Genna saw something move.

"Wystan! *What* are you—"

A dark figure on all fours was shredding books, tearing pages from the spines with its teeth and paws. To Genna, it looked to be a medium-sized dog. Pointed ears. Thick fur. At the sound of her fumbling for the light switch, the animal looked up, its eyes two flashes of phosphorescent green. It made a low growl, sniffed the air, and then returned to ripping. Genna barely moved as she scanned the room, under the bed, the closet, the jumbled chaos on the floor. In the loudest whisper she could manage, she said, "Wystan, sweetie, where are you? Mommy's here."

The animal had drawn closer and was growling again. Its teeth, now fully bared, slowly parted, almost seeming to grow larger—Genna fled. She yanked the door shut with a backward lunge that nearly knocked Roy over. Through the warmth of his chest, he radiated adrenaline and alarm.

The door began to thump. "Don't let it out!" Genna said. Roy held the doorknob while she ran through the house calling her son's name, upstairs then down to the basement and back up again. She found Roy standing in the open doorway of their son's bedroom.

The animal was gone. Wystan lay curled up, naked, profoundly asleep in the corner on a heap of tangled sheets, a mangled page in his damp fist.

It was not a dog they'd seen that night but a wolf. And it was not a wolf exactly—it was Wystan. There could be no denying it, however much they wanted to attribute what they'd seen to some shared sleep-deprivation mirage. Over the next month, the animal reappeared in Wystan's room at night, and Wystan disappeared, despite the new grates on the windows and the sliding bolt they'd installed on the door.

One afternoon, Genna and Wystan were in the forest a few minutes' drive from their house. They often went there: Genna had read that interacting with nature had a soothing effect on high-strung children. Wystan was walking some distance behind her, lobbing pinecones at trees and speeding them on with rocket-launcher sounds. He went silent, and as if in benediction of the respite, a rabbit crept-hopped onto the path up ahead.

"Wystan, look!" Genna said softly. But when she turned, behind her was only a little wolf, gray and grinning. The wolf darted past her and ran the rabbit down, clamping jaws on it and flinging it around like a brown fur beanbag before disappearing into the bushes. Genna found Wystan hours later. He was near the bank of a stream, bloodied, sucking his thumb in a daze.

Up until this daylight transformation, Genna and Roy had thought that the wolf would only come at night. They were thankful that Wystan had never turned while he was at preschool—that certainly would have tied the director's hands. Tied her hands, tied her feet, and thrown her in the river.

They took their son to their pediatrician, Dr. Conliffe. When Genna was booking the appointment, the receptionist asked the reason for the visit. "I think he might be having a severe allergic reaction," she said. She'd had to say something. She wondered if she also should have been booking meetings with an exorcist, a psychiatrist, a documentary crew? Lately, reality had been rippling underfoot.

And yet the pediatrician was quite calm. After examining Wystan and asking them a series of questions, she said, "Yes, I'd say this sounds like lycanthropy. He's definitely on the spectrum."

"On the—? Wystan, please be quiet. Mommy needs to talk to the doctor." The boy had discovered a basket of blocks in the corner of the examination room and was now smashing them together in accompaniment to "Itsy Bitsy Spider."

". . . of werewolf. Or bearnwolf, you might say, since he's under twelve." Dr. Conliffe tapped her pen against the counter.

". . . WENT UP THE WATER SPOUT!"

"Shh, Wystan!" Genna said, too loudly: he would only get louder.

". . . although you really don't find that many cases of adult onset."

". . . DOWN CAME THE RAIN . . ."

"Don't hit Daddy with the blocks, Wystan," Roy said, one hand shielding his face.

". . . but I'd like to run some tests, just to be sure. It's kind of a fashionable diagnosis these days."

Roy shook his head. "I've never heard of it. I mean, I've *heard* of it . . ."

"And don't go alarming yourselves with what's on the internet," Dr. Conliffe said. "It's full of misinformation.

Old wives' tales. There's treatment available. I'll walk you through it."

The doctors did not shoot Wystan through the heart with silver bullets; they medicated him.

Blue pills, twice daily on a full stomach. The drug was called Aconitem after *Aconitum*, the Latin name for wolfsbane. Only traces of the plant were present in the drug—Roy Googled this, notwithstanding Dr. Conliffe's warning—and Genna said it made her think of her shampoos' claims to being made of hibiscus or honey or what have you, even though they only contained some atom of these substances. Just shy of make-believe, but you bought it all the same.

The Aconitem needed a few weeks to take effect, so in the meantime, Wystan was placed on a closed ward at the hospital. Genna attended visiting hours and brought her laptop with her while Roy was at the office. "It's not a good idea for me to be taking time off right now," Roy said, and Genna agreed. Aconitem was newly developed and very expensive. They were fighting their insurance company to cover it.

"You'll just have to persuade them," Roy added. Genna wrote grant proposals for a living, but she didn't see how that put her in charge. She said she'd look into picking up more freelance work to help with the cash flow.

While Wystan was more likely to transform at night, there seemed to be no connection to the moon or its phases, no predictable triggers. When Genna finally did witness Wystan's transformation, it was under the fluorescent lighting of the hospital's glassed-in observation room, and it was not what she had expected—that he would drop to all fours, that parts of his body would bulge, stretch, and sprout fur like a time-lapse film of yogurt moldering in a fridge. Instead, he kind of shimmered, and she was not really sure what she was looking at. When she found her focus, the boy was gone and the wolf was there. "Even when you're watching a slow-motion film of it," one doctor explained, "your brain resists processing the information, and your eye transmits a message of blurriness."

The doctor was young, with a movie-star smile. "It's pretty cool, actually," he said. He kept on smiling right up until the point the wolf hurled itself at the glass and cracked it.

Several months passed with Wystan under treatment, and he stopped turning into a wolf. Instead, he turned into a different boy. So it seemed. He was no longer exasperating and defiant. He was listless and often cranky, but his behavior was far more manageable. His only lingering trace of aggression was a ravenous hunger. Genna fed him several times a day, and she made sure each meal contained some generous portion of animal protein, as they'd been advised. Also following advice, Wystan was staying at home with Genna, even though he preferred to spend most of his waking hours watching cartoons. So much screen time wasn't ideal, but it appeared to be the only way to engage his interest—to see him smile! To see some light in his eyes, even if it was only the reflected brightness of animated figures on a screen. He would not play with his cars, his trains, his action figures. Take him outside and he would just lie down, with no wish to kick a ball or dig in the sand. He would not do crafts. One time, Genna dressed him in a smock and propped him in front of a pallet she had dolloped with paint—high-quality acrylics, glistening like candy-colored snails. He sat, stared, and then smeared all the colors together to make a grayish brown. Slowly, he covered one page after another with overlapping brown stripes.

"Tell Mommy about this picture." Genna knew you weren't supposed to phrase the question as, *What's that supposed to be?*

"It's a picture."

"Yes, but can you tell me what's going on in the picture? Wystan? Can you look at Mommy and talk to her?"

"It's brown."

"I like the pattern, the textures. It looks a bit like fur. So what are those stripes? Is that a cage? It looks like—"

Wystan shoved against the table and pushed back his chair, causing the water glass to topple and flood the paintings. He pressed his palms into the murky puddle. When he raised his hands, little rivulets of paint bled down his wrists, disappearing into the cuffs of his smock.

Genna put one of the salvaged brown paintings up on the fridge, although later, she took it down. Every time she looked at it, she felt something like sorrow. But really, it was closer to rage.

"It's not your fault," Roy said.

"Right. I know it's not my *fault*, but it's still a question of *cause*," Genna said. They sat at their kitchen table, drinking beer on a Friday evening. Such leisurely rituals were possible now. They had been talking about the latest speculation in the scientific community regarding lycanthropy: some researchers linked it to a nascent gene possibly activated in utero by environmental factors. "I thought I was doing everything right. Prenatal vitamins, healthy diet. No alcohol, no caffeine. Exercise, but not too much exercise. No lunch meat. No Tylenol, no Nyquil, no retinol. No BPAs." Genna and Roy had already been through different versions of this conversation, dating back to Wystan's implacable colic. In those early days, all three of them had done a lot of crying and very little sleeping. Genna and Roy had made many bitter jokes about the olden times when such children would have been left exposed on a rock. Those jokes gradually gave way to running gags about selling Wystan to a sweatshop as he passed through his "terrorist twos" and "threenager" years.

"It's nothing we could have prevented," Roy said. The beer made a gentle sloshing sound as he tipped back his bottle to drink. Outside, on the lawn, fireflies drifted like cinders.

They knew that contrary to popular belief, infection did not occur through a werewolf attack. At least, contact with bodily fluids didn't appear to play a role, although werewolf-induced wounds could be severe and resist healing—the research was maddeningly murky. "It's not like some supercharged form of rabies," Dr. Conliffe had said, during one of their numerous office visits. "It's more complicated than that. It's in their DNA. That seems to be the case." One controversial theory had it that children evolved into werewolves because of maternal ambivalence, that it was a mutation brought on by a "profound yet unfulfilled wish for sincere attention and consistent validation." The author who had put forward this theory had been widely discredited as a crank with false medical credentials, yet the theory had persistent traction in certain circles.

"Blame the mother, blame the mother. It's so reductive," Roy said. "Like the father doesn't even exist."

"Yeah, what about all those lousy fathers out there?" Genna said. "Blame everybody!"

"I'm sure they're doing the best they can," Roy said. As he went to the fridge for another beer, Genna wondered who exactly was doing "their" best. And why that even mattered. She was familiar with the concept of "the good enough mother": did "good enough" allow for screaming at your child? How about the occasional spanking? Did it absolve a mother of resentment? She wished some invisible jury foreman could just finally read the verdict.

The doctors could give no clear prognosis. For the foreseeable future—and perhaps for his entire life—Wystan would have to be on medication. "We're keeping the wolf at bay," Dr. Conliffe said, without smiling. She was drawing blood from Wystan's arm while the boy observed, silent and still, pupils widening as the vial attached to the needle filled with red.

On the drive home, Genna said, "It's usually 'wolves at bay,' isn't it? 'Wolves' plural?" They were driving past a forest—the same forest where Wystan had his first daylight transformation. The scrolling sameness of the trees reminded Genna of the cheap cartoons she used to watch with recycled frames, every chase scene filled with déjà vu.

"Same thing, really," Roy said. He gave a quick glance to the rearview mirror to check on Wystan, who was

now asleep. Earlier, they'd planned to have a picnic as a treat after the doctor's appointment, but Wystan wouldn't move from his car seat. So he'd eaten his lunch there, and now the whole car smelled like beef and ketchup.

The wolves at bay. Genna imagined a pack of wolves running along a beach, gray sand under a gray sky. Bay of wolves. And then she began to play a game with herself, making a list in rapid succession: Wolf at the door. Crying wolf. Howling like a wolf. A wolf in sheep's clothing. Wolf down your food. Wolf whistle. Big bad wolf. Lone wolf. Thrown to the wolves. Pack mentality. Leader of the pack. Cub scouts. Genna almost laughed out loud at the last one. She pictured a little pack of werewolf boys, all dressed in blue and yellow, tearing into a scout leader. Would Wystan do better if he were with others who shared his condition? She wondered. So far, they had avoided support groups, along with any other kind of social interaction. There was danger, and there was pity, and they wanted neither, in any combination. Even before the onset of Wystan's lycanthropy, playdates had been fraught. Each one of them a countdown to a tantrum, a showdown, a breakage, a breakdown, an embarrassment.

The Aconitem triggered vivid nightmares. Yet another unpleasant side effect—but at least they provided some of the few times when Wystan would have a conversation. He always called for Genna. She would hold him and wait for him to be calm enough to speak.

"Mommy. My legs and arms fell off. You had to sew them back on but you wouldn't. They were all rotten. They're back on now."

"You're okay, little man. It was a bad dream. I've got you."

"It hurts."

"What hurts? Please tell me."

"I want to go home. When can I go home?"

"I don't understand your question, sweetie. You're home now. Do you hurt now?"

"If I'm a good boy, can I go home?"

"You *are* a good boy. You're safe here. We're doing everything we can to make you better, okay?"

Sometimes, during these night disturbances, he wouldn't wake up—he would just moan in an octave that seemed much too low for a boy his age. He sustained sounds that were not quite like words.

"Do you hear that?" Roy said.

"Yes. I've heard him do it before," Genna said. They lay on their backs in bed, speaking to the ceiling. The digital clock glowed 3:00 a.m.

"It's like he's trying to howl. Do you think?"

"No idea. You have to work in the morning—just put in your earplugs. He's fine."

He wasn't fine. Genna didn't think of Wystan as so much talking in the darkness as talking to the darkness. Could she intercept his messages? She wasn't sure she even wanted to.

As the insurance company continued to stonewall, Roy and Genna began to talk about taking Wystan off the Aconitem. They were draining his college fund, which they'd been building since before his birth, and next, they would drain their savings. But they knew stopping the meds wasn't a realistic option. Wystan was growing, and he would only get bigger; he would not get better. At least, he couldn't get better on his own. That much they accepted as true.

In any case, about a year in, the medication stopped working. From time to time, Wystan would flicker into a wolf and then back into a boy—like a faulty broadcast or an old-fashioned flipbook, slowed down. The week before this began to happen, Genna felt particularly edgy around Wystan, and looking back, she wondered if those flickers had at first appeared so quickly as to be subliminal or even superimposed: wolf/boy/wolf/boy. And then one night Wystan had a full-blown transformation. Roy and Genna woke up to crashing and banging, followed by a long, cadenced loo-ing.

◆◆◆

In Dr. Conliffe's office, Wystan had one block in each hand and held them pressed together as the adults spoke. On the doctor's recommendation, Genna and Roy had doubled Wystan's dosage, which only increased his lethargy. The wolf was not held at bay.

Dr. Conliffe confirmed the bad news. "This was always a possibility," she said. Reminded them, really. The medical professionals had been clear, in a small-print kind of way, that while a developed tolerance was not inevitable, it was not exactly rare. "We're going to adjust his meds and explore other options, but in the meantime it's important to stay away from him when he's in a lupine state," she added. The "other options" included possible placement in a long-term treatment facility. "And take this." She handed them a blue nylon bag imprinted with the Aconitem logo. "It's a wound kit. I got a bunch of free samples."

Back in the car, Roy pulled open the bag's drawstrings. "Are you fucking kidding me?" he said. It contained a packet of Band-Aids, a roll of gauze, a small pair of scissors, and a tube of ointment labelled "Antiseptic Gel."

"What, no shower cap?" Genna said. "No shoe polish cloth? Cheap assholes." From the back seat came a faint clacking. Wystan still had the blocks in his hands and was tapping them together, like he was a baby. Except that as a baby, he'd never been so subdued.

"We should watch our language," Roy said.

"Can't have you turning into a little potty mouth, now can we?" Genna said. "Can we, Wystan?" She hadn't meant to shout that last part. As she burst into tears, Wystan dropped his blocks and crossed his arms over his face, whimpering quietly.

They'd counted on sending Wystan to kindergarten in the fall—a delayed entry, at age six, with a designated classroom aide—but there could be no question of that now. He was officially unfit company for other kids.

"Well, it was never going to be easy with this kid, right?" Roy said.

With a wistfulness that caught Genna off guard, she remembered the very last time, pre-wolf, that Wystan acted out in public. They'd been at a park where he'd been throwing sand into other kids' faces over and over despite her reminders, pleas, and threats, and then he began screaming when she dragged him out of the sand pit and away from the park. He struggled so hard to escape her grip, she thought he'd dislocate his arm. She thought *she'd* dislocate his arm. The adrenaline flood she experienced was like euphoria wrapped in shame. From the strength of his struggle, you'd have thought she was abducting him. That her grip had the burn of acid. "What is *wrong* with your child? What is wrong with *you?*" No one actually said this, but she could hear all the other mothers thinking it as they ceased conversation with one another and looked on. At least now, she had an answer to those questions. Sort of.

The treatment facility was relatively new, and during the long car ride there, through the city and past the suburbs, Genna constructed a soothing image of their destination. Something charming, ad hoc, with combined shades of academia and Montessori. A Victorian mansion, staffed by gruff but kindly eccentrics. This was not the case—she knew just by the look of the place as it came into sight. It resembled a concrete egg carton with windows, all business despite its bucolic setting, fir trees standing at a distance from the parking lot as if intimidated. And the whole place smelled wrong, Genna thought, inhaling deeply as they approached the front doors: not bad but somehow neutralized.

While the family sat in the lobby, waiting for Wystan to be processed, three orderlies in white T-shirts passed by, large and stone-faced, like football players or bouncers, later followed by two doctors in lab coats, walking at a pace that did not invite conversation. Genna wondered if the staff members would all pass by again in the same order if she waited long enough. "I don't like it here," Wystan said flatly, without looking up from his iPad.

Neither Genna nor Roy asked him to elaborate.

Three other adults sat in the waiting area. Not a couch in sight, just armless individual chairs arranged around a coffee table laden with magazines that no one seemed inclined to read, even for the sake of avoiding eye contact. One woman stood by the service counter, arguing with an administrator through a hole in the glass partition: Her daughter, she insisted, was vegan. The facility's menu lacked appropriate alternatives.

"Yes, I understand, ma'am. But don't you worry. No such thing as a picky eater in this place!" The admin was plump and jolly, with tinge of the officious—much like a shopping-mall Mrs. Claus.

"She's not *picky*. She loves animals."

"I'm sure she does! Don't you worry, now. Please have a seat, and we'll be with you soon." (Be ready to tell Santa what you want for Christmas!)

The mother turned away from the glass with a look of immense fatigue. Genna could imagine an empty room, decorated with cat posters, teddy bears, glass figurines. All ripped and smashed to tatters and splinters. A little girl lycanthrope: now that was unusual. The afflicted were mostly boys. Genna was just working up the momentum to ask the weary mother about it when the admin lady called Wystan's name.

Genna approached the window and was handed various forms attached to a clipboard. At the same time, an orderly—a different one—came by with two boys in tow. He directed them to sit on a bench by a far wall while he paused and spoke into a walkie-talkie. The boys appeared to be twins, a bit older than Wystan. One had an eye patch, and the other had his arm in a cast. Both had fresh suture marks zigzagging their faces. Genna realized she was staring and quickly looked away, only to be intercepted by the orderly's gaze. He stepped close to her and said in a low voice, "They turned on each other."

The twins giggled. Wystan raised his head from his screen to glare at them, and the older boys stuck their tongues out in his direction, then pulled their lips back into wide smiles. Wystan grinned in return—it was like a grin: Genna flinched at the thought that he must be out of practice. Then Wystan tipped his head to the ceiling and began howling.

"Indoor voice, buddy. No! Get down!" Roy said. Wystan had jumped onto the table, scattering magazines; the two other boys were on their feet and howling too. Wystan leapt from chair to chair as Roy tried to catch him. The boys' first few yelps sounded like jokey imitations of wolves and of each other, but within seconds, it was as if they were lip-syncing a recording of actual animals, ululations overlapping, distorting. All three of the boys began to shimmer. An alarm shrieked, accompanied by the sound of doors slamming shut, and Genna had just enough time to grab the back of Wystan's hoodie before her vision went misty, then black.

In the next moment, Genna and Roy were side by side, propped up on gurneys. A nurse in floral scrubs was tapping Genna's arm and handing her a cup of juice.

"What happened?" Genna said.

The nurse explained that they had been subject to a safety measure: at a moment's notice, the inmates could be gassed into a stupor. All staff and visitors were equipped with respirators, fitted snugly right inside their nostrils.

"Why didn't you tell us? Why weren't *we* given respirators?"

"They're a purchasable option, if that's something you'd like to look into."

"They're expensive."

"Yes, I'm afraid so."

The blazer-clad facility liaison spieled as he walked Genna and Roy to Wystan's room, assuring them that the facility was "state of the art." While Wystan would be stimulated with educational toys and videos, he would at all times be isolated from the other children (who were in turn isolated from each other), and his primary points of contact would be with healthcare professionals. Genna and Roy had thought there might be classes, group activities, even occasional outings—something more along the lines of a traditional boarding school. In the middle of a long corridor lined with doors, the liaison stopped and swiped a key card. "Here we are!" he said. "Your son appears to have settled in already."

They all observed from the doorway. The room, filled with light from a large window, was painted a rosy beige and furnished with a bed and a desk-chair-computer that looked to be all of one piece. Wystan sat at the desk, tapping away at the keyboard. Onscreen, a pixelated figure leapt through a conveyor-belting landscape, vaulting from oversized mushrooms to elevated platforms. "We've been working on ways to help with their socialization," the liaison said. "We've had some success with monitored online interactions. Structured, goal-oriented play. Avatars and proxies." In one corner of the ceiling, a surveillance camera made a discreet, whirring pivot.

The video-game figure was dodging arrows thrown by a wolf floating on a cloud. Wystan was so deft in his keyboarding that Genna and Roy never got to see what happened when one of the arrows found its mark.

Back in the lobby, Genna could feel Roy watching her as she dug through her purse for a Kleenex. She wasn't crying anymore, but her nose wouldn't stop running. As she searched, Roy muttered a speculation that they'd been kept in the dark about the details of Wystan's care so that they'd be more likely to comply with the treatment. The very expensive treatment, which remained very expensive despite the government subsidy they'd received, thanks to Genna's grant-writing finesse.

"Well, we're not leaving him here," Genna said. "I don't trust this place."

"We have to at least give it a try."

"I don't want to *give it a try*. We can't leave him here."

"No, we can't. But we have to. What's the alternative? We can visit him, right?" That's what the liaison had said. And he'd told them that it was best not to say goodbye since it "might set him off." Wystan, that is. They needn't have worried: eyes locked on his video game, Wystan had all but ignored them and had shrugged off Genna's attempt at a hug with an irritated little growl. She didn't persist.

From the living room window, Genna watched a neighborhood cat traipse across their front lawn. The cat was large and orange and sometimes still left dead birds on their doorstep. Genna used to feed the cat tuna whenever it came to the door and meowed. She'd cut off all such encouragement around the time of Wystan's transformations. Now she wished Wystan were here so she could show him "Fat Kitty," consequences be damned. In the late afternoon sun, the trees' shadows stretched onto the road. Genna wondered what Wystan had eaten for dinner, what he would be having for his late snack. He'd been in the facility for several months now; almost a week had passed since she'd last seen him. The visiting hours were restricted, the drive long, and with her current workload, it was hard to squeeze in trips to the facility. She told herself these were the reasons. Each time she had visited Wystan, he'd barely acknowledged her presence, and yet she felt in him a deep, coiled unease, felt it through his very skin when he allowed her to touch him. *If I'm a good boy—*

Roy's faint reflection appeared beside hers in the window. "I was thinking we could get a pet," Genna said, without turning around. The ginger cat flopped down at the lawn's edge and stared back at Genna. It began licking its paw, washing its face.

"Don't we already have one?"

"Hilarious. You know, a cat." Outside, the creature suddenly sat up and froze. Then disappeared silkily through the hedge.

"Yes, we could get a cat. But I think we could do better than that." Roy circled Genna's waist with his arms and gently pressed his face against her hair. She leaned her head away.

"Don't you think our resources are at the absolute limit?" Genna felt Roy's arms unbuckle themselves, and she turned to face him. "Even if I can bring in more money. It's not just the money. It's too much of a risk."

"And so we should *only* have one like Wystan? I think that's a risk too."

"What exactly are we risking, Roy?"

"I don't know. Our happiness?"

"Because we're so incredibly happy now," Genna said. She could tell from Roy's face that her words tasted as burning-sour to him as they did to her. "Sorry. Sorry," she said. "I'm just so on edge all the time. It's like I've forgotten how to breathe properly."

"I hate bickering like this."

"So let's not." Genna gathered up her coat, grabbed her purse, and said, "We need a few things from the store. Milk, eggs. Text me if you think of anything else."

Genna slept in the car, waiting for the facility to open. Her phone, with the ringer turned down, had buzzed through the night. Genna assumed that Roy knew where she was and was angry with her. He'd be angrier still if he knew what she was about to do. Or maybe he already knew that too. For the past half hour she'd been watching staff arrive, and now, at 9:00 a.m., she crossed the parking lot and walked through the doors herself.

"I'm discharging my son," she said to the admin lady, the same lady the vegan-advocating mom had tangled with. A primal intuition whispered through Genna that she'd need to draw upon the deep core of her female self that was immune to bureaucratic authority.

After much waiting and argument, and much repetitious but tirelessly polite referencing of regulations, procedures, and impossibilities, the admin made a series of calls, produced papers for Genna sign, and finally released Wystan into Genna's custody, saying, "Not to be a broken record, but we really don't recommend this. You sure you don't want to sleep on it? He's going to be a real handful."

It took Genna and Wystan twenty minutes to make the short distance from the lobby to her car: he kept slowing down and stopping, like some toy with dying batteries. Genna was tempted to just pick him up and carry him, but he was a heavy boy. A big boy. She was determined not to be provoked.

"Get into the car please, sweetie, and I'll buckle you in. Wystan? I need you to get into the car now." The boy stood by the open car door. Genna gave him a light nudge. He reacted by swatting at her hand and moving further from the car.

"Car's over here, buddy. Wrong direction. Wystan? Get into the car. We can't go home until you get into the car."

"No!" He stamped his foot, and his face turned pink.

Genna felt her own face flush as they continued to argue, and she found herself laying hands on him, pushing him and feeling him push back.

"What, you want to stay here? Why is it so hard for you to just do what I ask? Get into the FUCKING CAR, Wystan!"

"NO!"

He pulled free of her and ran. Genna pelted after him, cursing her choice of high-heeled boots. He was surprisingly fast. Letting her weight fall onto the balls of her feet, she chased him across the parking lot, along the road, and then through the roadside ditch and into the woods.

Among the tall pines, she slowed to a walk and began calling his name. She'd lost him in the woods before, that morning of his first daylight transformation. Those woods had been all papery, peeling birch. She'd searched and searched, and then, for a moment, just a moment, she had stopped searching. She had closed her eyes and stood still, listening to the shush of the wind in the leaves, the air rolling over her skin with the softness of powder, and she had let herself feel what it would be like to not ever find him.

Genna saw the wolf as it leapt, moving in seconds from a flash in her periphery to a force upon her, slamming her to the ground. The creature snapped at her and then sunk its teeth into her forearm, raised in defense over her face. Its teeth were like burning nails, and it would not let go. *Wystan, if you bite Mommy—*

Genna tasted blood and fur and dirt when she bit into the wolf's front leg. She pressed her jaws together hard, but she did not, could not, bite deeply. And yet the wolf yelped and released her. Genna lay on the ground, feeling moist breath, cold muzzle, wet tongue upon her wounds. The canine whimpering gave way to a little boy's sobs. Eventually, she was able to look at him. Despite her torn flesh, she picked Wystan up and carried him, with his arms wrapped around her neck and his legs around her torso, all the way back to the car.

No one at the emergency room wanted to treat her, but at last some intern wearing three pairs of gloves was able to put in a few stitches. "I don't touch those wounds," Genna overheard one nurse saying. Everyone wanted to send her to the facility, but Genna refused. She didn't mention that she'd just come from there. She only told them that she'd been bitten by a werewolf, that she'd seen the creature shift shape to a young man right after it attacked her and fled. But that she may have been hallucinating.

"I'm supposed to file an incident report on this," the intern said. His tongue stuck out of the corner of his mouth as he taped gauze over the sutures. He hadn't scolded her for driving in her condition, but he did say that she and her son were very lucky. At this, Genna laughed, with brief, bitter giddiness. She said nothing about how she'd briefly lost consciousness and snapped to with the car rumbling along in a shallow ditch. She'd even forgotten to fasten Wystan's seatbelt. The intern had insisted on examining Wystan, despite Genna's assurance that the blood on him was all hers. He found no bite marks on Wystan: she'd made sure there were none as she'd shakily swabbed him with Wet-Naps outside the hospital. Throughout, Wystan had sucked his thumb with an intensity that bordered on theatrical. Now the intern looked from Genna to Wystan and then back to Genna. "I'm just going to step out for a few minutes, okay?"

◆◆◆

Back at the house, Genna locked Wystan in his room. He was asleep even before she pulled the blankets over him. She marveled, as she always did, at how beautiful he was in repose: long eyelashes; elegant, faintly etched eyebrows; velvet, baby-doll skin. He was exhausted. She was exhausted, but she still owed Roy a long explanation. A discussion of what she'd done, why she'd done it, and what they would do next.

Roy was waiting for her at the top of the stairs, apparently no longer content to seethe patiently in the living room.

"I fucked up," Genna began. "What? Why are you looking at me like that?"

She turned her head. Through their bedroom door, she could see herself in the mirror above the dresser, shimmering.

"What do we do?" Roy said. "What do we do!?"

For a few seconds, Roy stood motionless, gaping, and Genna was afraid that he was too afraid—for himself and for her—to leave her. She wanted to say something, to scream at him, but her mouth was overtaken with a sparkling pain, like a foot fallen asleep now forced into service. And then the moment unstuck, and Roy did flee the house, double-timing it down the stairs and out the door. Which he left wide open. Genna, Genna the wolf, ran right through it.

Genna would not be charged for her assault on the woman who'd been out walking her dog, nor would Roy be held to negligence charges. The woman likely would have sustained far worse injury had she not been carrying mace and had her dog not insisted on standing its ground. If Genna were a rabid animal, she'd have been put down. If she were insane, she'd have been evaluated, then incarcerated. According to public opinion, according to the law, she was neither; she was both. Ultimately, Genna decided that she wanted nothing to do with pills, with doctors, with medical opinion and intervention. She was offered placement on a special, privately sponsored reserve, and she took it. Wystan would go with her. Roy agreed to this, though not easily, not happily.

"You'll kill each other," Roy said.

"No, we won't."

"Please don't do this."

"How could you handle us both? How could you handle him on your own?"

"I can't be apart from you."

"You already are."

"I'm right here."

"Here for me? Or for me and Wystan? I guess we both know the answer to that question."

"Stop snapping at me. Just because you're—"

"A werewolf."

"It doesn't mean you have to play the part. You don't have to be so awful to me."

"I'm not." Genna couldn't find the words to say how much she loved him—to say that if she were in his place, she'd be helping pack the bags.

Genna and Wystan roamed their patch of the reserve. Their transformations had fallen into synch, and as a mother-child pair, they were compatible, or at least equally matched. They had a rudimentary cottage with spare furnishings: steel beds and chairs, some grubby blankets. Two separate bedrooms, each with a lock and a reinforced door. A small bathroom with a shower. Possessions were kept at a bare minimum because they would only get destroyed. Besides, the founders and benefactors of the reserve believed in the palliative effects of meditation and simplicity. Electric fences divided up the land into discrete territories, each separated by narrow corridors of no-man's land. Occasionally, at a distance, Genna spotted a lone figure in khakis, although aside from that, she never saw anyone else, wolf or otherwise. If Wystan ever saw anyone, he didn't mention it. Every three days, at a designated time, Genna and Wystan would have access to a hut at the corner of their territory, which was stocked with food. Soup kitchen-type odds and ends, Genna thought, that might be cobbled into passable meals. Genna and Wystan often supplemented the supplies by hunting rabbits and squirrels; she worked this out from the messy evidence left by her wolf-self. The hut also had a few supplies for "creative work" (yarn, paper, fabric, paint), perhaps the idea being that they might produce handicrafts for their own amusement or for sale. Genna was not so sure. She thought it all had the feel of an experiment that people were too embarrassed to abandon, even though enthusiasm for it had waned. A well-meaning but half-assed affair, run by moneyed hippies. She didn't mind. For the first time in many years, she felt free of judgment, expectations, and consequence.

And when I say "she," understand that I mean "me." I began this as a story about my little boy, but the maternal ego casts a long shadow, try as we may to be objective, to be selfless. And I wish I were writing this, but this is essentially a work in translation. Not that I'm writing this down in some werewolf-speak or barking this out to some transcriptionist—no, I am trying to think of how to say this, to translate thought into coherent words that others may touch and see and feel. I have tried to put pen to paper, in the little hut, but as soon as I get there, I forget how to hold the pen, forget how to form the letters. I have memories of writing in that hut, but when I return to the notebook, it's blank except for a few words that I've written before. No one's taking it—I'm sure of that. No one comes here. I refuse all visitors, even Roy. I think I'm a little more wolf-like each day. Hairier. My fingers are curling inward. I'm hunched. Time moves along like scenery flowing past a car.

But Wystan—he's thriving. Quite the chatterbox, although half the time, I'll be damned if I can remember what he talks to me about. I just know, in the moment, that I'm very proud of him. Or annoyed at what he's asking and that he won't shut up. One or all of those things is true. A while back, I agreed to let him spend extended periods of time off the reserve with his father. It's only fair. And clearly, it's been good for him. He has fewer and fewer instances of transformation. I didn't know it was possible that lycanthropy could recede—it's kind of news to the medical community—but apparently, it happens. Such facts stick to my memory, like burrs in fur.

Wystan's talking to me right now.

"Mom. You don't have to stay here. I don't blame you for anything. Why don't you come home?"

He's such a lovely boy, my son. His hair has turned a golden brown, and his cheekbones have emerged, lightly fuzzed. I can see that he's going to be tall like his father. I tell Wystan that he should not have come so close to nightfall, when I'm more likely to change, but he's not afraid of me. He never has been. That used to make me angry.

A big white moon is hanging in a corner of the sky, watching us. If I could find the words to tell Wystan, I would say that the moon has always been a symbol of barrenness, cold and dead. But tonight, I think it looks like a breast full of milk. As a baby, Wystan couldn't drink enough of my milk, and the more he drank, the more I made. He would cry, and when I went to feed him, milk would spurt from my nipples onto the floor, such abundance. The "letdown," it's termed, like it's some disappointment, but it wasn't: it felt like electricity, like a live current I could share. The moon—she's alone up there. More like an idea, like a phantom, than a massive celestial body in perpetual orbit around something even bigger than itself.

"Want to howl at the moon together?"

Wystan knows I'm just kidding because howling together even in jest might set us both off, and he's been doing so well. There is no ironic howling among the werewolves, you see. He asks me one more time to leave with him, and I say no, I won't. I can't. Not right now. I ask him to sit with me, out on the fresh grass, in the warm night air, so he can hold my paw/my hand/my paw/my hand until it's time for me to go back to the cottage and sleep.

MISCARRIAGES

You look familiar.

That is what the anesthesiologist says to me. She's petite, much younger than I expected, and has pale, smooth skin. I'm here to have a D&C. I had an abortion three years ago, but that was in another city. In a few minutes, this woman will take the clear plastic cup that she's now holding and place it over my nose and mouth; she will put me to sleep. I will have no memory of her doing so.

D&C is short for Dilation and Curettage. The initials are in the interest of delicacy as much as for convenience. It's the operation performed after a miscarriage, wherein the fetus (or dead baby, however you wish to think of it) is sucked out of your womb. A bit of vacuuming in preparation for the next tenant. If there will be one.

I don't have a reply for the anesthesiologist's remark, although I feel that I should. She sounds so casually certain. Oh, I say.

Maybe I just have one of those faces. I'm lying down on a padded table, dressed in a large, two-ply, green paper gown. A hose attached to a circular notch on the gown blows in warm air, inflating me like a pool toy, making me feel both comforted and a little silly. I'm wearing purple socks with teddy bears on them in a raised, rubberized pattern. The hospital provided them. These I will keep. I will wear them around the apartment for the next few days until the soles get dirty and I begin to worry about the state of the unswept floors.

The nurses have directed my husband, Sean, to another room that is filled with other patients' relatives, waiting. As a day-surgery patient, you're only allowed to bring one relative and no children under twelve. So in other words, no children. We'd read that on the slip of paper given to me by the nurse at my pre-op examination two days ago.

I guess they don't want a pack of crazy brats running around upsetting people, grinding cookies into the rug, Sean said, probably thinking of the sign we read on our first visit to the obstetrician's office, stating NO FOOD OR DRINKS. *But you can bring in that coffee, honey. It's got a lid,* the receptionist had told him as we hesitated in the doorway. Sean has an open kind of charm about him, so she probably would have let him bring in a melting popsicle.

Senbazuru

Because I am in my late thirties, I worry that I will never conceive again. I have this notion, following my miscarriage, that I will undertake an origami project of folding a thousand paper cranes. In grade school, my class read a story about a brave Japanese kid who folded a thousand cranes while in the hospital, hoping to get well. I remember feeling both impressed by and jealous of the kid's dignity. According to ancient lore, whoever folds a thousand paper cranes will be granted a wish. I imagine a cinematic time-passage montage: people will see me patiently creasing small pieces of paper, bending and unfolding with gentle, nimble precision. Tiny paper birds will accumulate in our apartment. White birds, birds with the faint blue lines of notebook paper, glossy magazine-scrap birds, birds folded from the silver paper discarded from cigarette packs. It will become a joke among my coworkers at the library and my friends that this is my zen fidget, my quiet party trick. And then, someday when I announce that I am pregnant again, I can explain what was with the months of folding. I will have a mobile of paper cranes for the baby's crib, perhaps even a framed print of a crane—a white bird stretched in flight against a powder-blue background—that people will mistake for a stork. Later, I will tell my child the story of my ongoing dedication, how I humbly willed him or her into existence.

I sit at my desk, turn on my laptop and look up how to fold a paper crane. I find a set of directions that consists of diagrams showing a step-by-step transformation of a square of paper into a bird with pointy wings. It seems simple enough, once I finally manage to cut a piece of paper into a perfect square (I've always found it difficult to cut straight lines). But as I start following the instructions, I can only get so far before I am stumped. I try a different website, a different set of diagrams. Again, I have a problem. Again, I try a different website. But each set of directions I find seems to leave out a crucial opening step or depict one step in abstract terms. (Where is that arrow pointing, exactly? What do they mean by *fold the outer corners to the center*? How?) The online videos I find feature people whose hands occasionally obscure their operations. I fold, re-fold, unfold, and rotate the paper, smoothing it out and pushing aside the books and notes cluttering my desk so I have more space to work, but I just can't replicate any of the instructions beyond a certain point. I leave my creased not-crane by the laptop. A paper diamond. A crumpled kite.

The kid in that story—I think she died at the end, even though she folded all those cranes. Radiation poisoning.

Womb-ah womb-ah womb-ah

Oh, my empty womb. I understand it's the size and shape of a pear. But when I think of it, it's hopelessly abstract—more in my head than in my torso. I can only picture a cross-section diagram, done in different shades of red, isolated against the contrasting white of a page. A scarlet light-bulb shape, with the pink fallopian tubes attached like alien arms, stretched in crucifixion. My friend Emmy knitted a uterus from a pattern she'd found in a feminist craft book. She shows it to me when I am hanging out with her one evening at her apartment. This is a year before my first pregnancy.

The fallopian tubes were the trickiest part, Emmy says. If you don't stitch them right, she explains, they won't stick out like they're supposed to. See? She tosses it to me, and I catch it. A fuzzy pink ball.

It's nice and squishy, I say and toss it back to her.

Isn't it? It's my wandering womb. She demonstrates by moving it from one place in her apartment to another—a bouncing path from bookshelf to countertop. Countertop to back of couch, nestled beside a sock monkey. She also has a pillow that is a stylized vagina made with beige velour and pink satin. I avoid sitting near it.

Blot

After the D&C, the maxi pad they put on me while I'm unconscious lives up to its name. It's thick, long, and fluffy. It strikes me as a relic from another era, a less elegant prototype. There's only a small spot of blood on it. I notice this as I'm getting dressed, readying myself to go home, still dreamy and slow with receding anesthetic. When I look back to the cot where I'd been lying, I'm surprised to see a large bloodstain on the sheet. It's like a Rorschach, and I need to read it. Is it two elephants walking side by side, one slightly ahead of the other? But no: diagnostic inkblots are symmetrical. This is just a blob. I cover it with a towel.

Rot

No one tells you that after you turn thirty-five, you start aging in dog years. I can see it in my own face, looking into the mirror right now. The wrinkles multiply and deepen. It looks like the skin over my knees is melting. I see the roots of the gray wires that have wandered in little by little among the younger silky strands of hair. Covering them with dye over and over is like spreading pesticide on a lawn for a few dandelions, but what the hell. I've found that if you pluck out the interlopers, they grow back in to resemble antennae. Their coarseness makes them stand straight up from your scalp. I try not to complain. Compared to what I'll look like at seventy-five, these are my fresh salad days. *When I was green in judgment, cold in blood.* It brings to mind those sad pre-cut salads in a plastic bag, wilting bits of arugula and radicchio that always look like they're two days away from being clotted slime. You must use them up quickly.

After the age of thirty-five, on average a woman becomes 50 percent less fertile. You are born with all the eggs you will ever produce. This seems incredible, inaccurate. Like something that was believed in the seventeenth century, some misogynist bit of hokum. But no, it is true. A man's supply of sperm, like blood, like skin, keeps endlessly renewing itself, refreshed like a web page.

Questionnaire

Was this your first pregnancy? The nurse asks.

No.

She's holding a clipboard, rolling through a series of questions concerning my medical history. High blood pressure? Strokes? Diabetes? Migraines? Allergies? Any piercings? Capped teeth? She goes quickly because it's a long list and the information is redundant. I've been over this before.

Do you have any living children?

No.

I'm so sorry, dear. That's very difficult. I hope it works out for you soon.

I don't tell her about the abortion. I want her to keep believing that I'm a good person.

Kitty

I have a dream that we already had a baby—a teeny tiny baby, more like a miniature person, like in *Thumbelina*. But in the dream, the cat had killed it. The dream isn't about this event, more like the dream is about this event being true. I have an image of the cat carrying a limp little corpse in its mouth, like a doll. Or a vole. That is not part of the dream. That is the part of the dream that I imagine when I'm awake because it was missing from the actual dream.

After I come home from the hospital (the actual hospital; this is not a dream I'm telling you about), I look at the cat as she sits beside me on the bed and think, *You are not a baby*. The cat stares back at me, absolute blankness in her melon-green eyes. She yawns, and her ears fold backward like insect wings. Her mouth a leer of fangs, briefly. She walks over to me and begins to purr, bumping her head against my hand. Sean and I have joked with people about the cat being a child substitute. It's something I need to joke about, often, in order to keep it sounding like shtick. The cat's ears pivot slightly, and then she runs off to the kitchen. Her footpads make thunking sounds on the hardwood floor. I've been overfeeding her again.

When I was a little girl, my family owned a black cat named Minou. I used to dress him up and push him around in my toy pram. He would struggle as I forced his paws through the sleeves of the little clothes, but once he was fully dressed, he became passive and resigned. My favorite game was to stand at the top of our steep driveway with Minou in the pram and then let it roll down the incline as I chased after it at a short distance, always catching onto the handle just before it reached the road.

Dear

Dear. All the nurses refer to me this way. Like I am a little girl. Like I am simple-minded and adorable. But really:

like I am fragile. Such efficient tenderness. Step on the scale, dear. You can put your coat over here, dear. Here's a gown for you, dear. That's right, dear. After it is all done, when I wake from the anesthetic, they will offer me juice and cookies.

The atmosphere is the same as when I had the abortion. The kindest of assembly lines. I remember sitting in a room full of women, all of us waiting to have the identical operation. It's a small space, more of a nook than an actual room, and we sit in a circle on wooden chairs. I look at everybody as they look elsewhere. An older Indian lady. A young Asian girl. A woman with blonde hair who looks a lot like me. No one talks. We all wear a uniform. Plush white terry-cloth bathrobes over open-backed cotton gowns. Paper slippers. I keep the gauzy white shower cap in my pocket. Only one of the women is wearing it already, stretched over her braids. A soap opera is playing at soft volume on a television set fixed high on a wall. I find it odd that a parenting magazine has found its way into the thick stack of reading material. I suppose some of the women here are parents already and just don't want more. Buncha sluts, I think to myself, but not at all with sincerity. I'm just trying to cheer myself up. Every twenty minutes, a smiling nurse comes and calls someone by her first name. Although the closed unit we're in is referred to as "outpatient surgery," no other kind of surgery besides abortions is performed here. A receptionist had to buzz me in through locked doors.

The baby would be Sean's. I am five weeks along, which is barely longer than Sean and I have been dating. He has won a prestigious internship with a lab in Europe, one that he's worked for years to obtain, one that can't be deferred. We cannot have a baby now. The decision is mine, and I know it's the correct one. Sean holds my hand, and we sit side by side on my green velvet couch. A love seat, ridiculously tiny, like the backseat of a vintage Beetle. It's the first piece of furniture that I bought with my own money, and I will drag it with me everywhere I live. We live: Sean and I will marry a year from now.

Somehow, when I tell him about the pregnancy, I expect him to be physically disgusted. But his face is gentle, like a man looking at a night sky.

Naming

When I get pregnant again, Sean and I celebrate. We make my favorite dinner, pasta puttanesca. Afterward, we move to the living room with our dishes of ice cream, and Sean gets comfortable by the coffee table with a pen and paper. Although it's our intention to draw up a list of names we want, what we compile is its opposite. We nix the names of ex-boyfriends and ex-girlfriends (even if the associations are positive). Followed by anything that smacks of pretension. And anything overly trendy. Him: anything too hard for girls (Veronica), too soft for boys (Tristan). Me: anything too soft for girls (Charlotte), too hard for boys (Carl). Sean records our non-choices in block letters, writing with his left hand and spooning ice cream with his right. For both of us, certain names have unreasonable yet unshakeable associations. Although our prejudices contradict each other's, we are in agreement that names, in themselves, have the power to bestow flaws and fates:

PHILLIP—Small penis
ABIGAIL—Cow
ALEXANDER—Jock
JULIE—Pedantic about board games
GABRIEL—Dope-smoking underachiever
HANNAH—Gives blow-jobs so people will like her (Is that true? Doesn't sound like the Hannah I knew.) (Maybe she just didn't want you to like her.)
ADAM—Weaselly tagalong
BRENDAN—Sneaky coward
MADELINE—Hypochondriac; fake gluten allergy
ANTHONY—Chronic bed wetter
OLIVIA—The kind of girl who poses for pictures with her toes pointing together
(What do you mean?)

(Like she thinks she's so *whimsical* and *precious*.)
KEVIN—Fatso
NATALIE—Clumsy
CONNOR—Will grow a beard to disguise the fact that he has no chin
MACKENZIE—Self-important tramp; never wears proper bra size
TYLER—Manic
ELIZABETH—Insufferable micromanager
IAN—Republican
(No, I'm pretty sure Ian's a communist.)
(Are you kidding? *Ian* is not only a Republican—he's a queer-bashing, closet-case Republican. That's who *Ian* is.)
LUCAS—Stupid; hates reading
MICHAEL—Needs a punch in the face
KAYLA—Bitter backstabber
ANN—Doormat
(I think Ann's kind of cute. You know: Annie. It's sweet.)
(It isn't sweet. She's got body odor. She's a martyr. She's the kind of kid you have to force other kids to play with. Trust me on this one.)
DANIEL—Wimp
JENNIFER—Horse-faced anorexic
We are worse than any schoolyard bullies with these names, with our shouting and laughing. Kids can be so cruel, people always say. Who are we fooling?

There are certain names that we dismiss without pejorative annotation. These are the names with vices that we each secretly find glamorous and strong. Scrapper. Smart-mouthed. Arrogant. Workaholic. Maneater. Ladykiller. Ambitious. Ruthless. Cold. Selfish.

Nameless

I am now eleven weeks pregnant, and Sean and I are at the obstetrician's office for my first ultrasound. In the waiting room, Sean sips his coffee, and I talk about preserving the ultrasound image so we can show it to people later. The paper it gets printed on, I understand, degrades quickly, so we should make a photocopy.

In the room with the ultrasound monitor, the technician asks me to shift a little further down on the padded recliner. My feet are in stirrups, and a paper sheet is tented over my knees.

All set? Now, I'll take this, and you can reach through and help me guide it in, she says. The wand looks a bit like a microphone, and I think about (just think about) pretending to sing into it (*Feelings! Whoa, whoa, whoa*); I realize that I've made this joke before with a vibrator, with the same song. The paper sheet doesn't really cover me, but no matter: I wonder who I'm preserving my modesty for. Sean sits on a high stool, by my side. Maybe all these paper sheets will seem silly in fifty years. Then again, maybe they're a recent feature. My mother, who once worked as an obstetrics nurse, tells me that they used to shave off women's pubic hair and strap their arms down during delivery. I'm not so sure about the strapping the arms down part. My mother's been known to fabricate. Not maliciously and perhaps not even consciously. I suspect her brain splits the difference between the disbelief she anticipates and the truth.

The monitor on my right shows a grainy image, which moves a little as the technician gently pivots the wand. In the center of the screen is a large, black kidney-bean shape, framed by flecks of gray and white like static snow on a television. I wait for her to interpret the image. What is the head, what is the body.

Normally, at this point, we would see growth in the fetus. But I'm afraid a fetus hasn't developed. I'm so sorry. I know that's not the news you wanted to hear.

The technician hands me a stack of tissues, and in three seconds, I need them. After soaking them, I stack them and line up the edges, like it's important. I cannot look at her, or my husband as he rubs my back, or the obstetrician who comes in to confirm the bad news. I have let everybody down. My body has lied to everyone. I am my mother's child.

Birdie

Nine weeks into my pregnancy, I talk to my mother over the phone about my fear of miscarriage. So many of my friends have lost babies; I'm aware that it's a possibility.

If you're still barfing and your boobs are sore, those are good signs, she says. I can hear her television on in the background. She likes to watch the Silver Screen Classics movie channel at night while she sorts through grocery store fliers and clips interesting articles from the newspaper.

How far along were you when you miscarried, Mom? I know that she did, at least once. I have it in my mind that she had a stillbirth, but I don't trust that archival entry.

My mother tells me that she miscarried in the hospital at five months. A boy baby.

I press for details. Did you get to see it?

He looked like a little bird that had fallen from the nest.

This is the most poetic thing my mother has ever said. It is also, to my knowledge, the only poetic thing my mother has ever said. She's sentimental, but that's not the same thing.

If he had lived, I probably wouldn't be here. My brother would have had an older brother, and my sister would have had another younger one. Maybe I would have been that little boy. Later on, I look up images of developing fetuses in *What to Expect When You're Expecting*. A baby at five months would be the size of a mango (the book is fond of fruit comparisons). It must have died sooner.

The Case of the Blighted Ovum

Blighted ovum. It sounds like something you'd encounter on the blasted heath, something that would prowl the moor. But it also sounds right, in that it sounds awful.

Following the ultrasound, the obstetrician explains: With a blighted ovum, although an egg is fertilized and implants, the embryo stops growing. Or it never grows at all. The placenta, however, continues to develop and continues to secrete hormones.

In other words, my fetus is a phantom. It is a poltergeist, setting objects in motion when there is no one in the room, making malicious mischief.

I think back on the weeks of feeling pregnant but not being pregnant. Once, after drinking a glass of water, I had to run from the room to vomit. I kept a plastic bag of crystallized ginger in my purse, to nibble on when I felt queasy. I loved the fiery sweet taste, the melting grit of the sugar against my teeth. Even the burble of the coffee maker in the morning made me feel sick; like a properly cautious mother-to-be, I'd given up caffeine anyway— although I missed it, I needed it, I was so damn tired all the time. I felt dazed but rather pleased with myself. Sometimes I practiced putting my hand on my lower abdomen in a demure, protective gesture. My secret. I felt like the hostess of a surprise party, hiding behind a couch, poised to spring out and toss glittering confetti.

Old Model

My college boyfriend, Brian, is showing me the vintage reproduction anatomy model that he's ordered off the Internet. It's a ten-inch, yellow-white, nude woman, reclining on a bed as if sleeping, as if dreaming or perhaps thinking: her expression suggests rhapsody. Her neck arches, and her right leg is slightly bent. She is beautiful, with brown wavy hair spread loose over her shoulders, framing her upper body.

The eighteenth-century original was life size. Can you imagine? Brian asks. And this one's plastic instead of wax. He taps his model's miniature plastic thigh, lightly. Brian is a pre-med student with a minor in art history, so he's interested in these things.

But this is the best part, he says. With his index finger and thumb, he lifts away the top layer of her torso, a panel of breasts and belly. Underneath are colored replicas of organs: gray lungs, a red heart, a brown uterus. He lifts each of these out, and places them beside the model on his desk. She looks like one of Jack the Ripper's victims, poor thing.

And look. Brian uncaps the uterus to reveal a tiny beige fetus. She's pregnant!

She's suspiciously attractive, I say, trying to extract the baby. It's fastened in place.

There were lots of models like these, Brian says. Pretty cadavers. They're called *medical Venuses*.

Yes, a woman like a dug-out canoe, very sexy, I say. Although it is erotic, in a way. Brian and I share a daydream—I'm not sure who communicated it or thought of it first—about him cutting me open on an operating table. Not hurting me but seeing what other people could never see. A literal intimacy. He will write a poem about it, except that he will be the one on the table, dissected by an unseen hand.

Despite his original plans to become a plastic surgeon, Brian is now in pediatrics. We keep in touch, from time to time. He's married and has twin girls. I saw the photos in a group email.

Secret

At least I know I can get pregnant. Now that I've miscarried, I no longer have to remind myself never to let those words slip to Mom.

How can I tell my Catholic mother that I had an abortion? It is a mortal sin, such willful destruction of God's property. It is too much to tell. Given my mother's tendency for exaggeration, maybe the amount of mercy she already begs God for on my behalf will be in appropriate proportion. That's not a cheap shot, by the way.

Nothing

The time that has passed while I was under anesthetic is not like time spent sleeping. It is a pure absence of existence. The film has been cut and thrown away. I have no dreams to serve as souvenirs. I have been somewhere else, somewhere empty.

Of course, that is not the case. I've been put under by the petite anesthesiologist and have lain on a padded table while the obstetrician and nurses tended to my body, while they reached into me and cleaned me out.

Coming off the anesthetic, I feel euphoric, like I'm being rocked in the bottom of a boat on a lake, warm under a lattice of leaves and clouds. The nurses have likely smoothed the edges with morphine. I'm lying in a cot, now in a different place from the operating area, swaddled in cotton blankets, with curtains drawn around the cot to make a small room. Through a crack in the curtains, I can see the nursing station. A stout woman in lavender scrubs is making entries on a computer screen. Sean is standing to one side of my cot, and the obstetrician is standing to the other. Sean has always said that the man looks like Walt Whitman, with a little Jerry Garcia thrown in: a hippie intellectual.

It's good that you opted to have the D&C because there was a lot to come out. We got it all, the doctor says. The operation went well. You won't remember any of this conversation, he adds, smiling. He's partly correct. I don't remember any of it until Sean tells me what he said hours later, when we're at home.

Trying

I'm drunk on my own hormones. For a change, Sean adds. Oh, ha haa, I say, putting a touch of British into the last syllable. But he's right. There were some bad old days. Not that Sean was there for them: he just heard. That was back when we both would have considered each other un-dateable, living rather loose and large. Now we're married and trying for a baby. We're ready this time. I've been off and on the pill for almost twenty years, but now I'm off. My last pack of pills is housed in the medicine cabinet, each blister pocket empty.

I'm having a feng shui consultation with my friend Celine. She walks around our apartment, making comments and offering suggestions as I take notes on a pink spiral pad that I bought at the dollar store for this very occasion.

You should really think about moving the bed so that your feet don't face the door. That's a classic feng shui no-no. It means death. Bad for baby-making. Celine squats to look under the bed and laughs as she nearly loses her balance, teetering on her cork-wedge sandals. And also, she says, you need to clear out all the stuff you've got stashed under here so the *chi* can circulate. What are those—old magazines? Get rid of them. Clutter's bad. Blocks energy.

Celine suggests that we buy some plants for in the bedroom and also for the other rooms in the apartment.

Live things are good! But make sure you water them. Keep them healthy. Nothing like a shelf full of shriveled plants to put the kibosh on fertility, Celine says. She then tells me about a recent consult she did for another woman trying to conceive.

So I was walking through her house, and one of the first things I see, right off, is that she has a rotting pomegranate right smack-dab in the middle of her Children and Creativity area. Really! How long has that been there, I'm thinking. Talk about a *symbol*.

Huh, I say. But I wonder: Who eats pomegranates? Not that I'm doubting Celine's story.

Pomegranate

I have eaten a whole pomegranate once in my life. My mother brought a few home from the supermarket, moved by some rare whim. She placed one on a plate in front of me at the kitchen table, and I examined it, running my hands over its shiny red hide, tauter than an apple's, gathered at the top in points like a tiny crown. Give it here, my mother said and slit the fruit with a paring knife. She let me bend open the cut seam, which produced a faintly hollow cracking noise, and I marveled at the exposed seeds. I thought they looked like ruby teeth, clustered together in some luxuriously eccentric profusion. My mother tucked a linen dishcloth around my neck. It's messy, she said.

This was long before I read about Persephone. Her marriage and bargain with death. Her bereft mother. In the mythology book I won years later, as a prize for proficiency in Classics, there are charcoal illustrations of Persephone emerging from the underworld, her arms extending upward from a hole in the ground, reaching toward a weeping Demeter, and of the pomegranate, with the fatal seeds extracted and piled to one side.

(I ate all the seeds of the pomegranate, sucking each one white, a drop's worth of juice at a time. It's not that they were sweet but that they were so beautiful and so many.)

THE RABBITS

Ye Pregnant Wives, whose Wish it is, and Care
To bring your Issue, and to breed it Fair,
On what you look, on what you think, beware.

—Claude Quillet, *Callipaedia, or, An Art How*
to Have Handsome Children, 1709

There was nothing remarkable about the rabbits I gave birth to, other than the fact that I'd given birth to them. Little dun-colored rabbits with eyes glistening like wet stones. I'd had fifteen, over the course of as many days. They weren't velvety, like most newborn rabbits, but softly furred, more like rabbits a few weeks old. As rabbits tend to do, they slept in a pile, their bellies moving in gentle waves over my quilt.

My mother-in-law helped deliver them, although nearly all slipped out with little pushing. I know that in all her years as midwife, she's seen many strange things—twins fused together at the shoulders; babies born with teeth, with both sexes, with pincers like lobster claws instead of hands; a drunkard's baby covered in birthmarks like spilled wine—but nothing like this. She was silent on the matter. That's her way: thin white lips pressed shut. My husband was the one who couldn't stop talking.

"If only you'd been thinking of gold, not bloody rabbits!" Joshua said, smiling. He supposed that it would really amount to the same thing—that we'd be famous and grow rich so he could retire from the clothier's business. "Just imagine the food you could provide. At a special price!" Other rabbits were on their way. I could feel them leaping in my womb. I wasn't sure how to look on these rabbits, if I should consider them as victuals or even as special pets, like those kept by wealthy ladies.

"Rabbits. Dear little rabbits," was all I could say. I petted each one in turn before I slept at last, my hands on my restless middle.

After my short nap, Joshua brought me a steaming meat pie, fresh from the baker's, he said. When he told me it was rabbit, I shot up in bed and gave a cry, startling the bundles of fur around me from their slumber. I counted them, to be sure.

"Isn't this what you wanted?" he asked.

I'd been going on and on about rabbit pie, about rabbits in general, for weeks, ever since I'd been startled by one on my way home from the market. We tried to trap it, the other women and I, but it became more of a game as the rabbit darted this way and that, and soon we were laughing too hard to keep up. I'd been newly pregnant then, full of cravings and hoping for a boy.

"Not anymore," I said.

We decided to house the rabbits in a hutch that Joshua built out back so they wouldn't keep getting lost under the furniture or be trampled underfoot. I've always liked rabbits, as far as animals go. They spoil the garden with their nibbling thievery—still, they're tender things.

I had reason to resent these particular rabbits. True, they were living babies of a kind, even if they weren't my own kind. Not long after I'd chased that rabbit in the field, I awoke to find that my nightgown was wet through to the sheets, and although I'd slept deeply, I'd had terrible dreams filled with darkness, birds, screams, a rabbit caught in a snare, pulling and thrashing so that the wire cut deep into its neck. Joshua dozed beside me. I lay still, hoping that the slickness between my legs was sweat, that my bladder had misbehaved during the night.

When I finally lifted the blanket, I saw that it was all red underneath. He was not the first one I'd lost, but he'd lasted the longest; I so believed he would endure. My little boy gone, drowned in that shallow pool.

The following day, I felt a movement in my womb, and that's when the rabbits came.

I considered sewing clothes for them, but Joshua thought that would be a mistake. "We don't want anyone thinking you're mad," he said. I'm good at turning out tiny sleeves and such, but I took his point. I didn't give them names, either. They were just "the rabbits." Joshua promised that they'd be well looked after, with plenty of fresh straw in their hutch, while I stayed in bed, waiting to labor more.

The neighbors' tongues had been clacking about this whole business. Joshua didn't discourage it—he said the shop was bustling with sudden customers eager for more than just cloth. Word spread beyond our village, and some wit did up a broadside, the usual doggerel with smudged illustration: "Mary Tofte, Rabbet-Mother." Joshua flapped one in front of me.

"Penny a piece!" Meaning, those pennies should be ours.

"I don't look anything like that," I said.

"Nice job on the rabbits, though," he said.

"They're moving again," I said. "Really moving— come lay your hand there!"

I was thankful that in all the gossip, I hadn't heard any murmurs of this being the devil's work. Really, I wondered, would the devil busy himself with a trace of rabbits? On the other hand, I wasn't so sure that it was a miracle, although I knew it wasn't my place to say so. As I understand it, there are some things that He watches and some things that He does, and it's not for us to sort out which is which.

My mother-in-law helped me with the next two rabbits. And the two after that, which I assumed, surely, would be the last of the litter. It's odd: I'd gotten used to the feel of the rabbits, with their wriggling and their springy feet, but I could not get used to the touch of that woman's cold hands groping about me.

She carried away the last couple of rabbits, one struggling bit of fur clamped under each elbow, only to return a few minutes later. "You've got a visitor," she said. This surprised me. For the last few days, she'd been shooing away the gawkers who'd turned up at our door. A "man-midwife," she called our guest, making him sound like some bizarre mongrel. She could have just said he was a gentleman doctor because that's what he looked like, with a powdered wig, gold spectacles, and a large leather bag. His hat and coat were well cut, even if they were rather shabby.

He introduced himself as Dr. Howard, and my mother-in-law took away his hat.

Although Dr. Howard was disappointed that he'd missed the birthing, he was pleased when I said I'd let him examine me and my most recent rabbits. He drew a chair up to my bedside and asked me many questions, beginning with whether I had spoken to anyone else— any other medical men—about my condition.

No. I hadn't.

Dr. Howard clapped his hands together as if he were praying and bent to press his smiling lips against his fingertips. He asked whether I'd ever had any other unusual births. "Any sooterkins, as you housewives call them? Small, malformed, partly animal in appearance?"

"Nothing like that, sir."

"Any deformities in your other children? Harelips, for example?"

"We haven't had any children."

"How long have you been married?"

"Ten years."

He asked, hesitantly, were my husband and I having regular relations? In the regular way?

I almost giggled. A louse crawled through one of the curls in his wig, and all at once I felt terribly sad. I found myself telling him that the little ones I'd so wanted wouldn't grow in me. Because this was truth: I'd tried to be rich soil, offered myself to be tilled and sown, but all that took root in me wouldn't thrive in the open air.

All except one, briefly. James, who was so tiny, too early. Too eager to join the world, Joshua said. Oh, but I knew: too eager to leave it, to get his time here over and done with. He had the foggy blue eyes of an old man. His skin so thin—it was wrinkled like an old man's—and tinted orange-yellow. Mama's bitty carrot, I called him, barely strong enough to suckle. He slept too much, and then he didn't wake up. My breasts hardened, became rocks weeping milk, alongside my keening. "You'll have more," my mother-in-law said at the time. "There's nothing wrong with you."

Dr. Howard gave me his own embroidered handkerchief to dry my eyes, then said he'd like to begin the physical examination. I nodded, pulled aside the blankets, and turned my head toward the window. Clouds crept by, like a vaporous menagerie. Rabbits, rabbits, rabbits . . .

Afterward, Dr. Howard told me that my fixed preoccupation with rabbits was causing them to continue gestating rapidly within me.

"To continue . . . ?"

"More are growing," he said, "even now."

What choice did I have but to think of rabbits?

I was taken by carriage to Dr. Howard's own house, where, as Dr. Howard explained, he could keep me under close observation and provide me with all the benefits of his expertise. Joshua promised to visit as soon as he could get away from the shop. The room I'd been placed in was elegant, but like the doctor's clothes, it seemed to be barely resisting the embrace of ruin: the enormous drapes and bed curtains showed the haphazard lace-making of moths. I wondered what my mother-in-law would think. At home, she would clean the same surfaces again and again, wordlessly telling me what she thought of my own housekeeping.

Within two days I felt the return of movement inside me, just as Dr. Howard had predicted. This time it didn't feel like the squirming that had preceded all the other births but more like the stabs of indigestion. I moaned and twisted until Dr. Howard gave me a pungent medicine to drink. He even took a tiny dose of it himself. I was still feeling heavy-headed when he brought a group of gentlemen to my bedside. They were elderly men of fashion—scented with perfumes, ruffles bursting from their coat sleeves like cream from pastry—but Dr. Howard announced them as physicians. "The king's own surgeon is here," Dr. Howard whispered in my ear while he propped me up on pillows.

In his address to the assembled company, Dr. Howard claimed that he'd delivered all but one of the rabbits. Somehow, I couldn't bring myself to contradict him in front of the other doctors—maybe I felt caught up in his obvious desire to impress them.

"There are those who would dismiss the theory of maternal impression as the stuff of wives' tales," he said. "But surely even old wives can express an understanding of a true natural phenomenon, if they witness it often enough."

The men laughed, nodded, and murmured. Each, in turn, laid his hands on my belly. The medicine I'd taken earlier appeared to have made the rabbits drowsy, and they moved sluggishly in response to the doctors' tappings and squeezes.

"Now, gentlemen," Dr. Howard called over the overlapping conversations' steady rise in volume, "please don't stray far from the house. Mrs. Toft will be delivering soon."

I felt uncomfortable about being exposed to all those men, and I told Dr. Howard so in private. He patted my shoulder and called me a good girl. "Don't worry," he said. "They're men of science. They won't see a naked woman but a machine of flesh, operating as it was designed to do. Or in this case, with a fascinating variation."

When the drug wore off, the cramps came back, climbing toward rhythmic pain. It was all I could do to hold off until the doctors had returned, as Dr. Howard implored me to do.

The rabbits were born dead, the sad, tiny things. The runts of the litter—I'd seen that before. They smelled putrid. The drapes had to be drawn back, the windows opened. In the restored light, I saw the doctors' faces, their eyes narrowed above handkerchiefs pressed to noses. I wished them all away from me, everyone, that instant.

One tall doctor began speaking slowly, with formality, as if to someone transcribing his words. I felt like I was watching him from far away.

". . . yet in your lecture 'A Brief Dissertation on an Extraordinary Delivery of Rabbits,'" he was saying, "you spoke of the precocious development and marked vitality of the animals."

My vision blurred, but I recognized Dr. Howard's voice. "As the illustrious Dr. Ahlers has implied, this is a new manifestation. It is of note that Mrs. Toft had been speaking of dead children, very recently. And now her morbid thoughts have clearly converged with her rabbit obsession."

I felt a hand cupped behind my head and a drink brought to my lips: I'd been crying out. The taste of the drug was familiar, and I drank deeply, despite its bitterness.

When I opened my eyes again, it was dark outside. My bed linen had been changed, and someone had put me in a fresh nightgown. I was grateful for that. Dr. Howard stood by my bedside, scribbling in a little notebook. With each looped movement of his pencil, I imagined him drawing rabbits' ears, over and over.

"Well, that's the last of them," I said. Dr. Howard looked up from his book. "The rabbits, I mean."

"Perhaps," he said, and went back to scribbling.

Later, Dr. Howard's housekeeper came into my room, carrying a bowl of stew. It reeked of rabbit, and I told her that I had no appetite. All the same, she left the dish uncovered on a tray by my bed. As I clapped the lid back over the meat, I saw that the china had a motif of rabbits, chasing one another around the rim. I rolled over in bed, away from the untouched meal, and a picture on the wall, one that hadn't been there before, caught my eye. I had to squint to make out the scene: a gentleman in hunting attire strode across a field of heather, followed by his servant, over whose back dangled three dead hares. With my head beneath the covers, I almost didn't hear the door opening.

Joshua had come to visit me, at last. He carried with him two rabbits in a cage. "I thought you might want to see them," he said. "Maybe hold them for a bit."

"You brought these from home?" These rabbits were gray. Not dun-colored as I remembered them.

"Yes." Joshua wouldn't look at me.

"Please take them away," I said.

Over the next three days, different doctors returned to question me about my rabbit pregnancies and births. "Monstrous," one doctor called them, although he assured me it was a medical term. Sometimes as many as three men visited at once; during every interview, Dr. Howard hovered in the background, clasping and unclasping his hands. I became tired of saying the same things so many times over. I felt like an actress, mouthing speeches, except that I was never able to leave the stage. I tried to correct the notion that Dr. Howard had been midwife to the first rabbits, but it was as if no one heard me when I spoke of my mother-in-law, so I stopped mentioning her. The king's surgeon, Dr. Ahlers, visited me twice, and he grew no friendlier with our lengthening acquaintance. He kept using words that I couldn't understand, kept asking complicated questions that unrolled in several directions at once, like a basketful of bobbins kicked to the floor, and when I asked him to please repeat what he'd asked, he'd move on to the next query.

I'd passed some bloody tissue—the afterbirth, I thought, much delayed. Dr. Howard believed otherwise. "Altogether, it adds up to another rabbit," he said. Still, he said I was well enough to get dressed and receive Joshua in the sitting room for his next visit, slivered in between sessions with the doctors.

Joshua began by telling me how well the shop was doing, how he'd barely been able to spare this time away, and I said that I should come home to help him with the customers. He insisted I stay put, and I said that I was sick of the whole business of staying put.

"You need the doctor's care," Joshua said.

"What about your mother? Didn't she see to me well enough before all this?"

Joshua leaned in from his chair and lowered his voice. "Howard says he'll pay us. 'Handsomely' was how he put it. He may not be good for it now, but he will be soon. This doctor's no fool. To him, you're a great discovery."

An embroidered rabbit smirked up at me from a cushion. In the next moment, I was on my feet trying to rip the thing in two.

"Stop it, Mary! What are you doing?" Joshua held my arms by the wrists. "This isn't like you. Sit down now!" He urged me to govern myself, and I urged him to shut his mouth, and then he took me by the shoulders and tried to push me down onto the settee.

I was bleeding—I could feel it soaking through my skirts. Suddenly I was dizzy and had to sit down, even though it meant ruining the furniture.

That evening, my mother-in-law arrived unannounced. A little maid trailed behind her, saying that the master would be angry with her when he returned, which would be soon, that she would be beaten. My mother-in-law turned to her and said, "Bring us a roasting pan of warm salted water, big enough to crouch in."

Having a soak brought relief to my flesh. That part of my body had been the focus of so much attention and yet had been offered so little comfort. My mother-in-law knelt on the floor beside me to pour in more warm water. She frowned when I clung to her and wouldn't let go.

"Ann, I want to go home," I said. "All the meat they give me is rabbit, I'm sure of it." I asked her if she thought I was cursed. I begged her to help make the rabbits go away. She had to pick my fingers off her arms. Her hands, as always, so cold.

"Dry yourself off and get dressed, best you can," she said. I'd had to lean on her to make it as far as the bed. She would take me home, she promised; she needed to arrange transportation and then she'd come back for me.

"Hurry," I said.

I waited and waited. Once, I thought I heard her calling me from the street below. When I went to the window to look, I saw no one except a poor woman in rags, begging to the air. And someone must have turned the lock on my door because the knob wouldn't give, no matter how much I rattled it. I felt too weak to go anywhere on my own, anyway.

The next time my door opened, two men in blue coats walked through and ordered me to go with them. I lost one of my shoes as they dragged me away on my wobbly legs. I was taken to a court of law or a chamber within some place of learning—I wasn't sure. The ceilings were high, the floors polished stone, and the bench they allowed me to rest on was hard wood. I felt so light-headed. I wasn't asked or allowed to speak on my own behalf. Instead, others, many of them the doctors who'd questioned me before, spoke about me. Dr. Howard was nowhere in sight. The voices of the doctors swirled around me like a cloud of gnats, and I muttered my own words, my head bent, my hand over my mouth.

"Esteemed colleagues, I must report that dissected, they show to be regular rabbits. The lungs float in water, which proves that they had breathed air. It is a fact: no infant of whatever species, in utero, breathes air."

I can breathe nothing in this room.

"Mothers produce milk to feed their offspring, whether they be monsters or no. If she's been pregnant, where is her milk?"

All cried out for Mama's bitty carrot.

"We have found a quantity of scat in the digestive tracts of two rabbits, and furthermore, this scat contains straw. Clearly, these animals had run in the fields."

My womb has been a green field through which they have run.

◆◆◆

Here is my confession, all that I told the doctors, miserably, after many repetitions to get it just right:

I'd put dead rabbits inside myself and then made a show of excreting them from my womb before Dr. Howard's company. A travelling woman had taught me how to do this, following the loss of my child, when my womb still allowed access. My plan was to create a spectacle of myself and thereby gain notoriety and work this to my advantage. The live rabbits were props, purchased to help sustain the illusion, to support the story that I'd been so intently building.

Did I say these things? I'm ashamed to have told them such lies. I couldn't find a way around it. Dr. Howard had never delivered any rabbits—that truth was a relief to tell, but they seemed to give me no credit for it. They badgered me until I wept and even then continued to press me; they wouldn't let me sleep or eat. Worst of all, they showed me the scissors, the pointed implements that they would put into me to slice and probe so that they could get to the bottom of the matter. Those are the words they used. So I made something out of all the stories they thrust at me, all that they insisted must be true, and they were pleased to deliver of me their very own monster.

I put my signature on a document, and it was done, after so many hours. Then I sat quietly, my clothing unfresh and befouled with blood beneath, feeling like a small animal amidst those men with their delicate attire and poised speech. One doctor, who had not been part of the interrogation, told a page to bring me a drink of water.

"She's exhausted and clearly confused, the poor creature," the gentleman said. "She's not well."

But another man said, "Don't be tricked. Everything about her is counterfeit."

Cony, cunning, cunny, cuntry woman. Merry Tuft. I've heard it all now. The jailers slide the latest broadsheets under the door of my cell and delight in reciting choice bits of verse, just in case I refuse to read them. As I understand it, my husband will be punished. My mother-in-law will be punished. Dr. Howard is disgraced, and that is how men of his stature are punished. The manner in which I'm awaiting my punishment, whatever it may be, is already punishment.

Aches twist through the core of my body, which has emptied out, finally. The rabbits have stopped coming. All I pass now is blood and more blood. No one's told me what charges have been brought against me, exactly. I'd so gladly trade what little food they give me for a few drops of Dr. Howard's sleeping medicine.

The pictures on the broadsheets get worse and worse. Rabbits bursting through a bush-trimmed doorway that resembles a woman's hairy slit. Me on my back with my legs in the air, a leering doctor into me up to his elbow. The latest one shows me attempting to fornicate with a rabbit in an alleyway. The rabbit is huge, dressed like a man, his red penis hanging out of his pants.

Baby rabbits rot in the corner of my cell. The jailer said that my little children came to play with me, and he threw them in. They hit the wall: I wonder if they'd been alive before that.

A fever has come over me, and I'm hot and cold, though sometimes numb. This is a strange kind of mercy because it allows me something like sleep. Sometimes the cell spins around me like I'm tied to a wheel, and I have to grip the straw hard to make it stop.

I can feel a new ripening. I know Joshua and I can make a child this time who will live. The meaning of the rabbits is finally clear to me—that anything is possible. I seem to remember reading in the Bible that He created the monstrous Leviathan to show that He could, for the sport of it. And now rabbits. In me and of me. This is not the worldly presumption of interpretation but a fact that I observe in all humility.

I've finally been given some medicine to soothe me. The kind doctor, the one who gave me water, came to visit. My only visitor. He brought water this time, too, but to bathe me. "One last look around, for old time's sake, Doctor?" I asked and laughed. He didn't laugh. He mentioned an infection and said he was sorry.

Nobody answers when I call out. There's food and water, only I can't say how long it's been there. Too sick to eat, the medicine all gone. Sometimes I think that the world has died and gone away, and there's only me in this room, waiting.

Tiny feet passed by my cell the other day. Orange-yellow feet moving across the slit beneath my door. Oh, my poor James. Too young for a place like this.

The little ones in the corner are sleeping, heaped in a pile as babies tend to do. I can see their bellies moving, in the dark.

I'm gestating now, and even though my womb is ruined, I will shit out a race that will punish all who deserve it. You have no idea. I asked for so little and have been given so much torment. The truth is, the truth is, the truth is, I am fertile with pain.

The stones all around me, touching me, are quiet and cold.

DIRT

The house and all its dirt waited for my touch. I was parked by the curb with the engine running. I wanted to go in because I wanted to get on with it. I also wanted to drive away, go fast and far until I ran out of gas, until I dropped off the edge of the earth. But the earth is round—so round and round we go. And there I was, back again, in my disintegrating Chevy Malibu with my rubber gloves, bucket, and dollar-store cleaning products all riding shotgun.

I switched off the engine and pushed my head against the steering wheel, pressure just shy of sounding the horn. It was time to face the filth.

I went to college, and somehow, never mind my talent for detours, I imagined that I'd have a house of my own by now. That I'd be paying off a mortgage, planting a garden, maybe remodeling a kitchen. That is to say, I didn't expect to end up cleaning other people's houses. While my résumés circulated like so much debris in an asteroid field, I couldn't have John paying the rent all by himself. Have him doling out cash to me—an allowance—from his slim salary as an adjunct. I wanted to be a kept woman only in the sense of not being dumped.

John didn't laugh at that one. No keep earned there. "You're too hard on yourself," he said.

"You have to say that," I said.

"There's no penance to be done. You made the choice you needed to make. No call for martyrdom." He was smiling, but there was a tightness to it. Well, good.

Truth be told, I had the kind of cleverness that readily alchemizes into stupidity by way of vanity. Five years in a PhD program and nothing to show for it except a box of rambling notes. So this is indeed my penance for being so ineffectual, I'd tell myself as I scrubbed, wiped, scoured. The idea was that it was a temporary gig, a stopgap, and soon a real job would surface. Like a magical island. Or a dead body.

Hartley Spencer said he'd found me through my Craigslist ad, which I'd more or less forgotten about. Most people seemed to hear about me through word of mouth, as my name passed through a network of busy people with enough money to outsource the boring, time-burning business of keeping house. My email exchange with Hartley was terse, on his side—little more than a name, an address, a time. I'm one of those people still stuck on the idea that email should resemble the correspondence of yesteryear, with salutations, full sentences, grammar, etc. I need to just get over it and stop crafting epistles.

The picture I'd formed in my mind of this Hartley— young, maybe a snappy junior executive in a silk tie— began flickering as soon as I saw the house, with its unkempt lawn and peeling paint. I wondered if the neighbors ever complained.

The buzzer didn't work, so I knocked, knocked again, and finally the door was answered by a short, pale, potato-shaped guy of indeterminate age. He was balding on top, and his frizzy clown-wig hair stood out from the sides of his head. Amid the constellation of acne on his chin, an unpopped whitehead shone like Venus.

"Hi," I said. "Hartley Spencer?"

He hesitated, as if he were about to be accused.

"Yes," he decided.

"It's Sharon. We have an appointment today?"

"Oh," he said. "Oh." His eyes looked past me to the street and then zigzagged over me, down and up. "Should I pay you now?"

"Sure." And then as I took the bills that he extended to me, stiff-armed, I added, "Thank you." I never knew if that was the appropriate thing to say. "I'm going to start in the kitchen," I said. The house smelled of B.O., must, and microwaved nachos. It looked like it had been furnished with cast-off hotel furniture: that weird blend of indestructible and cheap-looking, all dull gloss, pleather, and acrylic tweed.

"Okay," he said. "It's through here." He sat down at the kitchen table, presumably to watch me work, so I started with the dirty dishes piled in the sink. Whatever, dude. A little while back, I'd cleaned for an old lady who followed me around the house. She would sit with her tea and a book, affecting the premise that she just happened to be there, in the background. Whenever I moved on to a new room, she'd come drifting along, teacup rattling, and settle herself within a sight line. "You missed a spot." She actually said that, and at first I thought she might be kidding. Not the case. She was supervising from behind the fourth wall. After a few weeks she turned me out for using the bathroom. "I will have no locked doors in this house!" she said. I wondered who she was really talking to.

But this guy, he was silent. Near silent. Between intermittent blasts from the faucet, I could hear him breathing. I moved on to the counters.

"I thought you'd be dressed differently," he said.

"Different how?" I was wearing yoga pants and a hoodie, with the sleeves pushed up. Perfectly presentable. He kept quiet as I sprayed a cabinet and then scrubbed at the goo around the knob. "Like . . . wearing a uniform?"

"Maybe. Yes, I think that could be nice."

"I'm just a freelancer." *Freelancer.* God, my diction—the vestigial tale of my pretension. "I'm not with a company."

And just then it all became very clear, and I stopped scrubbing. As I've already admitted, I'm not as sharp as

I used to think I was. I heard myself ask, "So, what kind of uniform? A French maid?"

Blushing did not become him. He looked like he'd been scalded.

"I think there's been some misunderstanding," I said. In the film of my life, during this scene there will be a subtitle underneath my dialogue, providing translation: "Fuck off, perv."

You'd think I would have hightailed it out of there. I did, but not before scheduling another session. Historically, I am terrible at recognizing and making exits; let me be completely up front about that. Lousy romances, lousy friendships—my shaggy-dog grad school experience. Oh, I stick it out, try to make it work. Blame it on my churchgoing mother, who wouldn't leave her shitty marriage; blame it on my private girls-school education, with its constant subtext of *Just who do you think you are?* Blame it on Rio, blame it on the rain. Hartley made me do all the haggling. I started at four times my fee, then lowered it in five-dollar increments until he finally unglued his gaze from the tabletop.

I drove home and reviewed the whole episode in my mind, doing my best not to talk to myself while at stoplights. *I thought you'd be dressed differently.* Why had he expected anything, and why hadn't I thought to ask why? At least he hadn't said, "I thought you'd be prettier," although maybe he'd been thinking that. Hell, it's what I think, whenever I catch a glimpse of myself. The way he'd scanned me on the doorstep, without even trying to be subtle. He was someone, I thought, who didn't have much of a relationship with his mirror, judging from his goofy hair and his unharvested zits. Granted, the lighting in that house was truly awful. My eyes hurt from all the squinting.

"You know, your English is *really* very good. You barely have any accent." A client, my next one, after Hartley, said this to me as I was unpacking my supplies. I just nodded. She seemed to have gotten the idea that I was a recent immigrant from Poland, although we'd never had a conversation about my background. We'd only ever talked about things like rinsing the recyclables and never using paper towels on the stainless steel.

"*Do widzenia*," she said, by way of farewell.

Her assumption seemed fitting, in a sidewise karmic fashion. John's parents had a Polish cleaning lady, and that's where I got the idea of cleaning houses. Aleksey was wiry, jovial, pretty; John's father had a bit of a crush on her. As she crashed the vacuum cleaner around the living room, she'd told me about how she used to be a stripper, how that was her first job in this country. In her current line of work, she appeared to have done all right. She used to give helpful, instructive Christmas presents to John's parents. A spoon rest. A fresh set of dishcloths. A deodorizing spray for their bathroom.

It wasn't exactly a French maid's uniform, but it was the best I could manage, both in terms of what I had in my closet and what I was willing to wear for Hartley. White T-shirt, black pencil skirt. Black flats. I looked like catering staff. It would have to do. Had I told John about any of this? I wanted to, but every time I tried, I didn't. Didn't actually try, that is.

Hartley preferred that I just clean the kitchen, and that was fine because the place seemed to have reverted to extreme filthiness within a week. Like I'd passed through a wormhole to a month's worth of splatter, crust, and neglect. Could he really be such a slob? Maybe it was part of his whole fetishistic deal. The cleaning session was a replay of the last time: I cleaned while he watched from his position at the table. Lather, rinse, repeat. Although this time I spot-scrubbed the sticky kitchen floor, and I gathered he especially liked this activity because I could hear his chair squeaking as he tried to be subtle about adjusting its angle. And I could hear his breathing change. I thought I heard him take a shot from an inhaler, but it's possible I was imagining that. As before, he'd paid me up front. This time he offered an envelope that had been sealed with so much Scotch tape, you'd have thought the contents included something alive and capable of escape. How canny of him to judge that I wouldn't want to mangle it open in front of him. I did that later, as I sat in my rust-mobile, parked around the corner. Inside the envelope, along with the cash, was a picture torn from what appeared to be a costume store catalogue. He had circled a picture of a girl in a French maid outfit, and on the picture he'd double-circled the high heels. A uniform. Fine. I'd worn stupider clothes, by choice and in public, back when I thought I was hot stuff.

The next week I turned up in the outfit, which I'd hidden beneath a jacket. The lace edging on the sleeves was so cheap it scratched my skin, and the asbestos-like fabric of the skirt had already put a run in my nylons. Yeah, nylons, courtesy of the 1990s. The shoes were just as dated—shiny, black cockroach killers from the Goodwill, with battle scars on the four-inch heels. I handed Hartley the receipts.

"You never finished cleaning that first time," he said. By the time I'd processed this non sequitur, I found that I was already cleaning, the moment of possible protest gone.

The kitchen table was sporting a tablecloth, and I thought maybe Hartley was trying to class the joint up. But the tablecloth was, like my dress, a sleazy facsimile. The real purpose of the vinyl draping became obvious soon enough. "Obvious" is the wrong word: evident. Maybe there's some change in barometric pressure when a dick gets pulled out of a pair of pants; I sensed something. And then, yes, it got obvious, and I pretended not to hear the little grunts. Boy, did I make those cabinets sparkle. Every time an image appeared in my brain, I just kept clicking the little x in the corner of the box. His slitty eyes—click— his busy hand—click—his purple cock—click.

Masturbation is supposed to be a punch line, but it's funnier in the abstract. As with so much in life. And even then. About a month ago, while on the job in another house, I came across some porn mags under a mattress. I'd been stuffing in the ends of some over-long sheets when I touched a stack of soft paper, and I just knew. The smut stash must have belonged to the teenage son since it was his bed. I only knew the boy from the awkward photos of him that sulked throughout the house: the camera hated him, and he hated it back. I'd never laid eyes on the parents, who for me were just disembodied objects (keys, emails, voices, notes, checks). They seemed nice enough, although something about all those photos struck me as protesting too much.

I spread the magazines on the carpet, making a fan shape of topless, puffy-haired women not so much smiling as near-panting. I considered flipping through them but didn't. The pages were orange-hued and brittle. It was all wrong. What teenager would rely on old magazines instead of a laptop, a tablet, or a phone? The posters on the bedroom walls weren't retro—they were out of date, and the place was far too groomed. This kid had moved out, all right. Had he died?

I wondered how long ago a different cleaning lady had emptied the fossilized Kleenexes from the trash. I was about to get rid of the magazines, but then I pushed them back into place. For all I knew, the parents would miss them.

The next week, Hartley was at it again. His usual position at the table, that vinyl tablecloth, hands where I couldn't see them. I was gathering up garbage—soda cans, Doritos bags, a plastic container half-filled with some desiccated yellow dip.

"It's pretty messy today. Did you have a party last night?"

"I'd prefer it if you didn't talk," he said. That few seconds' pause before he spoke, a bit of breathlessness, and I knew it. I kept cleaning, moving on to wiping down the filthy counters. If I turned around and made eye contact, we'd both burst into flames.

While waiting for him to finish, I started to work on the fridge, swabbing at an arterial spray of red sauce

on the door. When I opened it, the light did not come
on, although a cold stink curled forward like a rancid
invisible tongue from the contents, packed in to capacity.
I pulled open a vegetable crisper, saw plastic bags full of
green slime, closed it again. Closed the fridge. My high
heels were now hurting my feet, like I was balancing on
steel tent pegs. Finally, I said, "What you were doing . . .
That wasn't part of the original deal."

"It's my kitchen," he said.

I turned to look at him. He was flushed. Exertion,
embarrassment, but there was something else in his rigid
posture—in the silly, ugly, upside-down U of his mouth
and in the way he not only met my eyes but wouldn't look
away. These things said something else and said it louder.

"Okay then," I said. And in that moment, that's when
the instincts of a normal person kicked in: Get out of
there. Take your bucket and cheap soap, and get out. I
made as dignified an exit as I could, in my French maid
uniform that reeked of sweat.

Later, I got an email from Hartley. *I can give you more
money if that's what you want.* If that's what you want.
Yes, I wanted. Compensation. He was utterly ridiculous
to be paying for this; I'd always felt that. But he owed it
to me. The cons were that it was creepy and gross. The
significant pro was that it was easy money. Good money.
He never touched me, he barely talked, and he didn't
want us to talk, as he'd made clear.

I wrote back, *What fee did you have in mind?* Should
we have been in a café, writing down sums on napkins,
passing them back and forth? Did that only happen in
movies? Were we in a movie? You tell me.

We settled on a raise. I have no idea where he was
getting the money. While the house may have been
valuable real estate, it was slumping into decay. Maybe
he had a modest trust fund. Maybe he worked from
home and didn't care about things like interior décor
or curb appeal. He hadn't demonstrated any flashy or
generous impulses when it came to cash, but he didn't

seem to be short of it, either. Our appointments were for mid-afternoon, and if he ever had pressing business elsewhere, he never so much as alluded to it. From carrying in his mail, I knew that a married female relative bearing his last name (his mother?) had once lived there, but I could not tell where she had gone. Since I cleaned only the kitchen, I wasn't afforded the unobserved roving and licensed snooping that my regular gigs allowed. In my mind, Hartley existed in the house like a figure in a cuckoo clock, making fixed mechanical movements along a runner.

"What is this?" John asked. He'd come home from teaching and had gone into our bedroom to shed the dress shirt and tie he called his "teacher drag."

"What's what?" I rounded the corner from the living room. John stood by the bed, where the French maid uniform was spread out like some sad invitation. Oh, God. I'd hung the rumpled dress in the bathroom in an attempt to steam clean it while I showered, then had laid it on the bed and forgotten about it. Stupid, stupid, stupid.

"I found it in a secondhand store for five bucks. It's hilarious, right?"

"Hmm. Yeah, it's pretty tacky." John had yet to shift his bag from his shoulder.

"I thought I could go as myself for Halloween. Reveal my superhero identity."

"Go where?" he asked. He had a point. When was the last time I'd been to a costume party? When was the last time I'd even put on a dress? He sat down at the end of the bed—away from the dress. He said, "Can I talk to you about something? And don't take it the wrong way."

Never a good preface for any conversation.

"I know you're out there, every day, working hard. But I think maybe you need to stop . . . hiding. Where is this taking you, exactly?"

"To the bank. To deposit checks."

"You need something that lets you use your brain."

"I use my brain. In my own way, all day, no interruptions." This would have been the time to talk to John about Hartley, but talking about it would also have involved talking about why I hadn't talked about it. I guess I felt like metabolizing the shame was just part of the job.

I continued to show up at Hartley's each week at our scheduled time. The kitchen was configured like a set, with the sink, stove, and fridge all along one wall, and I confined my movements to that strip, keeping my back to my audience as much as possible. The tablecloth was becoming Jackson Pollocked with streaks and blobs, but I never tended to it. I spent about an hour each time, sometimes less. I'd become sure that Hartley was deliberately crapping up the kitchen before I arrived. No one could be that much of a pig. So many dirty dishes, so many spills in so many layers, so much untended garbage. Whenever possible, I ran the tap at full force so that I wouldn't have to hear him breathing. Or beating off.

"The fridge needs cleaning, on the inside," he said one day. He added, "It's still dirty."

I wanted to object, but it's hard to call someone on an unspoken rule—that I was cleaning, okay, but that I was also just "cleaning" and wasn't expected to venture all that sincerely into the workings of his real life. Like the maintenance and organization of his food supply. Also, that fridge stank like a festering wound.

Normally, cleaning someone else's fridge would involve a bit of Q&A. (How old is this sauce? Are you really going to eat this last slice of bologna? Even though it's green?) But I didn't want to violate the "no talking" rule, so I didn't consult Hartley. I just threw out anything obviously putrid, which was a lot. Toss, toss. Toss toss toss. *He must be loving this*, I thought. I tried to look without looking at what I was doing as I peeled back the lids of Tupperware and knocked the murky contents into a garbage bag, then threw the empty containers into the sink to let the water blast them clean. Something must have clogged the drain, and suddenly overflow was imminent—I switched off the gushing tap.

And then I heard Hartley yawn. I couldn't help whipping my head around to look at him. He was checking his phone. He looked up at me, expressionless.

"I'll be done in about ten, fifteen minutes," I said.

I started digging at the clog so I could get that water going again.

"You can stop now," he said.

"Oh. All right." *What's wrong? What am I doing wrong?* So what, he wasn't into it today. Not a problem. Not my problem.

But it bugged me, and it continued to bother me over the next few days. True, the costume was getting a little bedraggled. Puffed sleeves deflating, lace dragging— damn thing couldn't be washed without it further disintegrating. I knew I could just get a new outfit; I could make more of an effort with some makeup, a hairstyle . . . but if he wanted upgrades, I felt it was up to him to ask. I kept thinking back to the moment when I'd headed to the door: Hartley gave me a little smile, no teeth. Some reflex of pity or politeness made me smile back, although he was already turning away. His reflection in the hallway mirror showed me that he was still smiling. I wasn't sure if he knew that I could see him.

On the day of my next appointment with Hartley, it took me fifteen minutes to psych myself up to get out of the car. That was me, sitting there with the engine running, thinking of making a run for it, head pressed to the steering wheel, etc. Finally I unclenched the steering wheel and hauled myself to Hartley's doorstep. I hadn't even knocked when the door swung open, and Hartley was there, his doughy face a vague glow against the gloom.

I took it as a good sign that the kitchen had been studiously destroyed, with the usual spills, dirtied dishes, and soggy clutter strewn about. Hartley settled into his usual position at the table while I turned on the tap and started filling up my mop bucket. The floor needed a good wash; it had a movie-theater stickiness. I imagined myself getting fused there, like a mouse on a glue trap. The tiles would get slippery with the soap, which would be tricky for me in high heels, but Hartley would enjoy the show. Once the bucket was ready, I dipped and squeezed the mop, then started to push the damp gray mass over the floor; I felt like the old energy of the room was seeping back. The mop made soft click-clicks with every movement.

Hartley's chair suddenly scraped against the tiles. "I'm going out right now," he said.

"So . . . do you want me to finish?" I said. "I mean, I barely started."

Instead of looking at me, Hartley was looking at my mop, which I was leaning on more like a cane than a spear at that moment. There was that inscrutable little smile again—what I deemed his apology/smug face. It made me think of one of those pictures that appear to be either a duck or a rabbit, this one, that one, not a double perspective but a mutually exclusive choice.

"Yes, you can finish up in here and then clean the living room," he said, before walking across my wet floor and leaving the room.

I waited until I heard the front door close before I pried off my shoes and set back to work on the floor. You might think it would have been easier to clean without an audience a few feet from me, but without that element, the tasks were reduced to a flat essence of tedium and squalor. The kitchen had been dirtied just to make me undirty it. As I scrubbed and swabbed, I half wondered if a camera were hidden somewhere, capturing my movements. At first, I kept expecting Hartley to return, to make more requests, to observe me from a different angle—say, from the anonymous pleather ottoman in the living room, screened by the couch. By the time I'd finished in the kitchen, I suspected he might not be back any time soon. There wasn't much to do in the near-empty living room other than deal with the dust, which had lightly furred the vertical blinds, the coffee table, and the two matched end tables. No knickknacks, no books, no pictures in sight. The room, with its odd, hotel lobby-type furniture, seemed itself to be waiting for someone to acknowledge it as anything other than a placeholder for a space somebody cared about. Maybe Hartley mostly lived in the upstairs rooms. I put one foot on the stairs and considered heading up. Were those boxes or stacks of magazines lining the hallway? I could flick on a few lights, have a look around. Then I pictured myself standing in Hartley's bedroom as he stood staring at me from the doorframe, having glided noiselessly up the stairs, knowing just where to step without making any creaks. I turned, gathered my stuff, and walked out of the house, padding along in bare feet all the way to my car.

The next week, Hartley sent me an email cancelling our appointment. I had to contact him to suggest a different time. I sent him a follow-up email and then followed up on that one. *Don't wear the costume this time*, he wrote in response. So that was it: I would now be a wildly overpaid cleaning lady. Or, more likely, as with our last appointment, he would find some way to get his money's worth.

Two days later, I was standing on his doorstep, waiting. It had almost been a minute since my second bout of knocking. I was about to leave when Hartley opened the door.

"Come in," he said, in a high, soft voice.

He was dressed in a French maid's uniform. A much nicer one than I'd worn, more like a proper theatrical costume. The cut was conservative, covering his knees and arms, with a white ruffled apron tied at the waist. He wore a wig that echoed my own color and cut. I reflexively reached up and patted my own hair. Red lipstick, slightly smudged, appeared to be the only touch of makeup he'd applied.

I hustled inside—as if stepping over the threshold would return us to normal. Hartley was already walking to the kitchen. From the back, he looked matronly and slightly robotic, arms extended on invisible guard rails, ready to correct any wobble of his high heels.

"You sit there," he said, again in that soapy voice. I sat down at the kitchen table and smoothed my fingertips against the tablecloth, which was now white linen and pristine. A strong scent of artificial lemon hung in the air. For once, there was no grease on the stove, no pile of dirty dishes, no goop on the counters. Undeterred, Hartley pulled on a pair of pink rubber gloves and began making slow circles with a sponge on the kitchen cabinet. Okay then, I would watch this performance. I tried to think of myself in the role of dominatrix, watching her submissive run his paces, yet I was the one who felt embarrassed. Hartley seemed to be perfectly, sensually at ease as he mimed different chores, moving as if to music, throwing little shoulder heaves into his swabbing. At one point he crouched down on all fours and began to scrub the floor, swaying his hips with each swish of the rag. I couldn't tell if this is what he thought I'd looked like or what he thought I *should* have looked like; I settled on the latter. Every now and then, he would throw a quick glimpse in my direction, as if watching to see whether I was watching. So maybe *I'd* been doing it wrong, but *he* also was getting it wrong. At least I had sustained the illusion of unobserved action. Under that frilly apron, he was aroused, no doubt.

I was worried that Hartley would draw the whole show out, but after about an hour, he said, "Well, I guess that's it for today." That's what I had taken to saying about ten minutes after he'd gotten himself off. Hartley would then typically say nothing and stay seated.

I nodded and rose from the table. Hartley hadn't paid me at the start of our session, so at the door, I stuck my hand out and said, "The envelope, please." A little joke— surely we'd come that far. I'd decided to postpone any conversations about what this development would mean in terms of added fees.

"I think there must be some misunderstanding," he said. "I believe I'm the one who did the cleaning."

It was tempting to rip the wig off his head to try to wrench him out of character. In drag, he was bigger— taller in those heels, padded out in the chest; the tightness of the clothes emphasized the breadth of his shoulders and his girth. Even with the door closed, I could hear the wind rattling the leaves in the trees, and I couldn't wait to step into the fresh air.

"Yes, but I watched you," I said.

"You liked it."

"*You* liked it."

"You *liked* it," he said.

We were getting stuck, and I fumbled for the right lines in this script. Some jolt was required, I thought, so I said, "You liked it, you dirty slut. Now give me my money."

Hartley's eyes widened before narrowing, along with his red lips. "You need to leave," he said.

I agreed.

"What happened to you?" John asked. When I arrived home, he was sitting on the couch with his students' papers spread out on the coffee table. "Have you been crying?"

"No, I'm just exhausted. Long day. Some rich bitch lost her mind over a scratch in her hardwood. I should just carve some obscenity into her dining room table. Give her something to justify her level of outrage."

"Don't let those people get you down. They don't know who you are."

"I know. I know that. I'm going to have a little nap before dinner, okay?"

Once in the bedroom, I cracked open my laptop. For all my notions of online politesse, I'm leery of email as a place for discussion because it's a portal to crazy. All the same, I needed to talk to Hartley, and I wanted to choose my words carefully. I wrote, *Hartley, I don't like how that ended. While I appreciate the improvisatory nature of our last appointment, clear communication is always important. I performed a service for you in that I participated in a scenario of your own design, for your own enjoyment. Therefore, I should be paid for my time.*

He wrote back almost instantly. *The last girl wore lingerie.* He'd attached a picture.

I suppose he could have been lying. That girl could have been crouched in anybody's kitchen. But tell me, when has something that felt deeply shitty turned out not to be true? You know you don't have to think about that too hard for it to make sense.

I will tell you something true. My disastrous exit from the PhD program was years in the making. Oh, the hours I'd spent in my advisor's office, drinking the coffee he poured for me, smiling back at his smiling beard, listening to him talk about his latest investigation of Restoration comedy, about his days as a young theater wag. Meanwhile my chapters floundered, each one less coherent than the last. He would correct my typos and tell me to do more research. And I would oblige, increasingly less certain of what I was looking for, but I'd sit in the library, in the tweed skirt my advisor had so admired, determined to look like I knew what I was looking for. In the end I just couldn't keep going back to his office, drawn further into a labyrinth with hedges of paper and nothing but the pulse of ego at the center of it.

When I woke up from my nap, it was early evening. In the fading light, I rummaged in the bottom of the closet for my French maid's uniform. It was oily to the touch and so rumpled it was barely recognizable as a dress. From the next room, I could smell spaghetti sauce on simmer.

"Maybe I should have fucked my thesis supervisor after all," I said. I'd been standing in the living room, silently watching John as he sat on the couch grading papers. My sudden announcement made his pen skid.

John sighed and rubbed at the mark on the page, like that would help. "That guy," he said, "was just a useless asshole." And then he asked, "Why are you wearing that?"

"For your viewing pleasure."

"Right." He laughed, but it sounded more like someone reading the words *Ha-Ha.* "Look, your thesis was never—"

"You like it, big boy," I said and rustled the skirt.

"No really, I don't," he said. "It looks stupid." His mouth hung open, as if he hadn't actually expected to give voice to that last thought and wanted to gulp it back.

"I *am* stupid, John."

"No, right now you're *acting* stupid. There's a difference."

"Thank you for that incisive distinction, professor!" I got right up close to him, propelled by the sudden force of my anger, bumping the coffee table closer to his knees. He winced. "What a marvel of comfort you are!" I grabbed each puffed sleeve of the dress in a fist and pulled. "I wear this for a client," I said.

Up until this point, John's eyes had been sliding away from me, but now he looked at me dead on, blinking like the dress was full of some terrible light.

"Why would you do that?" He asked this with such tender frustration, and I couldn't supply an answer, even though I could have said, "For the money." I thought about the old story of the frog in a pot of water on a stove, gradually heating up, dying by degrees—the story that never quite works as a warning because don't we all think of ourselves as smarter than a frog? The story we don't quite believe because we all think that even a lowly creature has some threshold of preservation. And if not, well, doesn't she deserve what's happening?

"Smells like the sauce is burning. I'll go change," I said.

I want to tell you that it all worked out, that I got my shit together and lived happily ever after, but then I'd be getting way ahead of myself. In some version of this story, I go back to Hartley with offers of a new outfit, with lingerie. In some version, over time, I end up letting him touch me and, still later, sucking his dick for a fabulous fee. Of course, this only happened in my mind. Unbidden, these scenarios play out in jump cuts on the back wall of my consciousness, all oversaturated colors on gray stucco. In truth, I never had any dealings with Hartley after his email to me. My clients dropped off significantly after I stopped working for him, and although I can't help wondering if he had something to do with that, I don't know how. People just cancelled on me, citing vacations (that they never returned from), claiming revised household budgets, or saying nothing at all. My main occupation became, with renewed sincerity, looking for a job.

I threw out the French maid's uniform. "Threw out" makes it sound like a light gesture: I walked a few blocks from our apartment and pressed it down deep into a garbage can in an alley, as if it were some cursed object. Now and then I think about that dress. I imagine it nestled against trash in a landfill, somehow defying decomposition. Some shadow. Someone else's idea of sexy that had covered me like an ill-fitting skin.

A DOOM OF
HER OWN

While few parents would describe their little girl as average, that's what you are. Neither beautiful nor homely, neither brilliant nor stupid, you don't stand out: you have learned to follow instructions, which pleases your teachers. You have learned to worship Barbie, and pink is your favorite color, not black, as you once believed. You were given a pair of white gloves for your First Communion, and you wish that you could wear them always, as you understand women used to do, back in the day. You wish you had an English accent, like the self-possessed ladies in the black-and-white films you watch on television with your father. On occasion, you've even affected a slight lilt, but people have either mocked you or asked if you had a cold.

You've been reading about Greek gods and have developed a particular fascination with Artemis, the goddess of the hunt. When you ask your parents for a bow and arrow, they say no— such a toy is dangerous. Your mother tells you a story about being hit in the arm with a dart by a drunken uncle.

Today you have worn your favorite dress to school. It is purple with pink flowers and has a sewn-on sash that ties at the back. The sash is meant to be tied in a bow, but you prefer to let it dangle down, like a train. Stephen Bailey, who has a blotchy explosion of freckles, keeps walking behind you and pulling at the sash, saying you have a tail like a rat. Saying you have two pieces of poo coming from your bum. Finally you turn around and say, "Quit it!"

"Quit it!" he says in falsetto. "Quiiiit iiit! Quiiit iiit!"

If you give him a shove, turn to page 82.

If you start to cry, turn to page 99.

"Quick, get to the time machine!" Dr. Professor shouts. His lab coat flaps as he high-steps alongside you, pursued by a band of angry villagers.

"At least guns haven't been invented yet!" you shout.

"But stone throwing has—ouch!" Dr. Professor begins to duck and weave, as you do, under a sudden shower of airborne missiles. Fortunately, the Time Bender 3000 is exactly where you left it, camouflaged by a mesh of branches and leaves. You both tear off the coverings and climb into the circular module, securing the doors on either side. Stones have begun an alarming percussion on the machine's shell, and you worry that the windshield will shatter.

"If we can just get back to where we started, none of this mess would have happened!"

Dr. P. nods as he slaps the control console back to consciousness, flicking switches and pressing buttons in rapid sequence. He's about to hit the large green button labeled GO when he pauses.

"Are you sure you want to go back? You may never be able to go back to the exact same time that you left."

If you yell, "Yes, GO!" turn to page 85.

If you say, "Pick random coordinates! At the very least I'll avoid getting involved with that asshole Adrian!" go to page 101.

In the end, it is Adrian who confronts you. You are having a fight about a woman who was pressing herself against him at a party, and he says that you are paranoid. That he doesn't know how to feel about the fact that you've obviously been going through his things when he's not home. "I feel my privacy's been invaded," he says. You blow up and tell him the extent of your discoveries. All the racy photographs and billets-doux. The collection of panties.

"You're like the fucking Nazis, you know that? Your downfall is that you need to document everything."

"I can't believe you just called me a *Nazi*." Adrian has no respect for rhetorical clichés.

"You're right. I meant to say you're like a serial killer. With trophies." You're pleased with that one, even though it's essentially a paraphrase.

When you pack, you're not completely positive that all the underwear you pick up off the bedroom floor is yours. Just to be sure, you mash a suspiciously unfamiliar white nylon pair into the garbage beneath the sink.

On your way out the door, you remember that you left your watch on the bedside table. It was a gift from Adrian—very expensive.

If you go back to retrieve it, turn to page 75.

If you leave without it, turn to page 89.

In your twenties, you are as sleek as a kitten. You watch your calories, work out every day at the gym, and dye your hair blonde, blonder, blondest. You spend money on body-hugging clothes and discard items of your wardrobe that could ever be described as "comfy." You pay women to pour wax on you then rip it off, to euphemize the fuzzy area around your crotch into a bikini line.

You wear G-strings rather than panties, lest the tightness of your skirts and pants communicate anything other than a mannequin-like smoothness in your haunches. Every woman in the world is your competition.

You gain a reputation for being "good in bed." You are game for anything, any fantasy: you are a pseudo-bisexual show pony. You own boudoir accessories that typically feature as risqué punch lines in the background action of B-grade movies. Your sleek, flirtatious line of patter matches the cut of your satin trench coat as you sit in an upscale lounge, sipping an eighteen-dollar martini. This persona is as deep, as brittle, as the dark red lacquer on your nails.

To see what this persona attracts, turn to page 111.

If you'd like to cash in your chips on this persona, turn to page 95. Go ahead—see what happens.

"It's MEee it's mweee it's MeeeEE It's meeE!!" A bizarre voice screeches through different octaves, like a warped record being sped up and slowed down.

You've had enough of this. In your pocket is a lighter, and at the moment, you don't care about conserving its fuel. After a rapid series of clicks, you manage to produce a flame. In its tiny glow, you look across the room to see just who it is you're keeping company with.

It's you. Except half your face is missing. In your horror, you cannot find the breath to scream. You feel yourself growing dizzy, and you don't seem to remember where the door is. . . .

If you pick a direction and run, turn to page 94.

If you try to seek refuge under the furniture, turn to page 84.

The filet mignon was a bold choice. A selfish and reckless choice. "Never order the most expensive thing on the menu," your mother always told you. You order it rare because you wish to seem daring, a co-predator, a partner in sensual crime. It works. Adrian smiles knowingly as the pressure of your knife and fork makes the little parcel of meat bleed.

After dinner, you go to a fancy hotel and order fancy drinks in their fancy bar. Adrian suggests picking up another woman who is drinking alone. She looks out of place in her sexily cheap clothes, and Adrian concludes that she's a professional.

Later, in the hotel room, you look at her roots as she's going down on you and pray that she's not giving you VD.

If you manage an orgasm, turn to page 75.

If you fake an orgasm, turn to page 100.

The water is cold and dark and pulls at you like a hundred treacherous hands, but you thrash against it, kicking and flailing for the shore. As you try to swim upstream, on a diagonal, you are constantly being dragged downward—both under the water and closer to the direction of the falls. The pounding sound of the water's cascade gets ever louder. Worse yet, in the near distance you catch sight of what lies up ahead. Pointed, jagged rocks, spiking through the water's surface like a Kraken's teeth.

Maybe drowning, you think, would be better than being smashed apart.

If you let yourself be pulled under, go to page 84.

If you aim yourself for one of the rocks, go to page 106.

Of course you hit the ground.

It's called gravity, dear.

Really, you've been aiming for the ground all this time, so what did you expect?

The impact hurts with the magnified force of a belly flop. You are shocked when, unsteadily but slowly, you manage to pull yourself to a standing position. Just like that. No broken bones, very little blood. You expect applause for such a miracle. But the tent is deserted. Everything is dark except for a shrunken pool of light, partially covering the stage.

Although your body appears to have escaped serious damage, your costume is in ruins, spangles askew, your fishnet tights ripped—beyond repair. You don't need it anymore, anyway. Once you limp from the spotlight's glare, you can make out a tent flap blown open by a breeze. Muted sunlight over damp grass.

Before you leave, you turn and bow to the empty seats.

And I clap for you.

I clap for you loud and long.

THE END

Stephen seems shocked for a second, but then he shoves you back, hard. You return the shove, and soon you are both pushing each other back and forth in a fierce rhythm. Stephen punches you in the shoulder, and you are about to punch him back when you are jerked aside. Mrs. Scott, a teacher, grips you by your arm and barks your name, like she's identifying something that she's found infesting her cupboards.

"She started it!" another girl offers, stepping forward and extending a finger that almost touches your nose, she's standing so close to you. Mrs. Scott holds you by the one arm and grabs Stephen by the other and walks you both to the principal's office, pushing you ahead of her slightly with your arm angled uncomfortably upward in the socket. It's a disgrace to be handled as roughly as a boy—you understand this. You will both have to stay after school and write lines. You write, "I will control my temper." Stephen writes, "I will not fight at school."

Later on, when you want to join in the girls' skipping game, you have to be a "never ender." Turning the rope, but never taking a turn at skipping. This is your probation.

If you don't care, turn to page 110.

If you care, turn to page 104.

You come back from your trip to find the apartment empty. Of course: your boyfriend, Adrian, is at work. When you take your suitcase into the bedroom and begin to unpack, you notice a manila envelope on the dresser. In appearance it's just an ordinary, dog-eared envelope, but it has an aura of audaciously phony innocence, like a jar labeled "Peanuts" containing a coiled snake. A live snake. You tilt it from one end, and out spill pictures of other women. Naked, partially naked, sprawled, spreading. You recognize a few of them as his ex-girlfriends posing in lingerie and raised skirts, submissive for the camera. Looking at them is like looking at a projection of your own neediness and vanity. You are spying on the truth about yourself.

You understand that these pictures have provided him with inspiration in your absence. It's not that the photos in themselves shock you: you've even seen a few of them before. It's that they have been anthologized and left in your path.

When you confront him about it, he sighs. "They were just some things I was putting away," he explains, "because I thought they might upset you."

If you decide to leave him, turn to page 107.

If you decide to let it go, turn to page 88.

You're drinking a lot. It's mostly expensive wine bought by Adrian, but still. You, on your own, average a bottle a day. Sometimes two. Every morning you wake up hung over, tender with toxicity. You take several Tylenol and then sleep until noon. You tell yourself you will watch one hour, all right, two hours only, of television, and then you will work on your writing. But you watch television until dinnertime, which is when you begin drinking. In the evening, sometimes you have arguments with Adrian that you can't quite remember. For the first time in your life, you begin to experience alcoholic blackouts. Like this one:

To resume the story, turn to any random page between 73 and 111.

Dr. Professor slams the flat of his palm against the green GO button like a driver applying the horn in rush hour traffic. The Time Bender begins to spin, and a deep whirring drowns out the screams of the villagers, who, at that very moment, have drawn within cudgel's reach of the module. They are now just a blur of color; the blur takes on a glowing intensity before it fades and blends into a uniform blackness. It would all be very beautiful if it weren't so completely nauseating. You close your eyes and bite the tip of your tongue, trying to master your queasiness.

You've never quite gotten used to this.

When you open your eyes, the time machine has stopped moving. You are enveloped in a foggy darkness illuminated by tiny, twinkling crystals, which drift like falling snow. Do you actually see this or merely perceive it? You're not sure.

"Where are we?" you ask. But Dr. Professor is gone.

If you decide to get out, turn to page 83.

If you decide to go to another destination in time, turn to page 88.

The pumpkin ravioli turns out to be near flavorless, as if all its splendor had been spent in the adjectives describing it: "Maple-infused, puréed, roasted heirloom pumpkin enveloped in translucent, cracked pepper, whole wheat pasta, lightly tossed with saffron crème and finely slivered Parmesan."

The ravioli sits like a chore on your plate. As you slice and chew the bland, plump pillows, you worry about the state of your ass. How many calories in this meal? You are used to living on soup, tuna, lettuce, and coffee. This will not do.

"Don't you like your pasta?" Adrian asks.

"It's delicious," you say. "I'm just savoring it."

"Take your time," he says and smiles. "Then we'll have dessert."

Because of the fashionably late hour that you arrived at the restaurant, it's closing time when you have finished your meals. You are too hazy with wine to notice (or rather, to care) that the restaurant staff have become shifty and resentful of your lingering presence. No one is actually putting up chairs on tables, but they have polished all the tabletops near you twice.

As you finally leave, the lights are snapped off almost before the door shuts behind you. "What next?" Adrian asks. His smile has become a smirk.

There are no foregone conclusions with expensive, innuendo-laden meals purchased for you by men with acquisitive sexual histories. It would be nice to think that.

Turn to page 102.

Although you try your best to pilot the canoe to the shore, the current's forward pull is now too strong for you to fight against it. You throw your weight into a back-paddle, but the water snatches the wood right from your hands. All you can think to do is grip the sides of the canoe and hang on. Water sprays and splashes over you, filling the hull as you crash along in the rapid stream. Up ahead, a terrifying sight: a swarm of giant sharks is heading toward you. But no—you experience a ridiculous feeling of relief when you realize they are, in fact, jagged rocks that you will hit in seconds, seconds. . . .

BASH!!!

The canoe has wedged itself between two rocks. To either side of you, more rocks are spaced like beads in a shattered necklace, forming a zigzagging line that almost, but not quite, spans the river.

If you try to climb and swim from rock to rock, turn to page 106.

If you decide to push the canoe free and brave the falls, go to page 84.

Your torch is burning low, but you feel you must continue down the stone corridor. Somewhere in this ruin of a castle is the Marie Medamite Diamond, and you won't leave without it. The wounds on your legs will need seeing to soon. Nasty rats—if that's what they were. All your companions have turned back, telling you that you are mad (mad!) to go on.

You turn a corner and see a sliver of light, riding low in the surrounding darkness. You surmise that it's coming from under a door, up ahead and slightly on your right. A few more steps forward and you've reached it.

If you push open the door, turn to page 91.

If you knock first, turn to page 105.

You are standing in the center ring, dressed in fishnet tights and a spangled leotard. Ahead of you, a muscled young man in a beige bodysuit begins to climb a tall pole studded with rungs. He turns his head back to you and beckons with it, his handsome face creased with brief, quizzical impatience. This is it: you've been given the job as an acrobat. Although you should be happy, you aren't. You're terrified. You have no idea what you're doing. You've never been on a flying trapeze in your life. And yet, somehow, you managed to talk your way into this.

Your arms and legs are numb with fear as you scale the pole, which goes up several stories, almost to the very top of the tent. You imagine yourself as a robot, with limbs of tin propelled forward by remote command. Otherwise, it would not be possible to keep going.

Finally, you reach the tiny platform at the top. The young man in the bodysuit has already jumped, lightly, while holding a trapeze. In midair, he has moved so that he is dangling by his knees. You understand that when he swings back toward you, you are to jump into his arms.

You jump.

You are falling, falling, falling. There is no net.

To miss the ground, turn to page 81.

To plummet to your death, turn to page 90.

What are you thinking? I deliberately tried to make the choice obvious, and yet you're here. Weren't you listening? What's wrong with you?

Go back one page. Go back and do it right.

You push open the door with some difficulty: the wood is heavy and the hinges rusty. Before entering the room, you hesitate. Did you hear a scratching noise, see some movement bending the deep shadows? With a shaking arm, you move your torch in a slow arc. A brief twinkle on the far wall catches your eye. As you play your sputtering light over the spot once more, you see it again, that unmistakable, flickering dazzle.

If you still think he's going to marry you, go to page 95.

If you're beginning to have doubts, go to page 83.

You do not hate boys forever and ever. Junior high school changes that. Well, you still sort of hate them. But all the other girls seem to like them, so you try to follow suit. Okay, it's not hate, really. Let's call it fear. You have no idea what to say to them. You study your *Seventeen* and *Tiger Beat* magazines very carefully for clues. Sometimes, at the dentist's office, you look at more sophisticated magazines. *Cosmopolitan. Vogue. Elle. Mademoiselle.* You are awed by what awaits you. You wonder how you will manage it.

If you're eager to find out, turn to page 77.

If you decide to gather more notes, turn to page 103.

As hard as you scrabble against the grass and the fabric of the tent, you just can't pull it up high enough to fit your entire body through. You do not know whether to keep struggling through the gap in the tent or to pull out and look around for the tiger.

Your decision is made moot by the hot breath on your backside. You feel a large paw on the small of your back. This will not be pleasant. But you're prepared to bear it. After all, you joined the circus.

Turn to page 95.

You wake up with a throbbing head—you must have fallen in the dark and passed out. You see that you are lying in a dusty, ramshackle room strewn with broken chairs and the shredded remains of books. Light enters from between rotting velvet curtains, one of which must have fallen down during the night. Across from you, propped up on the scarred surface of a wooden table, is a mirror.

It is blackened on one side, the mercury foxed with age. Perhaps that was your doppelganger. An illusion. Or perhaps an omen.

When you locate the door, you find that it's open.

Turn to page 96.

You decide to move in with Adrian Shackleton Laroue, the man of your dreams, and let go of the lease on your apartment. You surrender to reveries about walking down the aisle with him, wearing a beautiful white dress, then retreating from the church into a life of adventurous bliss.

"You're the woman I've been waiting for," he tells you.

You have already spent most of the advance on your novel, so the timing is convenient. You won't have to get a day job. You couldn't anyway since, to join Adrian, you will be moving to a country where you aren't legally entitled to work. Funny, what a difference a border makes.

Adrian has recently landed a position at an investment bank and is subletting an apartment from a dot-com millionaire.

"I'm at the top of the food chain," he remarks.

If you have some idea what's in store for you but suppress it anyway, turn to page 88.

If you remain blind to the inevitable, turn to page 101.

Please turn to page 108 because I need to tell you something.

For the next few moments, the tiger stares at you with tiny green eyes as you jiggle and jump, then yawns and walks away. Maybe you just don't look appetizing. Have you considered that?

Turn to page 95.

A few years later, Stephen Bailey is run over by a drunk driver while walking home from school. You hear the news from your mother.

"Good," you say, without really thinking. She smacks you across the back of the head.

If you don't want her to hit you again, turn to page 103.

"Gonna cry-yi-yi," trills Stephen. It's part of some song he's heard on the radio, and he's made it into his trademark sneer. This makes you cry harder, as he knew it would. But the teacher appears and asks what's the matter.

It's hard for you to explain what happened without shaming yourself further—can you really repeat the word "poo"?—so you just say, in a choked voice, "He was teasing me." You have some satisfaction when Stephen is scolded, even though he is not given a detention.

If you decide to hate boys forever and ever, to page 92.

If you decide to just hate *this* boy, turn to page 98.

You are dressed as a clown, although you were hired to be an acrobat. You feel silly in the rubber nose, the floppy shoes, the yellow curly wig. You pictured yourself in fishnets and a satin-bodice leotard, sequins throwing off light into the cheering crowd as you rise to a standing position upon the saddle of a galloping white horse, arms outstretched, face serene. Well, at least you get to be a girl clown. You look in the mirror and apply an extra dab of white greasepaint to cover the black smudge near your left eye. Soon, you must walk over to the Big Top for your act.

Suddenly, the ringmaster rushes into the tent. His black moustache is wilting with sweat, and his silk top hat sits askew on his head.

"The tigers have broken loose!" he cries. "Sergio the Magnificent was doing his routine when the tigers turned on him! In his desperate rush to escape, he left the cage door open, and they ran after him and . . . tore him to pieces! Everyone in the audience was already screaming and panicking and climbing over each other to get to the exits when the animals turned to them and . . ." The ringmaster falls silent, looks over his shoulder, then runs away. You walk to where he stood, to see what scared him. Then you walk backward, slowly.

At the mouth of your tent is a large cat, orange and black and dripping blood from its muzzle.

If you decide to do a little dance in the hopes of distracting the tiger, turn to page 97.

If you turn and try to escape under the back edge of the tent, go to page 93.

The apartment that you share with Adrian is porous. It is not safe; it absorbs the unwelcome presence of other women. As you have become aware, first through accidental discoveries, then through more deliberate explorations, artifacts of Adrian's women are stashed everywhere in the apartment. They upset you, yet you can't stop looking at them. You can't stop looking *for* them. Astonishingly, there is always more, just a little bit more, to find. Where are they coming from? More letters. More photographs. A bag full of panties and stockings. Even, weirdly, a photograph of a used condom. You would snoop through his email if you knew his password. A strange fact: a disproportionate amount of the women write letters, and of them, a disproportionate amount write with fountain pens. They are an epistolary lot, a confessional, romantic lot. An immodest lot. So many of the photographs are nudes.

You should be writing your novel, but you are hopelessly blocked. You are, however, becoming an expert snoop.

If you finally confront Adrian, go to page 76.

If you say nothing, go to page 88.

You are in a fiberglass canoe on a river. On both sides of you, trees, dense and dark, crowd to the banks. Your progress forward is difficult. The water yields almost grudgingly to your inexpert stroke. Your knees hurt as you pull the paddle in a long, crooked slice. One side, then the other. One side, then the other. There are songs people sing when they canoe—"dip, dip, and swing . . . flashing with silver"—but you can only remember parts of them. You never actually went to summer camp. You become aware of a lightening of pressure—as if the water has become more agreeably liquid. Perhaps you are getting better at this. No, that's not it: the current in the water has picked up. Your paddling is quickly becoming irrelevant. In the distance, you hear a sound like drums, like amplified thunder. You are heading toward a waterfall.

If you decide to jump out and try to swim to the bank, turn to page 80.

If you decide to stay in the canoe and keep paddling, turn to page 87.

You are listening to your parents fight. As they stand in the kitchen and yell at each other, their voices are loud enough to be heard on the street outside the house. The fight began while you were sitting in the living room playing with the cat, and it continues as you walk past the kitchen on your way upstairs. Your father wears a three-piece suit in brown. Your mother wears a faded blue housecoat; her thick, black hair is cut like a man's. She has no self-consciousness about her lack of glamour, and you find this vicariously humiliating. To you, she has always looked old. You think, *No wonder dad cheated on her*. And also, *I will never be like her when I grow up.*

To avoid becoming like your mother when you grow up, turn to page 77.

To become just like your mother when you grow up, turn to page 111.

If you didn't care, you wouldn't be turning the rope for the other girls at recess. The girls decide that it's okay for you to join in the singing. By the time you're allowed back into jumping rope, you're out of practice. In the skipping rhyme that goes, "Ice cream soda, lemonade, and tarts, tell me the name of your sweetheart . . ." when they start singing the alphabet, you can only get to D before you snag the rope with your foot. But there are several boys with D names in your class, so no one can say for sure who it means. Besides, if you got as far as S, you might have to marry Stephen. The trick is to make it as far as U because no one's name starts with U, but you still get to stay in for a long time.

As the bell rings at the end of recess, you make a secret promise to yourself.

If you vow never to get married, turn to page 92.

If you vow to be a beautiful bride, turn to page 103.

Your knock is answered by a high-pitched cry: "Come in, come in!"

Pushing open the door, you step over the threshold and enter a dim chamber. You are straining to make out the features in the scant light—high ceilings, misshapen chairs, shelves filled with moldering books—when a damp gust of wind blows the door shut and extinguishes whatever weak light source was burning in the room. Your torch gutters and dies with a faint crackle. But not before you see a hunched figure skittering across a far corner. You are in perfect darkness. And you are not alone.

If you stumble for the door, turn to page 96.

If you shout, "Who's there?" turn to page 78.

You've taken to crying in restaurants. You cry while Adrian looks weary. Because of the long hours of Adrian's job, and because Adrian always insists on eating out, this is where you spend most of your time together, apart from in bed. White tablecloths to white sheets: surrender, surrender. The tears begin to flow after the second bottle of wine—there is always a second bottle of wine, sometimes a third—and after the conversation turns to your relationship. It is all a predictable chemical reaction.

"Sometimes, I need to be alone," he says.

He will not marry you. You are moving toward nothing.

"She's just a very sexual person. It has nothing to do with you. If you ever get a chance to meet her, I'm sure you'd like her," he says.

His former lovers will never completely recede into the background. They are a cursed harem of succubi. With new members every day.

"I love you, but I see myself as an independent person. This is going to sound really terrible, but I just don't need other people," he says.

You are stranded in a city where you have no friends, no job, and no money. Your book is going nowhere.

Plop, plop, plop go the little tears onto the white linen, joining the crumbs and sauce stains.

If you decide to leave him tonight, turn to page 107.

If you can't bring yourself to leave, turn to page 102.

In the morning, you are still there. And the next morning after that. And the one after that. You complain to girlfriends, long distance over the phone and over email. They are properly appalled and sympathetic, as always. This makes you feel better.

If you really, really decide to go, turn to page 89.

If you decide to stay, turn to page 90.

HE'S GOT A KNIFE, AND HE'S RIGHT BEHIND YOU!
PUT THIS DOWN AND RUN AWAY!!!!!!!!

GO THIS WAY. $\longrightarrow$

Wait, maybe that wasn't the killer.

Sorry about that.

Maybe you should go back to the beginning. There are probably some things you want to do differently anyway.

Turn to page 73.

It's hard not to care. Without friends you are vulnerable. And you can't be friends with the boys.

Stephen Bailey is not to be put off and seeks further opportunities to torment you. Finally, he does succeed in making you bawl. He has good instincts, that boy: one day, you wear brown velour overalls, and he makes loud suggestions that your bathroom etiquette is not what it should be. He says you look like something from the toilet, with legs. He holds his nose and fans the air, and soon, other kids do the same.

.

Turn to page 100.

You start dating a man who is a wolf in wolf's clothing. His name is Adrian Shackleton Laroue. He's a tall, tousle-haired investment banker with a private school pedigree. You have flirted with each other for years. Adrian has titillated you with stories of his outrageously confident sexual campaigns and maneuvers. You have titillated him by listening.

And now you are both in the same city, facing each other over a white tablecloth. As Adrian casually weaves resume highlights through witty anecdotes, you consider your options.

If you decide on the filet mignon, turn to page 79.

If you choose the pumpkin ravioli, turn to page 86.

SECONDHAND

Second Chances is part of a chain—it's one of those warehouse-sized depots full of used clothing, old furniture, and cast-off household junk. Scuffed shoes, sagging couches, Crock-Pots. All the flotsam of society. At the store, I wear a red vest over my T-shirt and a serious, professional expression over my face, a look that comes naturally. Even when I'm somewhere else shopping, other customers will think I'm an employee. I'll be wearing a coat, with a purse slung over my shoulder, flipping through a rack of clothes, and someone will come up to me and say, "Do you have this in a size 4?"

"For you? Dream on." I never have fun with people and say anything like that.

I usually hear myself saying, "Oh, I don't work here, sorry." It comes out like a pre-recording, and I give this slight, polite laugh.

Right now, I'm working in the women's section, returning clothes to their proper places on the long, subdivided racks that form narrow aisles across the store. Alanis Morissette plays over the loudspeakers, briefly interrupted by an announcement that today is Seniors' Day, 20 percent off. At the end of one aisle, I've parked a wheeled garment rack full of items from the changing room area. Everything is to be sorted by color, size, and category. I take a white silk shirt (nice, except for a faint pen mark) and hang it with the other light-colored, long-sleeved tops. I walk up the aisle and file a black sweater with a kitten (I think) done in sequins among the other sparkly, bedazzled knits. Holding a mauve and periwinkle flowered tunic, I'm briefly stumped. I decide it belongs best with the purple tops rather than the blue. Someone obviously was looking for retro chic and didn't quite find it: I heft an armload of polyester zip-front dresses from the garment rack. Collectively, they waft the chicken noodle-soup smell of vintage sweat.

I take a short break for lunch: a tuna sandwich with too much mayo that my boyfriend, Dylan, made for me despite his hangover. Dylan's a little younger than I am; he has bafflingly lucrative computer skills, so he has lots of free time. Sometimes he drops by the store to hang out. I tell him he's going to get me fired, but no one really cares. Everyone likes to look at him, truth be told. One time he sprang at me from the sleepwear racks wearing an old fox-fur coat, which he insisted he was going to buy. Even his good looks couldn't elevate the moth-eaten pelt. I said that I loved it. My sarcasm was pretty obvious, but he bought it for me anyway. He's always doing things like that. It's sweet when it isn't completely irritating.

I'm in the employees' break room finishing the last of my sandwich when the manager, Lynda, approaches me. She wears 1980s lady-executive clothes, ruffle-front blouses under peplum-waisted blazers with shoulder pads: rumor has it she burned out in Toronto's financial district ten years ago. Funny how as we move through the 90s, the 80s are starting to look like   the 70s—that is, sad and misguided, fashion-wise. "Sasha, you're on back room today," Lynda tells me, "with Vera."

I like that Vera has an old lady's name. She's not an old lady, but she's working on it, her pack-a-day habit already etching faint pucker lines around her twenty-three-year-old mouth. We're sorting through the bags, doing the initial cull of unwearable and unusable crap. Sometimes people mix in their garbage with their donations. We find wadded-up Kleenex. Dishes with dried food on them. And not just soiled clothes, *filthy* clothes, among them dirty underwear, crusty socks. But you also come across really nice things, like velvet jackets, brand-new hardcover books, even gold jewelry. You never know. When Vera and I have a big enough stack of acceptables on the sorting table, we'll start putting things on hangers on garment racks. The industrial gloves we wear for protection make our hands look oversized and waterlogged.

I'm pulling stuff out of a green garbage bag. From the feel and weight of it, this bag's all clothes. I'm in a bit of a trance, reaching into the bag's misshapen mouth, pulling and piling jeans, men's shirts, towels. And then I stop.

I've seen this little sweater before. The wool is light blue and a bit dingy beneath its aura of fuzz. Snowmen, holding black twig hands, make a pattern wrapping around the sweater's torso, and large lumpy snowflakes fall from the V-neck. I wore this sweater. I take off my gloves so I can touch it.

"What's up? You cut yourself?" asks Vera. She's stacking dishes in the Households cart. I hear them clacking as they settle against the glassware she's got stacked willy-nilly.

"I used to own this sweater."

"Yeah, sometimes I see clothes I used to have. I'll be, like, 'Hey, I remember wearing that!' and then I'm like, 'What the hell was I thinking?'" Vera laughs.

"No—I owned *this* one."

"Probably not the exact same sweater." Vera is speeding up, as if to compensate for my arrested motion.

"No, my Gramma made this."

"Huh. Okay, so maybe it is the same sweater. Freaky. Neat."

I stow the sweater beneath the table, behind some plastic bags. We're not supposed to do this—to save things. But everyone else does it. I just never have before. Earlier, I saw Vera stash a nice Louis Vuitton knockoff behind the garbage bins, so she isn't going to tell on me.

At home, I show the sweater to Dylan. I'm annoyed when he pretends to think it's a gift for him and tries to put it on. I snatch it back, a little too roughly. To mollify me, Dylan says he'll make dinner tonight. He raises his index finger, makes a suave saunter to the fridge, opens it, and then withdraws a bottle of wine, which he presents to me over his forearm, like a waiter. Goofball.

Later, Dylan is leaning slightly forward over his lasagna and nodding between bites, as if both in approval of the food and to accelerate his chewing. I usually don't mind, except this time, he's making noise.

"Slow down. You always eat like someone's going to take it away from you."

"Hey, in my house, if you didn't eat fast, you didn't eat much." Dylan smiles and wipes the corner of his mouth with a knuckle. He grew up with four siblings, two of them older brothers. "I used to envy kids like you. The only child! Sounds royal, doesn't it?"

I'm not really an only child. Or maybe I am. I don't talk to Dylan—or anyone—about my own brother, Ronan, older than me by two years. He went missing when he was ten.

In the morning, the little blue sweater is on the living room couch. Which is strange because I remembered folding it and putting it away.

"Did you take this from my dresser drawer?"

"If I did, I don't remember. But it's cute. You shouldn't hide it away." Dylan adjusts the strap of his messenger bag then heads out the door.

Today my assignment at work is to go through the racks and pick up clothes that have fallen to the floor or have migrated to the wrong section. I'm paired with Emma, a skinny art student who wears crazy, glamorous shit to work. Spangled miniskirts with 1960s sweater sets. Prom dresses under suede jackets. Silk palazzo pants and embroidered Mexican blouses. Combinations of clothing that really shouldn't work.

"This would look so beautiful on you, with your pale skin," she says, holding up a black lace shawl with tassels.

I smile. Emma is on a mission to make me over. I always like all the girly stuff she shows me, but I mostly stick to jeans and T-shirts.

There's a pile of dusty clothes under one of the racks, so I get down on my hands and knees to gather it up. As I dump the mass of fabric into a cart and begin to untangle it, my eye catches a word printed on a clothing tag in magic marker. I can just make out that it says, in bleeding block letters, "SASHA."

I'm holding in my hands a poncho that I wore when I was ten. It's orange-and-cream acrylic, with a matted fringe on the edges. I sneak it into the plus-sized women's evening clothes. When I go off shift, I retrieve it and buy it with my 30-percent-off employee discount. On the bus on the way home, holding the Second Chances plastic bag in my lap, I begin to cry. I think of how I used to flip the poncho back over my head, letting the neck band rest on my hairline, and pretend it was a large, luxuriant mane. All the girls would do that: the weight of the poncho felt a little elegant, like an eighteenth-century wig. We'd walk around like that at recess. Slightly ridiculous to each other but secretly confident of our own dignity. And then one day, a group of boys caught sight of us and ridiculed us. It broke the spell.

That night I give my mother a call. We don't speak all that often.

"Mom, what did you do with all our old clothes? I mean the things packed away in the cedar closet back on Fernwood?"

"Oh, I don't know. They might be in a box somewhere." I can hear the click of her lighter. On the exhale she says. "Sweetheart, I probably threw them out."

"Why would you throw out perfectly good clothes?"

"I don't mean in the garbage. I gave them to charity."

"I see."

"That boy still with you? Whatshisname—the handsome one. Clever."

"Yes, we're still together."

"Well, that's nice."

◆◆◆

After I hang up the phone, I go to look at the poncho, but it's no longer in the plastic bag. Dylan says he hasn't seen it, then goes back to tinkering with a cascade of code on his computer screen. After an hour of combing through the apartment, rifling through dirty clothes on the bedroom floor, weeding through the junk fallen to the bottom of the hall closet, I give up. I figure I must have dropped it somehow en route. We watch a little TV and finally decide to turn in. As I pull back the duvet, the poncho is there, clashing matter-of-factly with the flowered sheets.

"You *ass*hole."

"What?"

"Was it fun, watching me waste my time?"

"Sasha. Why would I do that?"

"Yeah. Why indeed? Grow up."

I snap off the light.

I'm on the lookout at work, combing through the racks for clothing I recognize. Over the course of the day, I find a pair of yellow pajamas with feet, a pointy-collared paisley shirt with pearl snaps, and a pair of blue North Star running shoes with white stripes, colored in with ballpoint.

"When you think about it, it's not that fucked up," says Dylan. He's come by to hang out with me while I'm on break. "Look. People are mass consumers. Buying, selling, tossing, buying all this shit they don't need. It's a disposable society. It's a corporate world." He begins to speak rapidly. "Second Chances is on the bandwagon, making big bucks by siphoning off all of everyone's extra junk and marketing it back to them at a profit like it's some huge favor. What does Second Chances actually pass on to charity? Two percent?"

"Twenty percent. I don't know. Ten."

"My point is it's no big surprise your own cast-offs come back to you."

"But that's crazy. Why *this* store? I didn't even grow up in this city. And shouldn't these clothes be long gone? Turned into rags or dumped in a landfill?"

Dylan shrugs. "How do you even know for sure it's all yours?"

I tell him that I just know.

"You know what you could do—you could make a quilt out of this stuff. You take a piece from this old thing, a piece from that one. Found art. You know? My mom's friend did that with a bunch of old concert T-shirts. I always thought it was a cool idea."

"Why would I do that? I don't even know how to sew."

"No, seriously."

"No. Seriously."

Shortly before my shift ends, I find my old Brownie uniform, buried between old nursing scrubs and marching band jackets. I recognize it from its armful of patches, earned for expertise in crafts and household tasks. My mother had to sew them three abreast, as opposed to the more typical two, because I'd earned so many.

I'm sitting on the living room floor, tracing over the Brownie patches with my finger. Each patch has a symbol, but they are proving too obscure to decipher: if the steaming pot is the cooking badge, what's the one that looks like an oven?

Look out! We're the jolly Pixies,
Helping others when in fixes.

The next morning, Dylan has to leave early. I walk into the kitchen after he's gone to work and find the Brownie uniform sitting at the kitchen table across from the yellow pajamas. A bowl of cereal is set in front of each of them. I try to appreciate the scene, but appreciation is not what I feel.

During the next week, more and more of my childhood clothes wash up at Second Chances. Among the things I find: brown corduroy overalls with orange mushroom patches on the knees; a bathing suit with a pattern of gray elephants; another paisley shirt; a pair of green bell-bottoms with a deep, falling hem on one leg; a gingham, full-length party dress; and a navy-blue parka. Vera begins to notice me hiding away little articles of clothing, and she asks if I'm pregnant. God knows why she jumped to that conclusion. Even though I assure her I'm not, she starts shoplifting baby clothes on my behalf. In the parking lot, she hands me smuggled bags full of sleepers. I wait till she's driven off in her Chevette to put them in the donation bin by the side of the store.

Dylan watches me sift through my clothing finds at home, and he tells me he's got a great concept for a creative project. I could photograph the clothes on little kids and then put them side by side with pictures of me when I was little. I could do a website, and he'd help me build it. I tell him to get away from me with his flaky ideas. These things are private.

"I wish you'd show me pictures of you wearing these clothes. I'll bet you were an adorable little kid."

"I wasn't anything special."

"Oh, come on. Every little kid's special."

"No, they're not."

Dylan tells me that I'm no fun, and in protest, he strips off all his clothes. I have to say he did manage to cheer me up, if only for a short time.

I begin to keep all my salvaged clothes in the bedroom dresser's bottom drawer that I've cleared out for this purpose. I place them in carefully folded layers.

Somehow, they never stay put.

I find the paisley shirts knotted together tightly at the sleeves, right to left, strewn across the hallway leading to the kitchen. I go to throw away eggshells and discover the gingham party dress, bunched in a ball, nesting in the plastic bags beside the trash can under the sink. I discover my tampons piled neatly by the bathroom sink, displaced by the elephant-pattern bathing suit, which is rolled up tightly in the Tampax box. Another time it's a pair of mittens on a string, one mitten placed on the knob on either side of the bedroom door. The brown corduroy overalls and the green bell-bottoms sprawl across Dylan's desk in the living room not once but twice—each time arranged with the legs spread apart, as if running. One day I come home from work and find the poncho standing up by the foot of the bed like a teepee. It's stuffed with all the pairs of pants, which are telescoped one inside the other.

Dylan and I have daily arguments, but I can never get him to admit to anything.

"Stop screwing around with my stuff! It was never funny in the first place, so why do you keep doing it? Just what are you trying to provoke?"

"For the last fucking time, I'm not *screwing around with your stuff*. You're the one who's acting out."

I tell Dylan that it's my apartment and that he needs to take his bullshit somewhere else, to his friends or I don't care where. When he leaves that evening, he doesn't slam the door like I thought he would.

In his sudden absence, I know that by banishing Dylan, I have banished an explanation. Our fights were a kind of comfort, and I miss them immediately. I have never felt easy sleeping alone: I down several beers by myself in front of the television before I'm finally feeling woozy enough to commit to oblivion. I awake later feeling the urgent need to pee, so I creak down the hall to the bathroom. I am barely awake except for my bladder; I'm aware of the toilet seat's chill and of the soft shadows, cast by the night-light. As I pat myself with toilet paper, I see the shower curtain flutter slightly. It does that all the time—just a breeze from the heat vent. I pull back the plastic and see a dark shape at the end of the tub. I flip on the bathroom light. It's my navy blue parka, huddled in a ball. "What are you doing here?" I ask. I pick it up with both hands and shake it. It's wet, although the tub, when I touch it, is dry and cold. Against the gray-white porcelain, my hand looks like someone else's.

I wring out the parka and hang it up over the shower curtain rod. I clutch the sodden fabric in my fists, and it comes back to me: playing with my brother, Ronan, in the snow. Sometimes snow would saturate our snow pants and make our mittens soggy. Our body heat, pumped high from activity, would melt it.

◆◆◆

In the snow, we make a tunnel, even though we are forbidden to do so. Our mother believes such forts will collapse and suffocate us. But we love the cold. We feel it differently. We move through it like astronauts, protected with our own portable atmosphere of warmth.

We call the tunnel a shortcut, but it's not a shortcut to anything. It's a tubular passage we've dug through a mound of snow that we heaped up ourselves in the middle of the backyard. We just like the sound of the word "shortcut." Secret and savvy. We're certain there's no way we'd squander the freedom of adulthood on being something as perversely boring as our parents. There's some game we're playing, some rascally us-against-them adventure. I can't remember.

The blue parka is still hanging where I left it when I go to take a shower the next day. I move it gently to the floor and keep watch on it through a crack in the curtain, even as the shampoo stings my eyes. At the store, I don't look for any of my old clothes, nor do I find any. Lynda sends me home early because she thinks I'm coming down with something and doesn't want her "best worker laid low by some bug." I don't really want to go home, but I tell myself I'd need to at some point, so what's the difference?

When I unlock the front door, I have a strange feeling that the sound of the key pushing the dead bolt has been unnaturally amplified. But maybe it always sounds like that, and I've never paid attention. I push open the door and step into the gloom. The entire apartment is dark, although I'm sure I left a few lights on.

"Stupid," I say and flip the switch by the door. At the far end of the hall, I see the North Star runners facing me, splayed in a broken V. There is something aggressive about their stillness; it seems they're poised, and at any moment, they'll take a step. The silence is the soundlessness of a record in a clean groove. I hold my breath as I wait for them to move.

They do not.

When Dylan returns home that evening, backpack in hand, I don't even let him get his coat off before I start telling him that I'm sorry I blamed him. That I know for sure it's the clothes moving around by themselves. That I'm completely freaked out.

"Sash—come here." He leads me to the kitchen table and sits me down, then pulls a chair around next to me. He holds my hands between his and strokes the backs of mine with his thumbs. "Sash, you're doing it. You're moving stuff, and you're just forgetting that you're doing it. You're stressing yourself out, and you're sleepwalking. I've heard you. It's you."

"No, it's not." I pull my hands away, even though Dylan tries to hang on.

When he joins me in bed later, I pretend to be sleeping. I can feel his anxious weight on the mattress, sense him looking at the back of my head in the dark. But when I finally turn over, he's asleep.

Lynda almost cries when I give her my notice the next day at work. She holds me and rocks me in a hug. Emma tells me we should hang out sometime, and Vera squeezes my arm and says, "I hope everything works out okay."

I am horrified by what I find at home.

Dylan is sitting at the kitchen table, which is covered with stacks of my childhood clothes. He's smiling and holding a large pair of scissors. In front of him is the navy parka, with one of its sleeves hacked to pieces. To his right is a pile of different colored squares of fabric: the remains of several articles of clothing.

"What the fuck are you doing?!" I shout at him. Dylan's smile vanishes instantly, and he puts down the scissors with sudden care, like they're made of glass.

"I'm—I'm making you a quilt. I thought we could work on it together. See? I'm setting it all up for you."

I have no words. I can only stare at the scraps on the table.

Dylan says, "But you were throwing it all out!"

I don't know what he's talking about.

"It was all bagged up, by the door with the recycling box, ready to go. I had to wash some of it because there were coffee grounds on it and crap. I just thought it would be nice."

"You are so fucking stupid. You're such a stupid fucking child."

The look on his face is unbearable. He has a book that he's obviously taken out from the library called *The Art of Quilting*. I can't stand to look at that either.

"I'm sorry I wrecked your clothes. Here, we can fix it. I can fix it."

But he can't. I begin to cry, and Dylan asks how he's supposed to help me when I never tell him anything.

Years ago, I watched my brother get into a stranger's car. I never told anyone. He went missing, and everyone thought he'd run away, like before, and when he didn't come back, they assumed the worst. I came home from the park without him, and I said that he'd run on ahead when I'd hurt my wrist. But we'd bickered. Girls couldn't be superheroes, he said. I remember I had been close to tears, humiliated by my brother's confident, singsong denials. We'd been arguing more and more those days, and at school he wouldn't talk to me. He walked away from me, leaving me alone in the park, and I followed at a distance on the sidewalk, kicking at fallen leaves. A green car pulled up beside Ronan, and I stopped when he stopped. I watched while he spoke with someone in the car and then walked around to the passenger side and got in. For all my goody-goody behavior, adults always liked him better. I went back to the park to climb the monkey bars, a steel half circle lined with rungs. I'd reached the top of the arch, climbing hand over hand, the bars cold against my palms, when I felt sick to my stomach. I briefly blacked out, lost my balance, and fell, taking most of my weight on my hand as I landed in the dirty sand. The park was not a nice place.

I'm alone in the apartment now. Dylan has left and will not be back. I stuff the clothes into garbage bags, mixing together the tattered remnants, the neatly trimmed fabric squares, and the clothes that Dylan didn't get to with the scissors, and leave them on the living room floor, piled like boulders. There's nothing in the apartment to drink but a half-filled bottle of rum left over from a party, so I finish that, glass after glass at the kitchen table, before I go to bed.

I wake up and hear a scratching sound. I get out of bed, walk into the hall, and see the Brownie uniform. It's dragging itself along the floorboards by one arm. For a second, I think, *See, it really is moving! I'm not crazy.* And then I feel crazy. I see that it's hurt. Its progress is painful, slow. The brown dress leaves a dark stain in its wake, and I follow because I feel there is no other choice. I no longer recognize the hallway or the room at the end of it.

All the clothes are there. They are floating, side by side, in formation. They begin to fall away, like tiles, piece by piece, and behind this wall of clothes, there is a darkness.

"Ronan," I say. I am digging through an enormous pile of clothes. No, it's a pile of leaves. We've been jumping in the pile of leaves. Night's going to fall, and we need to get back home. The leaves are wet and clumpy beneath my hands, like rags. I can feel him, I'll find him, I just need to keep digging. I take hold of his foot, but he is disappearing into the earth. I can't hang on, and it's all my fault. He's lost.

ALL THINGS BRIGHT AND BEAUTIFUL

I do paintings of people's dead pets. Which is not to say that I paint animal corpses: I do commemorative work for people who've recently lost their pets. People send me photographs, although there have been a few awkward misunderstandings: "Do you have a fridge?" one poor lady asked, standing on my doorstep, clutching a lumpy plastic bag. I also do portraits of living pets, but it's the memorial paintings that bring in the most money. What I lack in technique, I make up for in dedication. People are grateful; they just want a little something to hang on to. They want someone to take their grief seriously, which I do.

It's probably this same impulse to redeem that led me to set up an intervention for my brother, Clifford. He'd never been Cliff of Cliffy; always Clifford, as in *Clifford the Big Red Dog*, the children's story about the little puppy who grows to be the size of a house. My brother had become like that, oversized in my mind because I was so worried about his drinking. What would become of him? He'd been living in Berlin for the past ten years, barely getting by as a musician, drunk every time I talked to him—it had passed beyond "edgy rock 'n' roll lifestyle" to "holy god, he's drowning." Every year, I expected him to pack it in and come back to Ottawa, but he never did.

During his most recent visit home, I thought we should grab the opportunity to talk to him, as a family, about our concerns. I would fly in from Baltimore for the occasion.

I called my mother and explained how the intervention would work, how we'd each write a letter beforehand, and then we'd read them out loud to Clifford, one by one.

"Okay, dear," she said. "That sounds fine."

I wrapped up the call and turned to my preliminary sketch of Professeur Bonhomme. I'd never done a rabbit portrait before, and I was finding it trickier than I'd expected. It kept wanting to look like a cat. I couldn't get the ears right. When my phone buzzed, I answered it soon enough. It was my older sister, Kristen.

"So Mom just called me," she said. "She was really confused. She says she doesn't know what you were talking about."

"About what?"

"About the intervention. Which is funny because she practically invented the ambush."

I exhaled forcefully and slowly through my nose, like I did in yoga class. Kristen crunched on something. Celery, maybe.

"Can you explain it to her? Again? It's important," I said. Our mother had suffered two minor strokes and took a lot of pain medication for various complaints. She forgot things, or claimed to. Also, it was hard for me to know when Kristen was exaggerating Mom's befuddlement.

"Can't you?" Kristen said. "Make sure she understands what she's supposed to write in the letter, or she'll make it all about her. I'm not sure when I'm going to write mine. When're you flying in?"

"Saturday. I sent you a text."

"Okay, I see it. Gotta go. He's back."

Clifford was staying at her house, with my brother-in-law and two nephews. Kristen had called me earlier to complain about what a lousy houseguest he was being: rock star without a handler, diva without a trailer. My arrival was to be a surprise.

❖❖❖

The rabbit that took shape on the page looked slightly demented, or even demonic, with sly eyes and uncanny limbs. I crumpled up the sketch and tossed it into the basket to join its siblings.

My husband, Colin, came upstairs with a cup of chamomile tea for me—he must have heard all my sighing and scrunching. He pulled a page from the trash as I sipped.

"It looks like a loaf of bread with legs," I said.

"I read somewhere that Beatrix Potter used to boil rabbits to help her draw them better," Colin said. I pictured some Victorian occult ritual. He added, "Dead rabbits. You know, to study their anatomy beneath the skin."

Now there was a woman who didn't flinch from clarity. To expose and behold so plainly! Never mind coaching my mother to write her letter: I'd been wondering if I'd be able to tell my brother what I really needed to say. Without hurting us both.

Healing with Love: A Family Guide to Intervention
A successful intervention requires tight scripting. The purpose of the letter is to ensure that family members keep focused and not freeze up at the last moment or explode with spontaneous anger that may be detrimental to the process.

I'd found a book on Amazon—it had a sappy title but good reviews—and I'd soon fringed its pages with yellow Post-it notes. The author stressed that intervention letters should follow a specific formula: you should begin with *a statement of concern and love for the addict*, then mention a time when he was helpful to you. *(Gratitude is the last thing an addict expects to hear. It is instantly disarming.)* As I read this to Kristen earlier over the phone, she said, "When was the last time our brother was helpful to anyone? I mean, besides as a cautionary tale?"

Next, you should *provide factual statements about the addict's behavior, detailing instances when he was drunk/high and how it affected you.* In closing, you should *repeat your statements of love and concern and ask the addict to accept help.*

"Kiss, kick, kiss," Kristen said. "Got it." I'd heard her apply the phrase to office dynamics. She did promotions, brand management, that kind of thing.

"Except not so much 'kick.' You're supposed to avoid 'statements of recrimination, rage, and judgment.'"

"As in, 'Dear fuckhead, I'm tired of listening to your drunk, belligerent bullshit over the phone'? Or how about, 'You claim to be a musician, but really you're just a bum who knows how to play the guitar'?"

"No, that wouldn't be good, Kristen."

"Not to be undermining, but do we think this'll work just because we've seen it in movies?"

"What movies?" I said. I tried to help Kristen come up with examples.

"Is it a bad sign that we haven't even seen this work in movies?"

"It's better than doing nothing," I said.

Clifford had been hitting the bottle even harder since he'd been dumped by his long-term girlfriend. The evening phone calls had become more slurred. Darker. It would be the wee hours of the morning for him in Berlin, and he'd have been up all night, getting lit. One time, he was talking to me about the view from the balcony where he stood, and with every sentence, I was afraid that he would jump. He told me the air wasn't right. "Tastes like a nail," he said.

"What does one serve at an intervention?" Kristen asked. "Red or white?"

"Are you looking into caterers?"

"I'd guess white, in case people start throwing things."

We used to be an object-throwing household. Mom and Dad were, that is. They didn't throw things at each other, but they threw them to make an impact. Dishes, glasses, food, books, at the floor, the table, the cupboards, the walls. Dad would kick things aside—stray shoes, toys, the vacuum cleaner that was always out but seemingly never in use. (Still life: Hoover with undigested dust.)

Mom spent most of her days driving around the city, hunting bargains, scouring thrift stores, and buying in bulk. "Filling this place with rubbish," as Dad put it. Once he bought Mom an apology gift, a large silver locket. She pitched it out the front door. I found it later, combing through the grass while pretending to play with my Barbies because I imagined the neighbors were watching. During one particularly shrill fight, my mother threw money into the kitchen garbage. Green-gray stacks of twenties, bound together with elastics, held in a lidless, shallow box. The trash hadn't been changed in a while, so the money peeked out the top. I could see it from the living room, where my brother and I were watching *The Simpsons,* and I found the sight of the tossed money nauseating and frightening. Clifford got up, walked over to the garbage, reached in, and said, as he thumbed through the bills, "Hey, there's enough money here for an electric guitar."

Shortly afterward, Clifford got his wish. As loud as that guitar was, it didn't drown out the fights. I didn't recognize it at the time, but it was its own kind of screaming.

The nephews, fourteen-year-old Zachary and ten-year-old Liam, had long been in awe of Clifford. The last time I visited Ottawa, a year ago, I noticed they both had pictures of him on their desks, and Zachary had made a corkboard collage of various grainy photos of Clifford playing in Berlin bars. The center image featured him with a cigarette clenched in his mouth, holding his vintage Rickenbacker like it was a fainting woman. My brother-in-law, Jake, resented it. I could tell. On Jake's side of the family, people liked to tease each other about sports team preferences, voted Conservative, and in general did not find bohemianism impressive. I also resented it, to be honest.

I spoke to Colin about this while we made dinner. Maybe the pet-painting auntie couldn't hope for cachet, but what about him? "Don't you think it's unfair that he gets top billing as 'the cool uncle'?" I asked.

"He *is* the cool uncle. I'm an optometrist." Colin smiled and flipped the vegetables in the pan, failing to catch a few as if making a point. When he'd offered to come along to Ottawa, I said he shouldn't cancel his appointments—I knew he had a full slate and then some. I would just give his letter to Clifford. Colin had a lot of compassion for my brother: aside from being a decent person, Colin used to be, by his own report, not such a decent person when he drank all the time.

"I don't need the hero worship, but I think your brother does. And that's tough because he doesn't sound like he's making a very good impression now that they're old enough to understand what's going on," Colin said.

It was true. During the past week, Kristen said Zachary had started to ask what was wrong with his uncle Clifford, who was always "sick" in the mornings, "tired" in the evenings, and who left a party's worth of empties in his wake over the course of each day. I was so sure the letter Zachary would write, with Kristen's help, would be our ringer. Zachary had begun to retreat into the cave of adolescence, but I thought that this would draw him out—a licensed occasion to directly criticize an adult. I remembered him as the little kid who would never shut up, who had sound effects for every movement he made, who spoke for the mini macho-men action figures he shook in turn as they faced each other, who seemed to have no unexpressed thoughts. A lot like Clifford once was, actually.

I emailed my rabbit lady (as I'd come to think of my client), and told her the portrait was coming along beautifully, which didn't feel like a lie since I figured it would be true eventually. Then I emailed my father about the intervention plans. I'd have called him, but we almost never talked on the phone—even less since he and Mom separated two years earlier. Not that I bore a grudge against him on Mom's behalf: at a distance, they got along better than they ever had. Writing to Dad, I thought, would let me get my words just right. The cup of tea I'd parked by my laptop grew cold as I typed and retyped, telling Dad how I was worried about Clifford, who, over a year's worth of phone calls, had spoken to me sober only twice and had always sounded unhappy. *I want him to know that we care for him,* I wrote, *and that he doesn't have to live this way. If you'd like to be part of this, it would mean a lot to me—and of course it would mean a lot to Clifford.* I typed, deleted, and then restored the following: *But I know this kind of thing would probably make you very uncomfortable, so I can understand if you don't.* Dad was not one for tightly scripted emotional interactions, as the intervention would demand, and I figured it was best for him not to feel maneuvered. When we were growing up, Dad had been transparent only in his anger toward our mother. Otherwise, he'd been a sealed room. And years later, that's what he was still.

On rare occasions when Clifford and I were little, Dad would take us on long walks through the rambling fields north of our house. Overdressed by Mom in rubber boots and rain suits, we'd walk beside our father, crunching over yellow reeds fallen on damp ground, quieted by his quiet. Sometimes he would find things for us—old keys, a rusty watering can. The area used to be farmland, he explained, so such relics had been left behind. He'd also pick up rocks and identify them for us: pyrite, scoria, slate. You'd have thought they were dinosaur bones, we were so excited and reverential. One time he found a large piece of mica, which flaked in brittle, glittering layers. Dad said Clifford and I could share it, which both my brother and I knew meant that Clifford would hoard it and gloat, and I would whine and keep asking *When will it be my turn?* But instead of launching into this drama, we just nodded. We were reluctant to spoil something so special by bickering over it, particularly in front of our father, who would maybe never take us out again.

Dad emailed back. *I guess I'll see you on the weekend, luv yer dad.* That was all he wrote, and I knew there'd be no letter.

◆◆◆

My laptop began to turn into a disappointment generator. Shortly after I received Dad's email, Kristen wrote, saying that Zachary would not be writing a letter. Jake would be taking him and Liam to the movies on the evening we'd originally planned to talk to Clifford. Reading that, I felt like immediately emailing Kristen back, asking her how long she was going to continue breastfeeding the kid, but I didn't. She also wrote, *Jake says this is just kicking Clifford when he's down. What good will it do. We're just setting him up to fail. We dump our buckets on him and then he goes back to Germany. In a way it's only self-serving.*

Dumping your bucket was a frequent Kristenism, referring to the conveyance and relief of mental burden. I imagined a tin pail full of cool water being tipped over Clifford's head, like a baptism. Kristen obviously pictured bilge, slops, green paint. (*Avoid statements of recrimination, rage, and judgment.*) Kick, kick, kick. I thought maybe several days with Clifford had pushed her to the point where that's all she really felt like doing. Kristen had mentioned that there'd been frequent digs at her "bourgeois" lifestyle. She said that when she brought out photos from her family's recent trip to Disney World, Clifford actually began to pound his head on the table.

Mom called and told me that she'd already talked to my brother.

"What do you mean?" I said. "What did you do?"

Mom assured me that she hadn't let the cat out of the bag. I knew that in her cluttered apartment on the other end of the phone call, she was surrounded by bags: bags of magazines, bags of unsorted junk mail, bags of toys the nephews no longer played with, which she meant to take to the Goodwill.

"You didn't tell him I was coming, did you?"

"No, no."

"Because the surprise is part of the intervention's impact—"

"You know, Kristen and I think it would just sort of . . . make more sense for you to talk to him on your own."

"I see."

Watching my family scatter in this way reminded me of the time I was helping a neighbor put up "Lost Cat" posters, and the wind blew them from my hand into the street and over the sidewalk. The ones I managed to retrieve had shoe prints on them.

"Frances, I've already said what I want to say to him."

And what was that, I asked her.

"Well, I told him to grow up, get a suit, and act like an adult. He was going on and on about some new girl he's after, and I told him, 'What do you possibly have to offer anyone at this point? You've got no job, no money, no steady place to live, no plans.' He was *morose*, Frances. I think his *real* problem is that he needs psychiatric help. He's clinically depressed."

"I agree he's depressed. But I also think the depression is fueled by his drinking."

Despite being the daughter of an alcoholic, my mother, a teetotaler, didn't understand booze. She understood pills: these she took, and these she respected as prescribed and therefore legit. With alcohol, well, you were just making it all up, weren't you?

"Yes, but he needs psychiatric help," she said.

I felt myself becoming stubborn because I knew that by "psychiatric help" she didn't mean therapy, which she deemed "pissing in the wind," but Prozac, which she was on. Mom was capable of arguing in circles as long as you did your share of turning the wheel. Again, I said that I thought Clifford's depression stemmed from his alcoholism and that, in any case, he'd need to get his drinking under control before he did any other work on himself.

"He needs psychiatric help. That's his real problem," she said.

Clifford was still angry about the last time our mother pushed that agenda. As a child, he'd been "bouncy." That was her euphemism for "being hyperactive," aka having ADHD. Sometimes, when Mom was talking about his behavior, Clifford would get an impish look on his face and make a sound like a cartoon spring. *Boinnng!* Bouncy.

It sounded cute, like Tigger. Except that it had involved Clifford taking large doses of a now-discontinued drug, which gave him headaches, rashes, and disturbed sleep. For a time, Mom took him to see a shrink, a dark-haired woman named Dr. Stephanopoulus. One time I went with him to a session. In the doctor's office, we sat on a rug that was like a giant, flattened teddy bear and pretended to play. Or at least, I pretended to play—I was conscious of being observed. Clifford sat near the bear's head, pulling on its ears and spit-stuttering out starship gunner noises, and I sat behind him, operating imaginary equipment. "You can play, Clifford, but I also want you to talk to me," Dr. S. said.

"You're the only one he really listens to," my mother continued on the phone.

Years ago I told Mom that I thought my brother had been misdiagnosed, that I didn't think he really fit the ADHD profile. She said, "But he was always better with you. You calmed him down." It was like she was talking about an ill-behaved dog or a skittish horse.

So that's my job this weekend, I thought: the drunk whisperer.

After I got off the phone, I walked around the house, ranting. I felt like mixing a big batch of dark red and covering an entire canvas. Or a wall. Colin told me that I was shouting at him, and I apologized. What I really wanted was a drink, to take the edge off, but that edge was too sharp with irony: as Colin has pointed out, the only person who really needs a drink is a drunk. Instead, I sat at my easel and dabbed some paint on Professeur Bonhomme. I'd decided to pose him nestled in a bed of flowers, putting fewer demands on precision of form. It wasn't ideal to be starting a painting right before I had to leave, but I just needed some feeling of getting somewhere.

Later, Kristen emailed me a draft of her intervention letter. *Proofread pls and thx*, she wrote. So just like that, we were back in business, although with a reduced staff. I didn't mention Mom's bailing on Kristen's behalf. Maybe

Mom had misunderstood, or maybe Kristen had let our mother think what she wanted to think, to get her out of the way. I edited Kristen's letter, injecting compassionate phrases like *because we love you* and excising statements like *you shame yourself*.

It was colder in Ottawa than it was in Baltimore, and the leaves had already started to turn. In the Uber from the airport, I watched as we sped past masses of orange-and-red trees on sloping hillsides, set back at a distance from the fields that framed the highway. I called Kristen's phone: "The eagle has landed," I said.

"The fat man walks alone."

"I'll be there in about fifteen minutes. Is he suspicious?"

"Oddly, no. Even though I made him take a shower. You should be grateful."

Against the pale sky, a huge, splayed V of geese was flapping raggedly. Through the rolled-up window, over the sound of traffic, I could hear them honking, their voices overlapping in their strange, instinctual chorus of encouragement. Mom used to claim that every year as the geese passed over our house, they switched formation, as if triggered by some secret signal. I can't remember if I ever saw it happen.

After I arrived at Kristen's, I crept down to the basement where Clifford was playing *Fortnite* with Liam. At first, my brother only gave me a quick glance. He'd mistaken me for Kristen, who, in a squint, was my older double.

"Hi," I said.

"Hey," he said. And then—"Frankie!" he shouted as he jumped from the couch to give me a hug. Clifford was the only person who still called me Frankie. It used to be that or Frankus. Or Frankenstein. "Because your feet are so huge," he used to say. Or "because your teeth are green" or "because I made you in a lab."

"I thought you said you weren't coming," he said, patting my hair, followed by, "I saw some roadkill the other day. I thought of you."

"It's great to see you too."

"Baby fox by the side of the road, like it was sleeping."

He'd lost weight; I felt it in his ribs. And he looked incredibly tired, puffy-eyed and drawn, even though, according to Kristen, he slept like a housecat, in fourteen-hour stretches. I'd seen him three years ago at my wedding, and he'd looked worn but not so completely worn out. On the coffee table, beside the video game controller, were two crumpled cans of Guinness.

My parents, who showed up separately not long after I did, had also undergone physical transformations. It seemed that way, even though I'd visited them just last year; their aging was something I must have mentally airbrushed. They both were shorter, and while Dad had become more wizened, Mom had continued to round out. Like Jack Spratt and his wife, only their "between them both" was now limited to occasional family get-togethers. The nephews, too, had changed, Zachary especially, who was now a big lunk. Clifford and I marveled at our oldest nephew's height as he stumped shyly through the living room.

Clifford asked Mom to drive him to the grocery store. She was reluctant since she'd already settled into the couch with the newspaper. But when Liam joined the pressing, she sighed and drained the last of her soda. The silent understanding was that Mom would pay for whatever Clifford picked out. She was already giving Kristen extra grocery money for all the food he was consuming on his visit. "You're coming?" Clifford said to me. It wasn't a question.

At the grocery store, everything that Clifford threw into the cart said "hangover." Ketchup-flavored Pringles and bacon-flavored tortilla chips, three-layered nacho dip, Oreo cookies, six-packs of Coke and Dr Pepper, a school-bus-colored drink called SunnyD. None of it was to share with other people. That became clear when I asked Clifford whether he thought we should get some chip flavors that the boys might like and maybe some diet root beer for Kristen.

After we loaded up the car, Liam dragged Mom off to the hobby and games store further down the strip mall to buy collectible cards, and Clifford and I went to the liquor store. It felt totally wrong accompanying him, but there just didn't seem to be a graceful way out.

Standing among the shelves of bottles, Clifford couldn't decide between the small and the medium-sized vodka. He wanted to make Bloody Marys, but he'd gone through all of Kristen and Jake's supplies. While the bigger size was the better deal, neither bottle was cheap.

"Never mind, Clifford. Don't get either. Save your money." Mom's wallet had gone with her to the other store.

Clifford looked at me. "What for?"

As I understood it, ever since his girlfriend had kicked him out, he'd been couch surfing, unable to afford rent. He was looking into housing support.

In the end, he bought the medium-sized bottle. I bought nothing, even though the mini bottles by the cash register kept giving me the eye.

The last time I bought mini bottles, I got them for a photoshoot. It was in the early days in my pet portrait business, and for my pet store-owner client, I thought it would be cute to do a party scene using live guinea pigs and hamsters. Growing up, Clifford and I used to watch and mock a show called *Hammy the Hamster* that featured live rodents with voice-overs, loosely herded through miniature sets to make some kind of plot. My idea was I'd place the animals around a little table stacked with little prop snacks and drinks, and an adorable imitation of party chaos would ensue. But they kept wandering out of frame and wanting to leap off the platform, and all my shots were lousy. I was bitten twice. My only consolation at the end of the day was the damn mini bottles, which I downed in succession: Baileys, Grand Marnier, Southern Comfort, Jack Daniel's, Kahlúa, Johnny Walker. At the time, I told Clifford about the fiasco, and he said he remembered that stupid show. He said he heard they got the rodents to stay put when they needed them to by gluing them in place, but I said that didn't sound right.

Back at the house, I sat with Dad and Clifford out on the backyard deck as they smoked, drank Bloody Marys, and talked about travel. On separate occasions, years ago, Dad and I had both visited Clifford in Germany. Clifford had given the same tour to each of us, except that for our father he'd made the concession of walking slower. It seemed Clifford hadn't been swimming so deep in the booze at the time, but then, I was still in college, so binge drinking felt like a normal part of existence. Now, as the three of us chatted, I watched Clifford and Dad smoke and compared their styles—Dad plied his cigarette with anachronistic elegance while my brother pulled drags like someone speed-smoking on a coffee break. Wind stirred debris off the blue vinyl pool cover, and I began shivering in my thin jacket. I headed back into the kitchen, where Kristen was making dinner. By the sink where she was working, empty Guinness and Boddingtons cans stood in staggered assembly. Normally, the recycling was kept under the sink and the overflow was carried to the garage, but it seemed to me that Kristen would rather construct Exhibit A than preserve counter space.

"Give me a hand with this Yorkshire pudding," she said, and we fell into our usual routine of gabbing and cooking. We'd made so many meals together over the years; I was really the only person Kristen tolerated in her "one-person kitchen." As I'd grown older, our eight-year age difference had gradually evaporated. It wasn't something I would have predicted at age seven, back in a different kitchen where Kristen tugged my hair into braids while yelling at Clifford to get his shit together or we'd miss the bus.

After about twenty minutes, Clifford rounded the corner.

"Why aren't you outside?" he said.

"I'm just having a talk with Kristen. I'll be back out in a minute."

Clifford cast a broody look at the floor, then left.

"You're here for him," Kristen said. "I know that. Go on." Then it was her turn to look pouty. On my wedding day, despite being happy for me, my sister cried because she said she'd never had to share me with anybody before. Untrue. As a kid, I'd been Clifford's exclusive sidekick, but back then, Kristen had wanted no part of me.

After dinner, the house emptied out rapidly. With quiet efficiency, Jake corralled Zachary and Liam and informed them that they were going to a movie. Minutes later, Mom and Dad also cleared out. Usually they each did their old-person routine, taking forever to get out the door, making trips to the bathroom, saying goodbye multiple times, forgetting things, coming back, but this time, they exited crisply, stage left, like a couple of pros. Until that very last moment, I'd thought there was a small chance that Dad might stay.

In the vacuum that followed, it felt like there was only one event that could reasonably occur for time to move forward. Standing in the foyer, I raised my eyebrows at Kristen, and from her position on the living room couch across from Clifford, she nodded. As I pulled my letter from the zippered side pocket of my bag, Kristen began rooting in a side table drawer for hers. Page in hand, I sat beside Kristen on the couch and faced Clifford where he sat in an easy chair, a half-finished glass of ale resting on the arm.

"Yes?" he said, looking from me to Kristen and back.

At that moment, I felt sick—with nerves, with sorrow, with something else that was hard to name exactly.

"Dear Clifford," I began. The first part of the *statement of love and concern* was not so hard. It was easy to tell Clifford that I cared for him, that I admired his musical passion, and to say how his example of doing what he truly loved made me feel I like I could do my own thing, too, instead of applying to medical school like everyone had expected me to do. It was the recitation of damage that was difficult. "Over the past few years, almost every time you've called me, you've been drinking. You're drunk when you call, and as we talk, you're in the process of getting drunker. You start slurring your words, and the conversation becomes one-sided. You get stuck talking in circles, and you sound so troubled. One time when you called me, you were so drunk, you didn't even sound like yourself." What he'd sounded like, I thought at the time, was some version of himself calling from hell. "It was like you couldn't hear anything I said—nothing could get through because you weren't really there. It was scary."

When I finished, Clifford said nothing. The corners of his mouth turned down as if pulled by weights.

"Go on," he said, motioning to Kristen, who was clutching her letter against her chest.

I watched Kristen as she read, not Clifford as he listened, because I couldn't bear to look at him. At one point, Kristen stopped. She made an odd sound in her throat, like she'd swallowed something rotten. She pressed on. "Whenever my phone rang and I saw it was you calling, I'd add six hours. If it was after 9:00 p.m. in Germany, I wouldn't pick up. I HATED talking to you when you were drunk like that. And then when I asked you stop calling when you were drunk, you stopped calling altogether. Zachary has told me that he's very disappointed in you: he's seen all the empties, noticed all the hangovers. He doesn't ever want to visit you in Germany because he's afraid you'll get him drunk."

After she was done, Clifford said very quietly, "I'm sorry. I'm sorry I've made everyone feel this way. I'm sorry."

"I don't want you to be sorry," I said. "I want you to be happy. I want you to get better." I told him that Colin had also written a letter and asked if he wanted to read it. He did. Clifford read in silence, then carefully refolded the letter and tucked it alongside his seat cushion.

"So where are Mom and Dad's letters?" he asked. There was an archness to his tone, indicating that the question was rhetorical.

"They didn't write any," I said. It was hard to fathom that he'd want any more of this, that he'd want his full due, even in shares of pain.

It was at this point that we went off script because we'd run out of script, and as *Healing with Love: A Family Guide to Intervention* warns, improvising is dangerous. *The addict may begin to get defensive and seek any opportunity to pick a fight. Do not engage. The self-control of the intervention team is paramount.*

Kristen suggested that Clifford put his talents to profitable use and maybe consider writing music for commercials. She knew the business: it would be good money and provide him with a project, something to fill his days with other than drinking.

"Advertising," Clifford said, his eyes turning into slits, "isn't art. It's about sucking Satan's cock."

"Oh, you mean like I do," Kristen said.

"I didn't say that. You just did." Clifford half smiled, as though he were conscious of moving us back into script, though it was a different, older one. Kristen picked up her cue.

"Some of us have to work for a living," she said.

"If that's what you call a living," he said.

I could tell from the look on Kristen's face that she was experiencing a mental traffic jam, not knowing which line of rebuttal to start with first but also, no doubt, weighing the consequences of destroying whatever sympathetic connection we'd managed to create. I cut in.

"Clifford, how can you say that to Kristen?"

Clifford dropped my gaze, and for just a second, he seemed to soften. But it was too late. Kristen stood up and began shouting.

"You've had so much handed to you, you know that? You think the world owes you a living, but it's the other way round. You never appreciated the privileges you had. *Some of us* didn't get to go away to university because *some of us* went to private school. And fucking complained about it."

"Why didn't you just get a job?" Clifford looked past her and took a sip of his ale. He was vandalizing facts for calculated effect. Kristen had gotten a job and had paid for most of her tuition at a local college. It was Clifford who'd moved to Montreal and leeched off Mom and Dad for years while failing to complete his degree at McGill.

"I think I'm done for tonight," Kristen said in a voice flattened of emotion and walked briskly from the room.

Clifford looked at me and said, "This evening. The letters, it's like a—" He made a slow circular motion with his hand, then snapped his thumb against his index finger.

"Ouroboros?" I offered. "Snake eating its tail?"

"No. It's—what is it." He pulled his iPhone from his pocket and began tapping at it.

"An intervention," I said.

He was still tapping away. He didn't appear to hear me.

"An intervention," he said, looking up.

"Yes, Clifford. Hang on a sec, will you? I'll be right back."

I followed Kristen into the kitchen, to make sure she was okay. I caught her just as she was leaving the room. She had poured herself a full glass of wine and was obviously heading up to bed with the rest of the bottle.

"Don't judge me," she said. "Don't you say a fucking word."

Liam slept on a cot in Zachary's room that night, and I was grateful for his vacated bed. I lay on his Pokémon sheets, looked at the riot of anime posters on the walls, completely exhausted. As promised, I placed a phone call to Colin.

"So how'd it go?"

"Oh. A mixed success, I'd say."

I couldn't sleep, so I stared at the plastic stars glowing on Liam's ceiling, trying to impose constellations of my own invention: The Flayed Umbrella. The Half Nelson. The Spilled Teeth. Everything was coming out broken, and my thoughts turned to the lady who'd arrived on my doorstep that one time, clutching a lumpy plastic bag.

"Do you have a fridge?" she asked.

"Yes, yes, I do," I said. I knew exactly what was in that bag. We'd spoken earlier on the phone, but I hadn't been expecting her or what she was carrying.

The freezer compartment was jammed with ice and frozen meals and bags of half-rotted bananas I kept saying I was going to use for smoothies—no room there. The fridge was no better.

"How about I take some photos with my phone? And then you can take him home with you," I said.

She couldn't take him home, she said; she lived in an apartment and had no backyard to bury him in. She so wished she could. I ended up driving her to a park, and we performed a secret burial at dusk. She said that I shouldn't worry about the photos, that she'd send me some. I'd peeked in the bag, although I shouldn't have: the dog had been hit by a car and left by the curb. I never did the painting, which was just as well.

In the morning, Clifford and I went for a walk. He and Kristen weren't talking, so I gathered he hadn't apologized.

The path by the river had been paved since I'd last visited, and people whizzed by on bikes. Clifford and I sat on a bench looking out to the Gatineau Hills, watching the wind wrinkle the water's surface. The liquid appeared to move in slow motion, with such gentleness.

"What are these?" Clifford gestured with his chin to the tall purple flowers that grew in clusters bordering the tumble of rocks leading down to the water's edge. They were fading and going to seed.

"Loosestrife. It used to grow all over near the cottage, remember? And that's Queen Anne's Lace, I think."

"Those phone calls you talked about last night. They give you the wrong impression. I don't drink that much during the day. It's not like I stagger around drunk."

"I know you don't. But it's not about you looking or seeming drunk. Like we said, it's about you having a constant level of alcohol in your blood. It's a depressant, and you keep topping it up all the time. When was the last time you lived without it?"

"Now I feel like I can't even have one drink without people getting all upset."

"Then why is it so important for you to have a drink at all?"

"What else am I supposed to do, Frankie?"

When we returned to the house, I wanted Clifford to play the guitar. Zachary's acoustic, a recent purchase along with his lessons, leaned against a corner in the living room. Clifford would pick up the guitar, strum a few chords, and then put it back down. Every song I asked him to play, he claimed he didn't know, even "Three Little Birds," which was an easy song, the first he'd learned. I tried to coax him into playing by singing a few phrases from his favorite Beatles songs, but he wouldn't do it. I knew that in the same way that it's hard to dislike people who are feeding you, it's hard not to like people who are making music for you, and making music was something Clifford did well. I had some idea that he could pull everyone into the living room and that we'd have a few minutes of sharing something literally harmonious. The scattered chords he played added up to nothing, no tune that I recognized.

"Please take care of yourself," I said, when I finally had to leave on Sunday afternoon.

Clifford flew back to Berlin two days after I returned to Baltimore. I knew Kristen couldn't wait to debrief over the phone, so I gave her a call. She told me that she and Clifford were on speaking terms again but only superficially. There had been no heart to heart, no acknowledgment of the intervention evening's final ugliness.

"He's damaged goods, Kristen. Try not to take it personally." *Damaged goods.* I felt mean calling him that.

"I think we need a second intervention," she said, "about him being a total asshole."

"We'd have to write new letters."

"No, we could just rewrite our old letters: *I hated talking to you when you were an asshole.*"

"Yeah, that could work. *Every time you called me, you were an asshole*," I said.

"*. . . and you were in the process of becoming a bigger asshole*. Simple search and replace," Kristen said. "Well, he's your project now. I've had enough," she said, finally.

Damaged goods. It wasn't a dismissal. But I could understand Kristen's impulse to write him off. You can get hurt handling broken pieces.

My rabbit lady was thrilled with her portrait. I was relieved because I'd finished it in a rush shortly after I got back, feeling bad about having kept her waiting. "Oh, it's lovely! It's just like the end of *The Velveteen Rabbit*," she said, "when he becomes real."

Something about that struck me as nonsensical because Professeur Bonhomme had always been a real rabbit, and I'd turned him into a painting. Granted, I'd read that story long ago, and my strongest memory is of the part where the velveteen rabbit is thrown on a heap of other Scarlet Fever germ-infested toys to be burned. I remember feeling so frustrated: couldn't they have just given him a good wash? Clifford and I had read the same books as kids, and I wanted to ask him if he'd felt the same way.

But I couldn't ask him because I was waiting for him to get in touch. I hadn't spoken to him since I'd left Ottawa—by his choice. He'd emailed me to say that we should talk soon, maybe next week, but he wanted some time to sit with our letters. He attached a picture of what I realized must be the dead baby fox he'd seen by the side of the road. It did indeed look like it was sleeping. It never crossed my mind that we'd never speak again.

I was thinking about what else I might say to him. *Begin with a statement of love and concern.* Good advice for any conversation. I could ask him, Whatever happened to that chunk of mica Dad found for us that one time? I'm pretty sure it came home with us. And then? It must be buried in the house somewhere, he'd say. Unless it's lost, I'd say. And then we'd both picture it, shedding its brittle layers, fragile yet solid—that was the marvel of it—bright and beautiful. You can have it, he'd say, wherever it is. Put it on your bookshelf with all your other treasures.

Most of all, understand that you can't save anybody. That was what the intervention book said, what I read and then chose to ignore. Or was it *everybody*—that you can't save everybody? I can't remember, and I've misplaced the book.

ZOMBIES

The zombie community is fastidious. One faction insists, controversially, that zombies are mindless creatures who can't make the traditional moan for "brains." And that they don't even crave brains specifically but the flesh, blood, and organs of any living human.

This is what I've learned from scrolling through discussion threads. I'm going to take part in a zombie parade, and I wanted to find a few makeup tips. Next week, a throng of gore enthusiasts will dress up like corpses and march through the streets of Toronto, as they have for the past four years. It's not really my thing so much as my boyfriend, Gareth's.

Gareth already has a girlfriend. You could say I'm his other, unofficial girlfriend. But that would be like referring to zombies as "the semi-deceased." I used to sneer at people who claimed that things like this *just happened.* So disingenuous, I thought. With me and Gareth, at first it only seemed to be happening, and I'd convince myself that it wasn't going to and perhaps shouldn't, right up to the point where it was, in fact, happening. Then I let it. We've been involved for almost a year now.

Gareth and I first kissed with *Dawn of the Living Dead* playing in the background at the Bloor Cinema.

The whole place smelled like musty upholstery, and I had a popcorn husk stuck in my throat, but it was still lovely. His lips moved gently, like he was speaking slow secrets into my skin. For the time being, Gareth's girlfriend is away doing her MBA at Queen's while he's staying in Toronto to work on his MA in history. That film was our fourth date—the fourth in a series of horror film dates. Before *Tombs of the Blind Dead*, *Horror Express*, *Død Snø*, and the like, the first time Gareth and I spoke was at one of the departmental mixers. History and English were sharing a midterm party, and my fellow grad students and I had come out to disgrace ourselves with our usual out-of-proportion enthusiasm for free food and drink.

I recognized Gareth from an intro lit course I'd taken as an undergrad. He was handsome as ever, serene and unsweaty, even though the lounge was broiling and he was wearing a bulky cable-knit sweater. I remembered that sweater. He'd always looked freshly windblown, even during the year-end crunch when most of us looked like we'd been locked in the basement and fed lard sandwiches. He rarely said anything in class, which made him seem smarter.

Now Gareth was standing by the snack table, talking to some stubby guy in pleated pants. I glided over, carrying one of the last bottles of cheap red.

"People keep talking about how zombies are hot cultural currency right now," Gareth was saying, "but it's not like zombie films haven't been around for ages." He mentioned that he had an old-school collection of films— DVDs and even VHS cassettes of obscure, cult stuff, bootlegs and limited editions. I asked him if this illustrious collection was given prominent display in his home.

"Nope. No it is not. My girlfriend finally made me pack them all up." Gareth's smile was a modest slice of sexy.

He didn't recognize me. Not surprising: I used to be mousy. And forty pounds heavier. A fat mouse.

"Seems a bit huffy," I said. I hoped the tannins weren't blackening my teeth.

"She thinks it's all junk. I mean, I can see her point. It's definitely a guilty pleasure."

"Well, what about Shelley's *Frankenstein?*" I said. "Classic tale of the dead brought to life. Or *Beowulf.* Filled with supernatural cannibals." I was talking out of my ass, but Gareth smiled again, and I felt clever and pretty. I think I blushed.

"But those are books," began the stubby guy, quietly. Gareth shrugged, and then he and I turned to the snack table as if suddenly interested in a platter of cookies. Stubby drifted over to the chafing dishes.

"So what's she studying? This girlfriend."

"Business."

"Ah."

"I take it you like horror films?"

I hated them. During high school it had been the big thing: sleepover parties with slasher flicks. I'd spend the evening with my teeth clenched, alternatively bored and scared but pretending to be otherwise because I'd been lucky enough to be invited. Later, I was too afraid to walk the dark hallway at night to go to the bathroom. The horror kept repeating on me, like heartburn.

"Oh yes. Big fan," I said.

And so we went from there. Love me, love my dog. Gareth's dog just happened to be the undead.

I'm alone in a house with boarded-up windows. Dark creatures lurk outside, staining the night air with their obscene groans. I've been bitten, and it's only a matter of time before I turn. My unnatural cravings will overtake me. I bind the wound on my arm and conceal it beneath a fresh cardigan. I'm not bleeding, but when I stand in front of a full-length mirror, I'm displeased. I keep trying on different sweaters. Each one makes me look dumpier than the last. I'm wasting valuable time, but I can't stop fussing. That's how the dream ends.

Gareth was always worried that we might be seen by some of his girlfriend's friends, so it was just as well that the movies we went to were shown in broken-down, shit-shabby rep cinemas like the Bloor. If we didn't see a movie in the theater ("for the magnified experience," Gareth said), we'd often watch one from Gareth's collection. After which we'd ravage each other, bruise each other's hip bones. Sometimes we went to my tiny studio, but Gareth is allergic to my cat, Lily, and no matter how much I sticky-rollered the furniture, it was hard to escape the fur. If we went to Gareth's place, we had to deal with his roommate. Ubiquitous Ben, we called him. It felt like we could never watch a film on the flat-screen without him flopping onto the easy chair next to us; cook a meal without him lurking in the kitchen door frame, chatting away; or share a bottle of wine without him swigging a beer alongside us. I don't think he was trying to be a prick, but it just didn't seem to occur to him to give us our space. He sort of ran with the bogus conceit that Gareth and I were close pals, and he told no tales. Kind of a mixed blessing, you could say.

Over time, in some weird, Pavlovic way, I actually came around to liking horror films. I learned to associate campily grotesque dismemberment and bloody mayhem with seeing Gareth. With the taste and smell of Gareth's skin, like freshly baked bread. My friend Allison once told me that I could probably fall for any man if I just stood next to him long enough. Oh, you're funny, I told her. Months ago, I thought I might ask Allison if Gareth and I could use her cat hair-free apartment some time, but then I lost my nerve. For a nineteenth-century scholar, Allison has surprisingly little patience for "digressive bullshit" (her term), and I was starting to feel the chilly breeze of her disapproval.

"Do I have to be the only person to tell you this? It won't end well. Not for you," she said. We were nursing coffees at Futures Café and sharing a piece of sweating cheesecake.

"It's not like I have any illusions about what's going on," I said.

"Keep telling yourself that. You and Mr. Pants on Fire."

I stopped sawing at the cold crust, and Allison took the opportunity to scoop up the last of the raspberry syrup. "Are you judging me?" I asked her, joking/not joking.

She looked at up me, her fork poised.

"Yes, I am. I'm judging everything, all the time. That's what intelligent people do."

Allison's right to judge; she's right in her judgment. But I don't care. I can't help myself. I think about Gareth all the time. In my stupider moments, I think about us getting married. A wedding day, a white dress, a cake. It's just a fantasy.

Gareth and I are holed up in a cabin in the woods. What began as a rustic honeymoon has become an extended stay following strange meteor activity and the rise of the scavenging dead. "We may well be among the last uninfected people on earth," Gareth says.

I'm pregnant with his child and thus carry a great burden of hope for humanity. At least, I think I'm pregnant. Every time I look down at my belly, it's growing, but it's a different shape. Sometimes it's rounded and firm, sometimes it's slack and puffy, sometimes it even looks squarish. At some point, I realize I have a terrible eating disorder. I've been ingesting household waste without knowing it. It comes to me in a series of flashbacks as I'm pushing an old shoe past my lips.

Gareth compares me to Galina a lot. That's his girlfriend's name. *Galina.* At least one syllable too many for my taste—it's like she overstays her welcome in my mouth. The comparisons are always in my favor, which shapes my role as the anti-Galina. Except that the more Gareth complains about her, the more I secretly want to be like her. She seems filled with contradictions, which feel more glamorous than my designated identity as transparent good sport. Galina: a haughty, self-centered bitch . . . and yet an insecure mess. A bulimic. Obnoxiously aware of her own attractiveness. Driven and effective. Her family life dysfunctional, fraught with money problems.

She and Gareth have been dating since high school. Two years ago, she cheated on him.

"But that doesn't make this right," he emphasized. That's Gareth all over. Constant reminders of how bad we're being. So many guilt trips covering the same ground. From time to time, we'd resolve to be just friends. We'd send a few chaste emails back and forth. And then we'd have a friendly coffee, which would lead to dinner or a film, which would lead us back into bed. "If Galina ever found out, it would just kill her," he once said, as we rested against damp sheets. *Wouldn't that be nice*, I thought.

One time while Gareth was in the shower, I snooped through his room, looking for pictures of Galina. I already knew what she looked like—I'd seen pictures on his laptop—but I wanted to put my hands on an actual photograph of her. In the bottom of his desk drawer, I found a cache of old snapshots, dating back to his high school days. There he and Galina were, outfitted for the prom. The scarlet cummerbund of his white tuxedo exactly matched her crushed-velvet dress. Her face looked just as it does now, kittenish, like a Czech model's, her complexion free of any blemish. Beside her Gareth grinned, gazing at her like a boy who couldn't believe his luck. She faced the camera and offered a calm, close-lipped smile, the kind that I could never affect without my slight overbite cracking goofily through on one side. I flipped through the stack and found there was not a single unflattering image of her, even among the candids. I keep going back to those pictures, over and over, whenever he's in the shower. Each time I hope she's less beautiful than I remember.

In the early days of our affair, I remember thinking, *Poor guy just needs a damn break from this domineering, joyless shrew. He's smart and handsome—he doesn't need to be pushed around. He just feels loyalty*, I thought, *and that's admirable. It's none of my business.* And later: *he just has Stockholm syndrome.*

Only once did I put the question to him directly. Why didn't he just break up with her, get it over with?

"We have a lot of history," Gareth said, and then blew his nose. Unwisely, he'd been petting Lily. The cat kept trying to climb into his lap as he sat on my bed, cross-legged and naked. In the silence, I could hear Lily's purring. I started to look for my clothes on the floor.

"It's complicated," he added.

History. Complicated. These words were not invitations—they were crime-scene tape, detour signs. Keep Out, Road Closed.

"Go on," I said.

"I can't just end it, just like that." He spoke quietly and quickly. "Galina's actually very sensitive, even though she puts on this tough corporate-competence act. She used to want to be a pediatrician, you know that? She only started to get obsessed with money after her father got the family in debt. She was supposed to have this college fund . . . and then they found out he spent it all." Gareth said that after such betrayal, Galina had problems letting people in. "And now look what I'm doing."

I didn't make Gareth talk about it anymore. I just shoved Lily out of the way and kissed him.

Lately, I've been telling myself that Gareth and Galina can't possibly last much longer, but I won't have him citing me as the reason for their breakup. After all, I've impressed him as being independent. As being classy and principled— yes, despite our sneaking around. I want him to be with that version of me, not with some gropey-grabby, needy hysteric. That would never do. Sometimes Galina comes to visit Gareth in the city, and so I make myself scarce. Sometimes he goes to visit her. It's become harder for me to be nonchalant about those trips, but at least Gareth isn't around to see me struggle with the act. His last visit with her was over a month ago. I want this to be a good sign.

Brains, the zombie moans.

You aren't a real zombie, I tell him.

He's sitting in the corner of my studio apartment. He looks like a real zombie, with bloated flesh and a missing

eye, but for some reason, I believe he won't be one if I can present a good argument.
    Real zombies can't even talk, I insist.
    Well, you're talking.
    Well, I'm not a zombie.
    Yes, you are.
    No, I'm not. This is stupid.
    You started it.
    Our conversation continues along those lines, on and on. I feel like I can't give in, or he will tear me apart. Or something even worse, which I fear without really understanding.

In the past few days, I've been watching YouTube tutorials and reading webpages on how to transform yourself into a zombie. There are all kinds of tricks for mimicking damaged and decaying flesh. People demonstrate different techniques involving spirit gum, liquid latex, theater putty, and even Elmer's glue, which are combined with layers of dampened tissue paper and blends of makeup. Fake blood is a popular ingredient—although contention surrounds it. One vlogger urged, "Remember . . . zombie blood isn't red!!" Some people insist that it's black. Or gray. Or green. Because a zombie isn't alive. But fake blood, the kind with convincing viscosity, is hard to come by in colors other than red. (I know because I've already bought some.) As I read and watch all this, I consider that this is the problem with the internet: it creates a sense of community where rightly there should be isolation and shame.

    All this zombie makeup—the fabricated rot pockets, the oozing facial desecration—is the aggressive inversion of my usual routine of enhancement and camouflage. Which I maintain with tense devotion since Gareth's good looks make me self-conscious. A recent immigrant to the land of attractiveness, I feel like I'm in constant danger of being bounced, of lapsing into ugliness, the pimple crop thriving if I don't harvest its sebum, the eyebrows growing wild, straying beyond the topiary that I pluck them into, my flesh thickening back up like curdled yogurt. I worry about becoming unappealingly disheveled during sex, all my artful zit cover-up melting off. And yet as the Other Woman, I know I'm meant to be uninhibited and adventurous, coaxed by Gareth's frequent comments about Galina being sexually conservative. Oh, I've been a smug little Kama Sutran, all right. But being boring in bed, I realize, is the privilege of the beautiful.

Galina is dead. She is moaning softly, one arm extended. I'm running from her, but I can never put enough distance between myself and her. I stumble over tree roots. But it switches: I am the ghoul, scratching at a cabin door in some distant muscle memory of how such an apparatus works. Gareth and Galina are inside. Eventually my hand lands on the doorknob, and the door swings inward. Galina is in the living room, putting logs on the fire. I lurch toward her. She turns to face me with a look of disgust, and I stop, swaying in my tracks. I reek like spoiled meat. As she raises herself from a crouch, she drags the poker from the fire. The iron weight makes her sculpted bicep flex.

Oh shit, I think. Except that I can't think. That part of me doesn't work.

I call up Gareth. I've just watched a rather ingenious bit about faking a protruding arm bone with a sculpted white candle. I say that maybe when I come over before the zombie march on Saturday, I can show him how to do it.

"Well, about that," he says. He's just gotten off the phone with Galina. She's coming into town for the weekend. Turns out she wants to dress up and participate in the parade. Even though Gareth is producing signs of irritation (sighs, a flatness in his voice), I suspect he's actually pleased. Galina, clearly, is no dummy. She must sense she's losing him, and she's trying to draw him close again with an unexpected, generous gesture. Maybe she's learned this tactic from one of her team-building exercises at business school.

"Why does she want to be part of this?" I ask.

"Oh, I don't know. She probably figures it's finally cool enough for her. You know how she thinks of herself."

"Cool."

"Yeah. It's kind of a hipster event."

Where to start with this one. "Gareth, real hipsters wouldn't touch this with a ten-foot pole. This is full-on Renaissance Fair, Dungeons & Dragons, nerd fest, no irony, okay? For people who fancy themselves a little edgy, who used to be losers in high school. Or do you still think the Goths were the cool kids?" There are pictures of me wearing black lipstick, but I don't mention that at this moment.

Gareth says, "I wasn't a loser in high school."

"Fine. You were the coolest teenager on the planet. I'll bet you did yearbook."

"Why are you"—he seems hesitant to name my unfamiliar tone—"being so catty about this? Look, I'm really sorry. But all things in perspective, right? It's just a few days. And you can still come to the party."

Gareth's friend Claire is throwing a post-march bash at her apartment. I won't really know anybody there except Ben, whose friend, Gareth suggests, I can claim to be. Beard Ben. Galina can't stand him (she thinks he's a downwardly mobile slack-ass), so she'd never question him closely. I apologize for blowing up at Gareth, and I tell him that I'm just disappointed that I won't get to spend much time with him.

I don't tell him that I'd thought that maybe this party might be a coming-out event for us. As I've been counting the days since his last visit with Galina, I've been hoping that he'd finally introduce me to his friends—as his girl-friend. I have kept that little yearning screwed up tight in a jar, along with other concerns: floating specimens of denial.

It's not by accident that I see Gareth and Galina right now, in the near distance. It's Friday afternoon, and I'm loitering near the park outside Gareth's apartment complex. Actually, "loitering" is too genteel a word for what I'm doing: I'm crouched in the bushes, like some maniac. They've walked up to the edge of the sandy play-ground area, laughing, their clasped hands a swinging knot between them. In their free hands, they each hold a Starbucks drink. I can see she's wearing his cream cable-knit sweater, which complements her long, dark hair; Gareth is wearing his favorite suede jacket. I want to get closer, but I don't. Now he's pushing her on the swing, and she's shrieking with delight, her hair flying. As Gareth retrieves their coffees from the park bench, Galina hops off the swing and lands feet together, arms up, striking a pose like an Olympian. Gareth rewards her with a cheer and then a kiss. Oh, the fucking whimsy of it all. But I can't cheapen what I see, no matter what volume of bitterness I pour on it. They look happy. Like a real couple.

The sun is setting, and as Allison and I sit in her living room, windows open to the cooling air, I tell her my afternoon's sorry tale of stalkerdom. As instructed, I spare neither of us the details. Allison listens, sips her lemonade, nods, and adds a splash more gin. Then she has a story of her own to tell me.

She begins:

"So a friend of a friend was dating this girl. All his friends know about her is her name, Jen. He's spending a lot of time with her, but nobody ever gets to meet her. If they're doing a group activity, he never brings her along. They never see her with him at his usual haunts. He never talks about places he's taken her out to. Seems like he and the girl just hang out at his apartment all the time. So his friends start calling her 'Indoor Jen.' They wonder if maybe he's made her up, but they figure she's got to be real because he's so obviously into her. When someone finally does run into them together, turns out, no big shocker, she's a total dog.

"And that's you," Allison says. "You're Indoor Jen."

"Holy shit, Alli, why don't you just set me on fire? Fine, so I'm not a ten, but done up, I'm at least a solid seven."

"Fuck that. It's not about looks. It's about compartments. You think you're being all decadent and indulgent with this affair. But really, you need to be greedier. Much, much greedier."

◆◆◆

I've decided to go to the zombie march today after all.
Last night, I'd planned on bailing. And then this morning
I changed my plan: I need to talk to Gareth. I want him to
tell Galina about us. It's the least he can do. I'm going to
make a scene, and I don't care if it's in bad taste. It's long
overdue.

Even before I hit the parade route on Yonge Street, I
start spotting zombies. Zombies on the subway platforms.
Zombies in the subway cars. When I get out at the Yonge
and Bloor stop and walk up to street level, it's a full-on
zombie jamboree. Pride Day for the undead. There are
varying degrees of commitment: some people have just
splashed on a bit of fake blood, like me, but someone else
walks past with what looks like an open chest wound, his
exposed heart visibly pulsing, and I feel a ripple of nausea.
I have to loosen the collar of my ripped pussy-bow blouse.
Everywhere I look, there are people shuffling along in
tattered clothes, groaning and besmirched with gore. It's
like the site of some mass civil disaster. Déjà vu layers with
premonition in some horrible way, but I press on.

Because I took so long getting out of the house, there's
no one left at the meeting spot, and I have to find the
party alone. I can't get a hold of Gareth on his cell, and
I can't get a hold of Allison either. She said she might go
with me, as a Regency zombie, but I never really believed
she would. As I weave my way through the costumed
crowds, I start to recognize archetypes. The lawyer zombie is very popular. As are schoolgirl, cheerleader, and
hooker zombies. And soldier, cop, and doctor zombies.
But there are also Rastafarian zombies. Rockabilly retro-
kitsch zombies. Clown zombies. Lumberjack zombies. A
moaning zombie choir. I'm moving much faster than most
participants, who affect staggers and limps. More than
once, when I accidently bump into people, they growl and
make as if to lunge at me. I'm so not in the mood.

When I reach the apartment where the party is being
held, the place is already packed, with everyone talking
and laughing over the blaring music, mostly in zombie

drag. I scan the room for Gareth and spot him in a far corner. He's dressed as a businessman in a disheveled suit and tie, sporting an exposed piece of cranium as his special effect. And beside him is Galina, dressed as his executive counterpart. Their prom photo immediately comes to mind, and the smarmy, his-and-hers, corporate-chic outfits sting me. *What the* fuck, *Gareth.*

As I get closer I can see that Galina has enthusiastically applied the Halloween-costume slut principle to her outfit and is skimpily dressed in the remains of a suit jacket and skirt. Her black eye shadow and deep scarlet lips suggest haute couture. She's also wearing makeup on her torso to emphasize her ribs and clavicles. It seems doubtful to me that a businesswoman would be wearing the stockings and garter belt Galina models. I'm deeply regretful that I dressed in such haste. I perch my glasses on top of my head in an effort to appear hipper.

When I approach them, Gareth looks a little alarmed, but I play it cool for now. I ask him if Ben's around. Gareth tells me he's in the kitchen, and then he introduces me to Galina, who gives that close-lipped smile I've seen so often in her photos. She says, "So I'm guessing you're a librarian zombie? Fun."

"I'm fucking your boyfriend." I want to blurt those words out, but they stay stuck inside me. Both Gareth and Galina are pulled along into another conversation, then blocked from my view by other people. I'm supposed to be looking for Ben, so I head to the kitchen.

Ben is rifling through the fridge, clinking bottles. When he hands me a beer, he almost drops it, he's so drunk, plus he's dressed as a rugby player zombie with one arm. I maneuver him out to the main room where I can see Gareth. I half listen as Ben slurs about the fake arm he'd been carrying around as a prop, now lost. He'd been using it to poke people in the ass. To get rid of him, I ask him if he'll get me another beer, and I promise to look for his lost limb.

I try to wend my way to Gareth again, but I get waylaid by Claire, the party's hostess, a princess zombie. She's created a thematically appropriate buffet and is anxious to explain all the culinary jokes to anyone who will listen. ("See the kebabs? They're pork because that's what human flesh is supposed to taste like—get it? And we've got lady fingers, and of course zombie cocktails. . .") I nod, nod, nod, waiting for my head to fall off and roll under the buffet table. I finally catch Gareth's eye but only for a few seconds.

As I tilt the rest of my beer down my throat, I notice that a short woman dressed as undead trailer trash is looking at me—looking at me look at Gareth. Her large thighs spill from her bloodstained Daisy Dukes, a reminder of my old body type. Every time I glance her way, she gives me a sour little smirk. From the way I saw her hovering around Galina earlier, I assume she's her friend. Or maybe henchwoman: outshone by her hottie pal, I imagine she's decided to embrace being a sidekick and even elevate the role. I hear someone call her by name, Amber. *Just stay the hell out of my way, Amber.*

The party burbles around me, and I cast a look around for Galina, who has not been by Gareth's side for a while. She's standing on the balcony, face to face with some blond guy in an unbuttoned Hawaiian shirt. Right now, she's tracing a finger over the simulated laceration marks on his six-pack. They both laugh as he crumples up, ticklish.

"We have to talk," I say. I've managed to catch Gareth alone and literally corner him. Melodrama rolls off me like stink from an unwashed armpit; I remind myself this is no time for shame. "And not chat. *Talk.*"

"That's not a great idea at this particular moment." His eyes flick around the room. Out on the balcony, Galina's still deep in conversation with Surfer Zombie.

"Just five minutes."

We go to Claire's bedroom and pull the door shut. We sit side by side on the bed, and I start to spill my guts.

"So. I want to tell her. I'm going to tell Galina what's been going on and for how long. And then you have to choose. Me or her."

"Slow down, deep breaths, okay? Where's this coming from, all of a sudden? Look, I really care about you, and we have this amazing connection, but you know I'm not in a place right now where I can just—" He goes on and I feel like he's delivering some speech spliced together from other speeches, producing a montage of clichés. It strikes me that he always talks this way, and I can't listen to it anymore.

"I don't want to be your Indoor Jen!"

"What?"

"I'm saying you don't get to have both. And you don't get to keep lying."

His pupils are dilating, his eyes darkening to match the makeup smudged around his lids. His exposed cranial patch, a piece of molded white plastic, is beginning to skid. I can see he's rattled. But he's also being very careful. There's brittleness underfoot, and if he treads wrong, I will snap.

"Let's just be calm about this," he begins. He puts his hand on my arm. His fingertips press into me, and his palm arches slightly. It's a light touch, but somehow it feels like a push.

"Who says I'm not calm?" I'm shouting now, although I wasn't before, and hearing him say "sssshh!" makes me want to punch him in the face and draw real blood. Someone told me once that you should never argue naked. This is so much worse: arguing in stupid costumes.

Amber, the henchwoman, opens the door on us. "Oops! I thought this was the bathroom!" Her voice is singsongy, but she shoots me a mean look—and gives Gareth and even meaner look—before she shuts the door again. Gareth has now turned red.

"There's your cue," I say. "Run along now."

I get up and leave before Gareth has a chance to. Back in the living room with the other party guests, I walk up to Ben and give him a quick kiss.

"There," I say. "Now you're one of Gareth's zombie army." On the spot, I improvise some rules for a game that I claim is fully in progress. The kiss represents a bite. A bite turns you. There are competing teams at work, each with a leader. The object is to turn more people than your opponents.

"What's to stop people from cheating?" Ben asks. He hasn't sobered up any, but he's focusing. He loves a good game. Oblivious Ben.

"What's the point of playing if you're going to cheat?"

Within a few minutes, people at the party are going up to others and kissing them. Some give little pecks, some lingering smooches. In jest, with earnest lechery, in different gender combinations. It's a hit, this game, and the parameters renegotiate themselves as it moves along. I wonder how long it will take to implode. More than once, someone approaches me to turn me, and I start to get different names: "Jill's rotten crew!" "Now you're with Darren's undead!" Gareth has finally emerged from the bedroom, and now he's out on the balcony having a cigarette, which is something he almost never does. He's avoiding me, just as I'm avoiding him.

I feel a tap on my shoulder. It's Galina.

"Are you with Gareth?" she asks.

"God, no."

"Then I should turn you."

She gives me a kiss. It's a light, warm kiss, and her breath smells sweet, like chocolate liqueur, maybe from one of Claire's elaborate themed cocktails. When Galina pulls back, she gives me that close-lipped smile. I wonder, briefly, if she's playing to an audience, but she's not looking around to see if anyone's watching. I'm the one doing that. Galina's just an ordinary girl, being flirtatious and in the moment. Her gesture could be a supremely sly one, but I doubt it. Well, I'm not sure. Her composed beauty presents a neutrality that I cannot read. I do know this: Gareth won't be telling her a goddamn thing, and neither will I.

I stand outside the apartment building, shivering as droplets begin to spatter the sidewalk, blurring into a mass of gray. Rain is falling on all the living, the dead, and the undead of Toronto. So much for the parade.

I'm walking through a dark forest. The trees appear to be moving with me; the entire landscape has a nauseating liquidity. Directly ahead is a massive oak, and nailed to its trunk is a poster depicting a zombie. The zombie looks a lot like me, if I'd been buried in the ground for a few months. There are no words on the poster, but I understand it's a warning. I hear a crackle and turn: standing behind me is the girl from the poster.

"Pictures of me are always terrible," I say to her.

We fall to the ground as we struggle with one another, turning over and over in the dead leaves. I land a solid punch, and she rolls off me, rubbing her jaw. The tears that stream down her cheeks are black.

She's clearly starving, and I feel sorry for her. Incredibly sorry for her.

"Don't follow me," I say.

That's how the dream ends.

YOU ARE NOW IN
A DARK CHAMBER

The campaign had been a difficult one. Beset by vicious creatures and bad luck, the venturing party had sustained many a gruesome wound, and their resources were sorely depleted, their steeds long gone—eaten by owlbears. Something good needed to happen, like, soon.

George and his friends had been playing the same game for months; Dungeons & Dragons was like that. Nathan, who had lived next door to George since they were five, had designed the adventure, basing it on one of the many available booklets. As for George and the other boys, Bunty and Davis, much as they liked the idea of calling the shots, none of them actually wanted to be responsible for writing the multilevel backstories, mapping out the terrain, plotting potential scenarios, setting up all the details of the monsters and magical objects, and then guiding the party through the adventure. So Nathan was the Dungeon Master, the DM. "Deigned" was the high-rent verb that came to George's mind with regard to Nathan's role: he wore his authority like a cross between a hair shirt and a toreador's cape and kept his dice organized in a plastic tray. In the background, the furnace ticked while they all sat around the scuffed table, a dining room castoff exiled to the basement. "The rumpus room," Nathan's mother called it, with what sounded, to George, like hopefulness. It made Nathan cringe, every time. She would not buy him an Atari, but she was happy for him to host any number of "nice friends."

At last, after defeating the remnants of the orc army, forging a molten river of poison, scaling the crumbling fortress walls whilst fighting off harpies, the boys had managed to navigate past the ancient, curse-laden booby traps to the center of the throne room and crack open the chest containing—they could only assume—the Lost Treasure of Shenrobbah.

George's playing character, a half-elf wizard-fighter named Gargan the Grievous, claimed rights to the first rifle through the goods since it was his spell that had finally shattered the enchanted lock when strength had failed to do the job. Amidst the protests of his fellow adventurers, he pulled out a glittering gold belt and strapped it on.

". . . only to discover," Nathan said, rolling the dice, "that it is, in fact, a Girdle of Femininity/Masculinity, which instantly transposes the sex of the wearer. In this case, male becomes female. Henceforth, Gargan will be known as Gargana." Nathan sat smugly, his maps and notes screened by a propped-up folder.

"Fuck you! You can't do that!" George wasn't usually one to break protocol: for the most part, he managed a kind of courtly diction, echoing Nathan's. But this, George felt, sucked mightily.

Bunty was laughing so hard he could barely speak. Putting it on a little, George thought—as usual.

"Your paladin did advise caution," Nathan said.

"I did." Davis's character, Theo the Defender, was always advising caution. Actually, what he'd said, in a mumble, was, "Way to be greedy."

"I thought it was a Girdle of Giant Strength!" George said. That particular item had been rumored to be among Shenrobbah's riches.

"Nice *girdle*!" Bunty's character was a half-orc assassin named Hess (which stood for H.S., which stood for Hulk Smash.) "Now wait a minute—" Bunty composed himself, cleared his throat. "So is he a hot woman?" The covers of the D&D booklets typically featured Playboy-type women in metal breastplates and little else—Women Without Pants, they called them, or WWPs. The wistful look in Bunty's eye gave George the creeps.

"Before you squander any spells," Nathan said, "I should inform you that only a wish spell will reverse the power of the girdle. This is common lore."

"So I could resurrect from the dead easier."

"It's in the *Guide*," Nathan said. The *Dungeon Master's Guide* was, to Nathan, the word of God. That is, the word of one Gary Gygax, the game's creator.

"Show us . . . your tits!" Bunty was now drumming on the table with alternating fists.

"Show us yours. Oh, come on, Nathan." George had only recently recovered from a lycanthropy curse.

"Well . . . Theo does have access to a wish spell," Nathan said. "He actually has one left on his ring of wishes. The one he's been carrying for the past four adventures in his pyx. No doubt he's been waiting for the perfect moment to help his fellow man." That was Nathan's subtle reminder: paladins were categorized as "lawful good," which meant they were obliged to do the right thing or suffer loss of experience and stamina points.

Davis's character, Theo, had been called right out, and yet there he was making busy with the dregs of the potato chips, blotting them up from the snack bowl with a licked finger. George death-glared at him. "I cannot believe you would forsake your brother in arms."

"I've been saving that wish for a dire situation."

"This is it."

"Yeah, don't be such a cheap Charlie," said Bunty. "Give the guy his pecker back."

"Oh, all *right* already. Just don't come crying to me when we're all half-sunk in a gelatinous cube, being picked clean by boggles."

In their seventh-grade English class, George and Davis were not paying attention to the group presentation on

A Midsummer Night's Dream. Instead, they'd discovered a list of Shakespeare's other works at the back of their play copies and were busy creating alternate titles, taking turns with each passed note:

King Queer
The Merchant of Penis
Henry IV, Part 2: Electric Boogaloo
Hoary Old Anus
Two Gentlemen with Boners
Ream My O and Pooh You Get
The Tempest . . .
???
. . . of Steaming Jizz

Davis snorted, at which point they were busted by Mrs. Barnes. Her eyes narrowed as she read the confiscated list, then tucked it into her folder. George vaguely wondered whether it would become part of his permanent record. Davis sat flushed, hunched, as if chastened into a physically smaller version of himself.

After school, George and Davis headed to detention, and Nathan and Bunty headed to the bus. Nathan dragged a pencil along the row of lockers as they walked.

"Why didn't Shakespeare have dragons?" George said.

"Because dragons didn't exist, retard," said Bunty.

"I know that, *retard*. But he didn't know that. He was olden times."

"Maybe he did believe," Nathan said. The pencil snapped, and he dropped it like a spent pistol. "But how'd you get a dragon on stage? Without it looking totally stupid."

The boys went silent. George knew they would not speak of the school play they'd been conscripted to make props for after they'd all failed to land parts. Oh, how the parents had laughed when the boys lowered, on an ingeniously cantilevered system of ropes they'd spent weeks perfecting, The Dread Beast of the Land, and in that moment, the boys saw it for what it was: a huge papier-mâché turd. With horns. In the wings, the drama teacher was shaking, and no one but George noticed that he was snickering into his fist. George was so fascinated by this sudden unveiling of adult malice that he forgot to be angry.

"Would've be pretty cool if he did, though," Davis said.

"Yeah. It would be like, 'My lord, me thinketh thou dost not...' *Enter dragon*— FOOOM! BUKUSHHHHH! AAAAAAH!" George ran around pantomiming bodily conflagration, until Bunty made as if dousing him with a bucket of water. George dragged his hands down his cheeks in slo-mo, his face melting.

"Some guy probably found dinosaur bones back in the day. Blew everyone's minds, suckered everyone good," Nathan said.

George snorted. "Like he'd know any better."

"Oh, I think he would," Nathan said.

George paused mid-descent on the basement stairs and sat down, as if too weary to continue. He was late, but he hadn't missed anything: Bunty was pushing some point hard. "So guys," he was saying, "I made a new character for myself, and he's awesome! He's a gold dragon, so he can take human form!"

Davis sighed showily while Nathan explained why Bunty couldn't play a dragon. Bunty always had ideas that were stupid but nevertheless took a long time to defeat. Nathan once said that if Bunty's ideas were wandering monsters, they'd have 300 hit points and be protected by an anti-magic shell.

"What's with you?" Nathan asked, looking up at George on his perch. "You coming down or what?"

"There's a kid at school who wants to join the campaign," George said.

"What kid?" Nathan asked. His hand drifted into a protective position over the dice tray.

"Megan Kensworth."

"Who?" Davis squinted. "Oh, yeah, that weird girl with the teeth."

"Not happening."

"Nathan."

"You heard the man! No dogs allowed!" Bunty arf-arfed, then howled, head at full tilt.

George had never wanted to propose Megan's membership, but he'd been roped into it. Megan's mother had apparently been chatting with George's mother, and somehow, they'd ended up talking about the boys' game. George thought it might be his own fault for making D&D sound like some kind of educational extra-credit venture, eager to justify the time he might be conscripted to spend elsewhere. Megan was "having trouble fitting in" at school: this, George knew, was not so much adult code as misperception. Megan did fine with the unpopular losers, but she kept nipping around the edges of the cool kids' circle, which got her teased and snubbed and smacked down. One time George had watched a group of girls continually adjust their swift pacing and configuration—like a flock of birds he'd once seen flickering above a parking lot—so that Megan was always walking in front of or behind them.

"My mom's making me bring her along. It's this or I can't play." This information unbuckled a torrent of baffled protest and accusation so strong that George practically had to raise his arms to fend it off. "Why can't she join us? Haven't we always talked about having new members?" he said.

"*You've* talked about it," Nathan said.

"*We've* talked about it," George said. "Anyway. You know, she can be that one girl. There's always the one girl."

"True," Davis said.

"Some girl," Bunty said. He retched, finger aimed down his throat.

"She'd be a newbie at level one," Nathan said. "She'd either be dead weight or she'd get killed in less time than it took to set up her character, so why bother?" George thought about pointing out that Bunty had entered the game with a character he'd nominally inherited, already at level five, but for some reason that seemed unsayable.

"So we'll up her level," George said.

"You can't just *up her level*."

"Hey, I want to up my level!" said Bunty. "Why don't we all up our levels!"

"Because that would be stupid," George said, without turning away from Nathan. "Why couldn't we, just to get her started? It's not like—"

"If she gets to enter with levels that weren't earned, then I should get five new magical items," Bunty said.

"No one's getting any new magical items. Nathan, listen—"

"Three new magical items and a familiar."

"No, Bunty. If she's stuck at level one, then she won't be able to last in the game."

"Why can't she piss off"—Nathan flicked his wrist—"and start her own campaign?"

"Fine, so just three new magical items. I can live with that."

"Bunty, will you shut the fuck up!"

"Jeez man, take a chill pill! Take three—they're small!" Bunty said.

"Too bad George's *mom* wasn't on the pill," Nathan said.

Eventually, Davis shouted at everyone to stop shouting. Davis came from a home where there was no trace of his dad except fist marks in the wall, so sometimes people hollering at each other made him shake. Seeing his involuntary vibrating just wasn't funny, and it had a way of making the other boys, even Bunty, uncomfortable and decorous; George always privately marveled at how everyone would just kind of smarten up. Nathan grudgingly conceded that Megan could come on a trial basis only—level one but with a small bonus to her stats and a promise that he, as DM, would not "smoke her."

Either Megan Kensworth's teeth were too numerous or her mouth was too small. George wasn't sure: some of her teeth crossed over each other on the sides. All day, she'd been trying to catch his eye at school, not taking the hint. Finally, she caught up with him outside the boys' bathroom. He tried to shake her off, saying that he was late for class.

"Oh, okay. I like to get to class early, too, and get set up." She didn't carry a backpack like a normal person;

instead she wore a leather satchel, strap slung low across her chest, allowing the bag to slap against her thigh as she walked. George picked up his pace and managed to put some distance between himself and her. "Well, see you at Dungeons & Dragons!" She practically shouted this down the hall, which was fortunately near-deserted.

George spun around and made the classic "keep it down" gesture, like he was dribbling an invisible basketball: "Shhh!"

"What? Is it a secret?"

"Sort of." George cast a glance at two older boys several lockers down, laughing and shoving each other. "Uh, yeah. It's a secret."

"Oh!" Megan looked surprised and then delighted. "Right! Of course. Gotcha. See you soon!" She winked hard, as if her eye were biting down on something. Her raised cheek exposed a flash of snaggletooth.

Megan had changed into a dress, different from the corduroy jumper she'd worn to school, and just the sight of her frilled skirt made George feel extra embarrassed. She started chattering right away, saying that she didn't know the game, but she picked stuff up quickly. She already had ideas for her character—an elf named Qu'ella, a warrior maiden with magical talents. Megan's colored pencil portrait of Qu'ella depicted a blonde, pointy-eared figure on top of a unicorn. Both were draped in bejeweled chain mail and looked lean, as if they'd been stretched slightly. Bunty said something about the unicorn's horn resembling a dildo. From Megan's puzzled expression, it was clear she didn't know what that was; Davis blushed. An image popped into George's mind of Megan warily holding a dildo like it was some alien ice cream cone, then scratching her head with it, and he let out a giggle like a burp. Nathan was all business:

"You don't play a female character."

"Aren't there female characters in this game?" Megan blinked.

"Yes, but you don't play one."

"But I'm a girl."

"Yes, well, this is an exercise in imagination, right? So why don't you just *imagine* yourself as a male character?"

"Why can't I play as a girl?" Megan's mouth was hanging slightly open, showing a bit of her teeth.

"Okay, have it your way. Female characters have fewer hit points and lower strength."

"That's totally not fair."

"That's totally fact. Males are stronger than females."

"I bet I can beat you in an arm wrestle."

"I very much doubt that."

George didn't. Nathan's biceps were about the same width as his wrists.

"That's actually a great idea! You guys should arm wrestle!" Bunty said. He'd been flipping through a stray copy of *Good Housekeeping*, marker in hand, blackening the teeth of the smiling housewives.

"I'm not arm wrestling her," Nathan said.

"Megan, we're talking about adults," George said. "The prime of their species." He figured that Nathan had squirmed long enough: now Megan just needed to understand the game.

"That's stupid. Joan of Arc did just fine."

"Until she got burned at the stake," Davis said.

"Barbecued, baby!" Bunty snapped his fingers in Megan's face, causing her to rear back slightly.

"She was not barbecued. Nobody ate her," Megan said. "She was martyred. She had to be. She was a saint. You think Jesus wanted to be nailed to a cross? People do shitty things to good people, and saints have to take it."

There was a silence. "Why?" George said. Somehow, he felt the burden of shutting this down had shifted fully to him while the others now quietly evaluated his performance. "Why?" he repeated.

"Because they're better and stronger."

"That doesn't even make sense."

"It makes sense to me. You just think about it."

"Can we stop this blathering and get on with the campaign?" Nathan said. George was both relieved and annoyed at the interruption: he gave Nathan a glance like, *I got this*, but Nathan pressed on. "We need to stick to the rules, or the guide, the *Dungeon Master's Guide*," he said crisply, "means nothing." Nathan assumed his position at the head of the table, which cued everyone to take their seats, and they began to roll Megan's character into existence. There would be opportunity, Davis told Megan, for her to become more powerful through battle, and this seemed to mollify her.

Qu'ella met the party at an inn, where she'd been working as a serving wench. Megan thought this backstory was ridiculous, but Nathan said it was the only way their meeting her with the campaign underway would be plausible.

"How about she reveals her abilities when she breaks up a fight that's erupted among the patrons over the bill? People could be stabbing each other, tables flipped over, chairs flying around, but then she could cast this spell that—"

"How about you just let me tell the story?"

This was a problem with Megan, George knew: she kept wanting to butt in, to negotiate what the DM had already set in narrative stone. Her interruptions were a bad influence on Bunty, who used to confine his idiot suggestions more or less to the margins of the game ("Maybe it turns out it's all a dream . . . but then we realize we're all having the same dream!") but now seemed encouraged to blurt out stupid shit along the way ("I know! Why don't we add some wormholes? So we meet our future selves! And then fight them!"). Both had to be told repeatedly to shut up.

Still, Megan proved an okay addition to their party, a good sport. George was glad that the bad luck that plagued him seemed to rain down now on Qu'ella: most recently, she'd contracted a fungal infection that enlarged her nose and required an expensive herbal cure costing her all the jewels from her armor. She was always eager for violence of any kind. In the marching order, Qu'ella always went second to last, behind Gargan (George) and Theo (Davis), with Hess (Bunty) protecting the rear, as always; this represented a promotion for Theo. While all the other characters had lead figurines to represent them lined up on the table, Qu'ella was represented by the wheelbarrow from the Monopoly set. They wouldn't let her use the clay model she'd made, which was way off scale, towering over the rest of the party.

They'd battled a skeleton army, outmaneuvered trolls, and tangled with a displacer beast, a tentacled puma that projected its own image, leaving its opponents to thrust at an illusion while the real creature caught them unawares. The plethora of rats had been easy enough to crush underfoot, although it took multiple rolls to finish the task. Morale was high. Now the party found itself emerging from the end of a subterranean passage.

"You are now in a dark chamber with a low ceiling. On the far wall, there is a tapestry, which appears tattered and water damaged, rendering it of little value."

"Let's check behind it to see if there's a hidden tunnel," George said.

"Wait! Don't touch it!" Megan said. "Burn it!"

Nathan continued: "As you step closer, there appear to be ancient runes bordering the tapestry."

"Okay, Qu'ella, do your thing," Davis said. Comprehension of ancient languages was among Qu'ella's abilities; Megan had made a big deal of insisting on it.

"Nope, not doing it. It's a—trap!" Megan extended her arm, finger pointing at Nathan, who scowled into his screen. George knew immediately something was up.

"What the what?" Bunty said.

"'*Appear* to be ancient runes'? Seems a little dodgy, don't you think? Can Hess and I detect any heat coming off that thing with our infravision?"

"I don't take orders from you," Bunty said. George assumed Bunty was not only playing up his character's orc side but also objecting on principle, that principle being dislike. Debate followed, but as Davis/Theo emphasized, "It can't hurt to be careful." George/Gargan agreed. Heat was in fact emanating from the tapestry in waves, indicating the presence of a large living creature, and so Qu'ella cast her "Burning Hands" spell.

"With the impact of the spell," Nathan said, "the rotten fabric smolders, then ignites, and then begins emitting piercing screams. . . ." The tapestry, as it turned out, was actually a mimic, a monster prone to assuming the form of something that invited touch, only to stick fast and then club the victim with a giant pseudopod. As the creature burned, it put up only a feeble fight and was finished off with a quick thump from Gargan/George's broadsword.

Megan smiled at Nathan, her witchy teeth a distracting band of off-white. She said, "Told you I learned quick. You never let us have too much fun before you sic some crazy surprise on us."

"The 'crazy surprise'"—Nathan dug at the air with two fingers—"is the whole point."

Megan kept smiling, which George thought was a tactical error. "I probably shouldn't tell you this," she said, "but you can just about set your watch by it."

"I thought mimics could only be metal or wood," George said. Megan was right about picking up stuff quickly, although she didn't notice that Nathan was fudging the rules here. Such corrections, no doubt, were soon to come.

"We have to get rid of her," Nathan said. He and George sat in the deserted playground, striking matches then blowing them out. They pretended to wish they had cigarettes to light and smoke.

"She's not *so* bad," said George. "Better than I thought she'd be. You still pissed about the necromancer thing?" Two weeks ago, at the very start of a new adventure, Megan had spoiled an elaborate setup that Nathan had spent hours crafting: a town's governor, Aloysius Fost, was enlisting the group's help to recover a magical orb that had fallen into the hands of a necromancer. But Nathan had barely finished delivering Fost's spiel before Megan said, "I think this guy's a bad-news bear, and we shouldn't trust him. I want to use my Detect Evil spell on him," with the result that the group learned (as they were not meant to until far, far into the adventure) that, yes, Fost was really a rival necromancer in disguise, with his own dark agenda.

"We need to kill her off," Nathan said.

"She'll just want to make up a new character."

"Tell her we've decided to wrap up the game." Nathan began flicking lit matches into the dry grass. Little patches flared up then smoldered.

"Like she'd believe us. Quit doing that, pyro."

"Tell her she can't come anymore."

"That won't end well," George said.

"So?" Nathan said, scuffing at the smoking grass. "So she cries. Boo hoody-hoo. So what?"

"My mom—"

"You think she really cares? It was perfect the way it was before. And now Megan's wrecking everything."

George nodded, slowly. She was certainly making life difficult, getting bossy and pushing her luck when no one had wanted her to be there in the first place. One week, Megan had shown up with some other girl, who tried to show around her sketch of an elf before they basically stampeded her back up the stairs. Megan got all huffy. She said she thought the game could stand to be less "clique-y," and she suggested that they take turns being the DM, or at least offer up a turn to anyone who wanted to design an adventure. She said she'd bought some books and was already sketching out a realm. As she spoke, she seemed oblivious to Nathan going all red in the face, all black in the eyes, until he finally, quietly detonated with a poison-gas burst of "*No.*" This had always been Nathan's thing, and she was trying to take it away from him—to take it away from all of them. Worst of all, people at school seemed to know about their Dungeons & Dragons activities, which somehow evolved in taunts from "Dweebs and Dickholes" to "Cum-Eating Faggots." Some people had heard about D&D before, but it didn't make being singled out as known practitioners any easier. Word got out that at the PTA, some parents had raised a concern about Satanic cult activities, with "this D&D club" being a gateway mode of recruitment. George had to endure a mortifying, confusing conversation with his mother: "You don't ever …tie each other up or anything like that, do you?" George guessed that Nathan had suffered a similar fate from the way Nathan's mother announced herself heading down to the basement to throw in a load of laundry, which was something she started doing more and more frequently. The sight of Nathan's father grimly unboxing a VHS in the living room also seemed somehow pointed. Was an Atari soon to follow? The question left a little jagged star in George's stomach. Everything seemed so fraught. What would really happen if they gave Megan a turn at DM? Would it all fall apart, or would it be interesting, you know, just to see?

George had thought Megan might not show up, and he was just trying to name how he felt about that when she arrived, breathlessly descending, satchel flapping, full of sunny apology for keeping the boys waiting. She took her seat, and they plunged into the world of the game.

They had not resumed their campaign for long before Qu'ella was separated from the group. For once, they'd let her lead the party; her leadership was key, since they found themselves in a diplomatically fraught situation, potentially requiring the character's skills with language. Tathrak, Lord of the Drow, had invited them to a banquet, with the possibility of negotiating a truce, an alliance against the Frost Giants. The lord was neither to be trusted nor his wishes defied. No sooner had they reached the end of a narrow, torch-lit corridor than a door slammed directly behind Qu'ella, leaving her trapped in a windowless chamber with Tathrak and his entourage—an assemblage of misshapen humanoid hybrids he'd created with his dark arts. In an instant, any pretense of civility evaporated as the group turned on her, weapons drawn.

"So!" Megan said. She leaned forward in her seat and swung her braid over her shoulder. She'd recently taken to wearing braids because she said they made her feel more "elfin." ("*Elven*," Nathan had corrected.) "I can't say this betrayal was entirely unexpected." She'd also been doing her best lately to match Nathan's dignified diction. "Now I will truly do battle! I cast a fireball!"

Behind his DM screen, Nathan rolled the dice. "The spell fails," he said.

"Completely? Not a single opponent took damage?" Megan said.

"Completely."

Qu'ella fought her attackers, but luck was not with her, not ever. George wondered about those odds but didn't question Nathan as he cast the dice. Roll after roll, her hit points dwindled, her strength faltered, until Nathan said, "You are overwhelmed utterly by their superior numbers. Your sword clatters uselessly to the ground, and the lord and his rank minions set upon you. You are stripped of your armor and then," Nathan paused, "your clothes."

"What?" Megan said.

"The other members of your party hear your muffled screams and try to break down the door," Nathan rolled the dice, "but they are not successful. Meanwhile, in the darkened chamber, some foul rag has been stuffed into your mouth, and you are staked to the ground. Tathrak's soldiers form a line, jostling one another, casting their deformed shadows against the wall."

"Will they kill her?" Davis asked. He was vibrating slightly, and his hands had disappeared underneath the table. George figured they were tucked under his thighs. His own palms were suddenly slick with sweat.

Again, Nathan rolled the dice. "There's a 90-percent chance they will sate their lust and then discard her."

"Ha-haa. You're gonna get ray-aped," Bunty chanted.

"No I'm not!" Megan shouted—so loud that Bunty startled. She pounded the table, and he jumped again. "Gargan, cast a spell. Make it a good one."

"Unfortunately, the chamber has been sealed in an anti-magic shell," Nathan said.

"How would they know that? Wouldn't they try anyway?" Megan said.

"It seems," Nathan said softly, "in the midst of your ordeal, they have been offered a large sum of treasure in exchange for you. And they've accepted."

"No they haven't. You're making that up. When did that happen? That's not how the story goes. Guys?"

No one said anything, and it was as if they really were sealed off from her in some dark corridor. George had a vision of gold coins spilling from a filthy burlap sack, slumped against a stone wall. He should say something. He should—

"Well. I don't like this game." Megan stood up, one fist closed around her braid. "You guys"—her voice broke with tears—"are MEAN!"

George looked at the little playing figures bouncing on the table as she thundered up the stairs. One of them, Gargan, toppled when she slammed the door. *Just stay down*, George thought.

Davis, at this point, was full-on quaking.

"See. I'd told you she'd cry," Nathan said. They waited a few moments to see if Nathan's mother would intercept Megan and then they'd be in trouble. Nothing.

"Nathan, you're a dick," Davis said.

"Oh, *I'm* a dick? I didn't see you rushing to her rescue, *Theo the Defender*."

"I guess we're all *mean*." Bunty singsonged the last word, but his falsetto sounded faltering, unsure.

"Yeah, well, it shouldn't have gone like that," George said. "It was shitty." Davis's head had started to bobble, as if he were one of those horrible shrunken celebrity dolls. With a slightly formal air of calm, George turned to Nathan, and Nathan mirrored his action:

"I was going," Nathan said, "for realism."

"We're playing a game," George said, "with wizards and orcs."

"It was an act of war. Terrible things happen. Worse things than that," Nathan said. George had known Nathan a long time: shame was in there somewhere, like a nickel in a ceramic piggy bank, and maybe if you shook him hard enough, or broke him, it would come out. *You cheated. You've always cheated.* And George let it happen.

Nathan shrugged. "It's just a game. Get over it. She's gone now. You're welcome."

"Look, she brought cookies," Bunty said, pointing to a side table. Each cookie was decorated with a lopsided "D" in chocolate chips. Nathan picked up the plate, ripped off the plastic wrap, and began eating them doggedly, like he was destroying evidence. They all watched him for a moment, then joined him—Bunty, Davis, then, reluctantly, George.

"Girls talk," Bunty said and bit into his second cookie. He had older sisters. He didn't elaborate, and George was pretty sure he didn't know what he was talking about. Who would Megan tell, and how would she explain it, anyway? It was done, and they'd all move on.

At school, Megan was putting up posters advertising something called the Fantasy Club. George felt sorry for all the crap she'd take for that name and for how all the posters would get torn down, every last cloaked enchantress, every last blood-dripping sword, but at least she looked happy in this moment. Two other girls were helping her, tearing off pieces of masking tape and making loops. So she'd finally settled in with her own kind. One girl had an elastic harness of headgear bunching up her hair in the back; the other one was both tall and chubby—an ogress. Megan was definitely in charge, and it suited her, George thought.

George had come to this conclusion about Megan: her teeth were weird, but she was not ugly. Her clothes were all wrong, and she had a funny look about her generally, but she might fix up okay. George had seen girls pull themselves together, reconfigure and transform. Guys changed, too, but the change was less dramatic, less impressive. And less important.

The poster the girls had just finished taping up began to wilt off the wall, and they all gave a cry then began giggling. Megan turned her head and caught George watching her, loitering unconvincingly by the drinking fountain. He gave a spazzy little wave; she nodded, then returned to smoothing the poster's corners. It had been more than a month since they'd acknowledged each other's presence, so it felt like a big deal to George.

"Megan, wait up." George caught up with Megan at the bike rack, just as she was wedging her satchel into her bike's flowered basket.

"What do you want?" she said. Her voice sounded all hard, like she was imitating someone tougher than her. The phoniness put George off, and he revised the nice greeting he was going to give her.

"Well, hello to you, too," he said.

"You want 'hello'?" Megan turned to him, her face in an unfamiliar furrow. "You guys were total jerks to me."

"Don't take it so personally."

"What, you guys being total jerks?"

"No, I mean, it's just—how the game is sometimes."

"Oh, please. I am a *person*. So I take things *per*sonally," she enunciated. For emphasis, she shook her head and threw her hands open: *Duh.* "You guys sold me out. Like I was garbage. You sold me."

If he were Nathan, George thought, he'd throw her words back at her with a smirk: why would we sell garbage? But he wasn't Nathan. "You can't take everything that way. It's not all about you. You know?" George said.

"What are you talking about? It's not *not* about me. Right?"

George said nothing. They could go on like this, he realized, back and forth, back and forth, forever. She was worse than Bunty, who could at least be brought around, even if by torturously slow degrees. The Russians would launch the nukes, and she'd still be there, an animated radioactive skeleton, arguing with the cockroaches and the blast shadows.

"Right," Megan said again, as if to reply for George, then returned to giving her oversized satchel a shove.

Was she crying? George put his hand on her back, and the way she flinched at his touch—immediately, without seeming to choose to make her point—surprised him.

He watched her as she rode off, backside raised from the banana seat, the frame rocking back and forth under her as she worked the pedals, satchel listing precariously with each sideways bob of the basket. To think he'd been worried that Megan might ask him to join her club. It was probably just for girls anyway, in an unspoken way, which made it even more so. If it lasted. George turned back to the school: there was something he needed to do.

In the hallway, Mrs. Barnes spread tape across the corners of a Fantasy Club poster while George held it in place. "That should do it!" she said and gave it a little pat, adding, "Very nice." The artwork was really quite impressive, in its own way, and Megan had spared no effort with the gold and silver colored pencils. George waited until Mrs. Barnes had disappeared from view before he took the poster down. The teacher had come across him just when he'd peeled it from the wall, and she'd assumed he was putting it up. George held the poster up for a moment before he folded it and stuffed it into his backpack, joining all the others he'd pulled off the walls. Even though the halls were emptied and dark, it was risky, this mission. A mission of mercy. He would spare Megan the heartache of seeing her all posters systematically desecrated, spare her all the mockery that would come her way, all the sneering, just when she was finally finding her footing amongst so many slippery, jagged rocks. It was, he told himself, the least he could do.

CHARYBDIS

I.

Some details remain clear. His penis was shockingly small. "Micropenis," she later learned, is the medical term for such a small-sized member. Tiny and slightly tapered, like a finger. In girth, leaning more toward pinkie than index. And that was fully erect: she hadn't seen it flaccid. When she pulled down his boxer shorts, he smiled, closed his eyes, and tucked his palms behind his head—all as if to say, "Behold!" Pot smoke and music leaked in from the hallway outside her dorm room ("Wish You Were Here" was playing on repeat—or is that just the song she remembers?), and she wished she could join her hallmates in oblivion.

She'd been lukewarm on having sex with him in the first place, and now she felt a disconcerting mix of pity, ever-renewing surprise, and resentment. Still: she fellated him, had intercourse with him, and, as she recalls, her vagina barely registered his presence. She'd been on top; she went into full service mode, affecting a kind of concentration and efficiency that passed for enjoyment. She can picture herself narrowing her eyes and sucking in her cheeks. In truth, she had sex with him because she wanted him to leave. It's not that she didn't like him, she just . . . felt squirmy about his attraction to her. But then they had sex, and his penis was tiny, and he didn't leave, wouldn't take a hint. The thought of him lying there all night, wedged against her in her narrow bed, emanating smugness, and then wanting to have sex again in the morning was unbearable. Hours later, she finally got him out the door, but she can't remember how. She must have invented some excuse about an early-morning class—no, she must have invented some better claim on her time because everyone skipped early-morning classes. Unfortunately, that part of her memory is missing, so she can't quite defeat the feeling of some sliver of herself being stuck there forever, marooned on damp sheets with him and his tiny penis.

II.

In the years since, she has seen penises that small. On her young sons, twins, who used to charge around the house pantsless, innocent as putti, their little privates like sculpted marzipan fruit, blush-tinted and smooth. "You're outnumbered!" people would say, meaning she was the sole female in the house. And yet she felt amplified, not diminished. If anything, the little boys were part of her entourage, which included the two cats (both toms, incidentally). Whatever room she was in, they were bound to populate, the cats materializing from some portal, the boys in noisy, competitive orbit, never quite managing to stay in whatever room she might banish them to. They loved Daddy, but Mommy's sandwiches always tasted better.

Now those boys are older and properly clothed, the cats buried in some other city. There must have been a day when her sons' privates became fully private, a day that slipped by silently, like the last day she breastfed them, the last day she was called "Mommy" and not "Mom" by either of them, the last day she read to them. All invisible milestones on a one-way path.

III.

That evening was over twenty years ago. What brought that tiny penis to mind now? Of all the things to remember. Possibly, it was sparked by something she found online, some sleazy story she couldn't help reading. About the president's Mario Kart-mushroom penis. About the over-sized celebrity who modestly revised the claim that his girlfriend had made earlier in the press. His penis, he said, just looks big to her because "she has such small hands." How poetic.

Something else she has read online: we only remember because we reimagine. So how many copies of copies of copies has she made, a flipbook of penises, a matchbox-sized tome, plied by a thumb, filed in some mental junk drawer?

IV.

There had been no foreshadowing of the micropenis, no distant rustlings on the college grapevine, not the slightest suggestion of any lack of confidence from the man himself. Au contraire! He was fine-featured, with amber eyes and flowing, Byronic hair. Not tall but not short either, his body well proportioned, lightly muscular—quite common for that age, the time before everyone hit the metabolic speed bump of their late twenties and discovered that they couldn't consume all the beer and pizza they wanted. Before they all softened but also became more substantial. In her mind, he is tanned and relaxed, sitting at a wooden table in the sun, and (in this scene where she is not trapped with him in bed, sticky and souring) a version of herself is seated across from him, likewise taut with youth.

He was a recent graduate, working temp jobs in IT, and they had mutual acquaintances at college. Over the summer, they had fallen into a kind of friendship, meeting in cafes and talking. Those were the days when she was rich in time but otherwise broke. Adrift but unpanicked about her future—it all seemed so inevitably bright. Someone would sort it out, notice her, make an offer, pick up the tab. She had a large roster of people she could meet up with and have endless coffees and pints of beer, and he was on it. He was smart and funny but not crush material: he would want to be her boyfriend, and she didn't want that. There hadn't actually been much in the way of flirtation, which, she now thinks, may have been a form of flirtation on his part. Later that summer, he'd gone with his family to vacation in France, and he wrote her letters and sent postcards, which she'd read carelessly and kept absentmindedly. They are stored along with all other written correspondence from friends over the years and her undergraduate papers that now seem like something written by another person. She has revisited those papers but not the letters.

V.

Someone had once given her a box of pasta shaped like penises—all rendered in artful loops of dried semolina. It must have been for her bachelorette party. Standard dirty fare, but what was the joke, exactly? As a bride, she'd be eating dick by the bowlful, ha ha ha? Or maybe it was a tribute to all the dicks she'd eaten, a ritual farewell. She imagines the pasta was sold alongside chocolate lollipops and cake forms in the same genre, beside the furry handcuffs and dice suggesting sexual positions. The lewd jokes seem like a holdover from an earlier time: there's now no pretense that marriage is some kind of bold initiation into the world of sex, the first time a woman will see some man naked and aroused.

She's sure she eventually ate that box of pasta—she's pragmatic, after all. She has a mental image of those penises in hot water, softening and expanding.

VI.

Strangely, she remembers that she spoke with him about penis size, in the pillow talk aftermath of sex. How had she managed such a masterpiece of diplomacy? Such arts are lost to her now, such courtesan subtleties; she can't recall how she phrased her questions. Maybe she hadn't been subtle, but he was clearly oblivious to having a micropenis, so such questions wouldn't have seemed like hurtful hints.

He said something like, "My dad was really open about sex stuff, and nudity wasn't a big deal in my family, so I never had any hang-ups."

Surely, all fathers must seem Brobdinagian to their sons, hairy and huge, and all sons must think themselves tiny in comparison. But no doubt they make some unconscious adjustment for scale, in the secret, genius way all children have.

VII.

"Objects in the mirror are closer than they appear"— that phrase always makes her mind stutter. The first time she ever noticed it, as a novice driver, she had to slow it down to parse it, and to this day, it resists her cognitive flow. What they mean to say is, "This mirror makes things looks small and thus far away. But, dear reader, they are not!" All things behind you are subject to optical illusion.

VIII.

Not long after her encounter with the micropenis, she told her friend, Gavin, all about it. Gavin, one of two gay men she knew at that time in her life, considered himself to be a connoisseur of penises, and so she was sure that he'd be an appreciative audience. That he would help her workshop this messy experience into a snappy little anecdote. "Hmmm," he finally said, as if pondering some philosophical Question of the Ages. "You know, maybe your vagina's just TOO BIG!" They burst out laughing at the very notion. No vagina is too big. Or too small, too hairy, too gross; there are no standards, no possible way to disappoint, to disqualify. Any port in a storm, and it's always raining. "I suppose," she said, "if you're giving her head, it's a different matter." Standards would apply then, they conceded, but only then. Oral sex was a favor, something you offered a girlfriend, a crush, a catch, not someone you were just getting your rocks off with. It required an outlay of stamina and skill while the penis was sidelined. "Cunnilingus": even the word sounded embarrassing, like "panties." They agreed "panties" sounded dirty, and not in a good way.

IX.

"You know what sounds stupider? 'Blow job.'" Gavin said.

"Maybe the idea is that you're, like, inflating him?" she said.

"'Going down on her.' Sounds like the opposite. Like you're insulting her."

"Or like you're using her as an elevator."

She imagines them having this repartee, although she's pretty sure she's rounding Gavin up a little, too eager to make him her sassy gay friend when, really, he'd been more of an acquaintance she exoticized. That fall, she'd returned to school for her senior year to find that friendships and priorities had shifted in such a way as to leave her wide social circle still intact but with few true allies. That was probably why she was so open to hanging out with Mr. Micropenis, even though she knew, at the time, that she should seize this opportunity to create distance between them, that he could not be allowed to lay claim to her, to pull her prematurely out of the golden sphere of campus life and into the world of rent and responsibility, a world where a low-paying job was not just a summer's lark but an enduring identity. It all sounded dirty, and not in a good way. But he made her feel less like she was a suddenly fading star, less like everything she'd cultivated was worthless currency, and so, yes, she was available for a movie, a meal, a drink.

X.

Mr. Micropenis. He is deserving of a name, and of course his parents gave him one. But to name him is to reveal him, to summon him, bad magic. To give him any name is to bring him into kinship with those of the same name, which would surely be unfair.

XI.

In college, she lived in an all-female dorm, and one evening in her sophomore year, she and her floormates came up with nicknames for their vaginas. This was in response to a rumor about boys in the residence across the street christening their dicks. The girls tried to outdo each other with weirdness and grossness, and looking back on it, she's not sure if it was an exercise in irony, internalized misogyny, or both: The Snapper. My Tuna. Mrs. Gash. Captain Beefheart. Hot Pocket. Furburger. She named hers Charybdis, from the *Odyssey*. She was taking a Classics course as a GPA booster, and it was fascinating news to her that the ancient Greeks had so many female monsters. Charybdis: a sucking, wet void, a destroyer of men. In some myths, Charybdis is a voracious beast, hoovering back seawater three times a day and then belching it forth, creating deadly whirlpools; elsewhere, she's imagined as the whirlpool itself. Her nebulousness seemed fitting, given what she represented—woman's dark interior. It wasn't flattering, but at least it was epic.

Swashbuckling dirty talk with her floormates aside, she did not feel that she was epic. More than a decade past her first encounter with *Our Bodies, Ourselves*, but also a decade or more from childbirth, she still felt there was something grudging about the vagina. She admired the clarity of the penis, how unambiguously it seemed to communicate feelings and intentions: I like you! I want to have sex with you! I'm enjoying myself! I'm done now! The economy of the architecture, the vulnerability of the equipment, which shapeshifted with a touch of fraudulence and comedy—all that was, she had to admit, very winning. She'd been with boys who, one time or another, could not get hard (beer, anxiety), and she'd found their dismay so misplaced because it wasn't like the condition was permanent.

XII.

All these horny, yearning songs on the radio—they don't apply to her anymore. She has aged out of that program, a middle-aged mom, driving through suburbia, ferrying groceries to her stable family unit, her youthful, carnal chaos miles and miles and miles behind her. She drives carefully, so as not to run over any kids/dogs/cats/squirrels/rabbits/any combination in pursuit or flight. Nurturer on wheels, guardian of all the tender, stupid things. Oh baby, I want you so bad, I'm burning for you, it cuts like a knife, why do you treat me this way, you broke my heart, we broke my bed, my crotch is on fire ooo ooo ooo, etc. She sings along, but it's not nostalgia exactly, maybe more like regression because many of these songs are new, and she has no business mouthing these anthems. This is the verbal equivalent of mom-dancing, and in a few years, her sons will deem it unacceptable, no doubt. Already, Dad is not allowed to sing. He does anyway—he likes the oldies—and turns the volume up so loud the dashboard vibrates. "Crazy Train," "Hell's Bells," and "I Won't Back Down" are particular favorites.

XIII.

Mr. Micropenis was angry. This came as a complete surprise. Even more of a surprise than the smallness of his penis. She remembers his anger with enduring clarity, despite the fact that so much else surrounding its revelation remains fuzzy.

After they'd had sex, during the days that followed, he mercifully didn't crowd her, but he was definitely keen to see her again. She recalls the confident tone of his phone messages, like he assumed their getting together was a foregone conclusion. She agreed to go see him at his apartment. She needed to talk to him, in person, about the way it had felt, having sex when she hadn't really wanted to: weird, like a mismatch of intentions, a wrong turn into an uncanny valley, a mistake she'd made with her body. These days, she now thinks, there is a better vocabulary for such gray areas, and men who wish to appear sensitive and enlightened know better than to act entitled.

In any case, the conversation did not go well. She fumbled and faltered, and as he drew her out, he did so with increasing coldness, his brow crinkling with mock confusion, a stern parent forcing a child to reiterate some preposterous lie. The relevant line of dialogue that stays with her is this: "So I was a mercy fuck."

The correct answer was, "Yes, close enough," and the correct move was to leave. Instead she got stuck, mired in her impulses to make it all nice again. His anger made her feel apologetic, and haven't women been wrestling with that script forever, but she also felt some shared embarrassment. On and on the conversation went, with each of them repeating different versions of their lines, the micropenis forming a strange subtext, both a non sequitur and the essential theme:

But how can you be angry with me when you have such a tiny penis?

Of course you're angry: you have a tiny penis.

This is because I have a tiny penis, isn't it?

Wait—are you saying I have a tiny penis?

Please accept my apologies for your tiny penis.

Oh, she'd been mealy-mouthed, backpedaling—no wonder she can't recall exactly what she said. Had she actually brought cookies to that awful meeting? Yes, she did—she really did. What a dope.

XIV.

Truth be told, over the course of her life, she had seen too many penises. Been naked too many times, with too many people. She'd been driven by desire and affection but also by curiosity. She slept with people out of a sense of acquisitiveness, like she was crossing entries off a list.

She slept with people she'd had an eye on, intriguing acquaintances drawn closer, not strangers—at least there was that. She slept with people because she was in the habit of sleeping with people, often on the first date. On two different occasions, two different men had said the exact same thing: "I hadn't been expecting this." Which at the time, she thought was bashfulness but she now recognizes as leeriness. Perhaps she had pressured them. Sometimes they smelled bad in the morning—funky breath, dirty clothes, stale sweat. One guy's armpits stank so bad, she lay there thinking up a comparison, finally settling on, "like something died and was buried in a coffin carved out of a huge salami." It made her giggle. They showered together and had sex under the pulse of the water, gleefully risking major mishap due to the slippery tub and incompatible pelvic heights.

She slept with people she didn't want to sleep with— Mr. Micropenis was not the first and not the last. She slept with people because she loved them. She'd had boyfriends and had not found monogamy a challenge: on the contrary, she basked in it.

It's not that she now finds promiscuity immoral but rather, in retrospect, spiritually expensive. She is not regretful but wistful. It was, for her, a careless way to live. She does not have an impressive mental archive of penises since all but the truly remarkable have faded from memory.

XV.

Turns out he's a serial killer.

She has already advised the students in her Intermediate Fiction class against twist endings. She further cautions them that if she has to read one more story where the twist ending is, "turns out he's a serial killer," she will, in fact, turn into a serial killer.

She wonders what Mr. Micropenis is up to now. He's probably not a serial killer. Although following their awful conversation, he did turn into a bit of a stalker.

She'd left his apartment too stunned to cry—that came later, alone—and she assumed that would be the last they'd see of each other. But two days later she saw him at a lecture she was attending in one of the university's great halls. Camille Paglia, the Jordan Peterson of her day, was to hold forth ("If civilization were left in female hands, we would still be living in grass huts"). She remembers the scene clearly: she'd been drawn to attend through a kind of dazzled pique, and she was just settling into her seat when she noticed him, Mr. Micropenis, determinedly picking his way through the students clotting up the aisles. He was beelining toward her, staring at her, his demeanor just shy of a man hacking through a jungle with a machete. His facial expression seemed unchanged from the last time she'd seen him, as if he were still lit by the fires of that indignation. With no wish to be scorched again, she grabbed her bookbag and bolted.

In the days following her escape, he left messages on her answering machine (an actual answering machine, like you see in cop shows), each one longer and more aggrieved than the last. "You now avoid me public places," he said, although there had only been that one near-meeting. There was also an uptick in pretentiousness: "I have a right to know what my crime is," he said, in a later message. She wondered if and when he might turn up at her dorm but was thankful that the ladies at the front desk were unholy bitches who begrudged entry to everyone, never mind some unaccompanied guy without an ID card. His messages filled whole tapes, which she switched out before they would revert to being taped over. He did not swear, name call, or threaten violence—but he did not relent.

Up until a few years ago, she still possessed those tapes, and she could have sourced some dead technology on eBay to review exactly what he'd said. But she had Marie Kondo-d the lot: they did not spark joy. When she came across them in a box full of college memorabilia, she knew exactly what they were, and they emanated some spiky, wounded energy.

XVI.

At the time, she told no one about his answering machine messages. Not the residence don, not the police, not a friend. The messages were not funny; they were simultaneously pathetic and scary, and she didn't know what to do with that weird intersection, which kept wanting to cancel itself out. Shame also formed part of the Venn diagram. Shame has its own powers of freezing the mind and tongue.

He continued to leave messages, and she continued to collect the tapes, which she stacked in a corner of her bookcase. The tapes were evidence, the tapes were talismanic, the tapes were synecdoche.

XVII.

Synecdoche, she reminds her students, is when a part represents the whole. The part is not a microcosm of the whole but a portion deemed to have symbolic significance. Examples she does not use:

Way to be a dick.

Let's get us some pussy.

You can be a real prick sometimes.

Don't be such a cunt.

XVIII.

She asks herself: Is it worse to be a cunt than a prick? By what degrees?

In insults, "prick" is roughly synonymous with "dick," although "prick" is meaner, more deliberate, and "dick" is stupider. Being a pussy or a cunt is worse than either of those things, although they are at opposite poles, the former being weak, the latter being overbearing and vicious. Men can be pussies and dicks and pricks, but only women can be cunts.

XIX.

She wonders what it was like for him, that moment when Mr. Micropenis was fully unveiled to himself, if there ever had been such a moment.

"How could he not have known?" her husband asks. (She has told him the whole story for the first time: fifteen years of marriage, and they have not run out of material. They are writers, emotional strip miners, and they will never run out of material.) "He *must* have known," her husband affirms.

"I just don't think he knew. Not consciously. I didn't say anything, not even when he was being a jerk, so maybe no one did. And it's not like guys compare erections, right?"

"No."

"Or check out each other's penises? Straight guys, I mean."

"No. You take the next urinal over, if you can."

"And where were his compensatory skills? None! He was totally selfish in bed. Blissfully unaware. That's what it seemed like."

"But there are things you know without even *wanting* to know or seeking them out. Facts and norms that are generally available. He must have known."

"He knew . . . and he didn't care?"

"Of course he cared! Every man cares. And from the sounds of it, this guy was an intense motherfucker, and he really, really cared."

XX.

After about a week, he stopped leaving messages. No tapering off, no shifting of tone, just all crescendo and then done, no more, the project abruptly abandoned. For months afterward, she still avoided being alone and travelled in protective packs of fellow students, which was easy enough to do on campus. Gradually, she lost the habit of scanning her surroundings, checking to see if he might lurch into her line of vision, waylay her outside some class, the dining hall, the library, the gym, especially after dark. That is to say, she was no longer on the lookout for him, but she remained vigilant, instinctually alert.

He disappeared from her life as obligingly as a flat character exiting a novel—that's her memory of the experience. The narrative trajectory of her life lifted up and out, plunged and extended, climbed and leveled. He was, she might say, a little bead far back on a very long string.

XXI.

He is looking at her right now, or rather, she is looking at him. She thinks she has found him, grace of Google. His professional smirk, the slightest suggestion of a sneer as he seems to rear back ironically from his beholder, makes her think, *Yes, this is the guy.* Mr. Micropenis. Well, Dr. Micropenis: he has a PhD and is a professor of economics at a small but reputable university. Less handsome, craggier, but still presentable. From the looks of his hair, which remains abundant, he seems to be of the opinion that he doesn't need to wash it daily. Social media reveals no trace of him, so she can't sleuth out whether or not he's married. He probably is, given that most people his age are; he has an aura of fulfillment of conventional expectations. Likely, he's fathered children. What does his wife think of his tiny penis? God, she'd love to know. She imagines that the wife is kind; that she doesn't care for sex; that she is a patient teacher, a frank and inventive lover; that she isn't shallow. She imagines the wife is like a loaded gun, waiting for the right moment to fire her devastating truth; she imagines the wife's love has made the tiny penis irrelevant; she imagines the wife will never be enough to reassure him because to reassure him is to diminish him.

He probably has a story he tells about his wife. A story about how they met is a standard one.

But what is the story he tells about *her*, his past whatever-she-was, if he tells any story at all? Possibly, she is an amalgamated character, merged in memory with other women who wronged him, a "crazy ex-girlfriend." (In her experience, men may claim women as "girlfriends" even if it was never true; the tag smooths out complications, boosts ego.) The crazy ex-girlfriend who ghosted him for no reason, no reason at all.

XXII.

"Someone must have told him," her husband says. "Not everyone is as nice as you."

"I suppose," she says.

And yet she isn't nice. Here she is, telling anyone who will listen.

CHANGELING

The courtyard is all green—green grass, green leaves shimmering, and buttery afternoon light fills the room. We were lucky this suite was available when the time came. As we sit in silence, my mother faces the window, her pale skin aglow, and I face her. You would never know that I've been itching to leave since the moment I arrived. But an hour has passed—I've been very disciplined—so I get up to say goodbye, my hand already sliding into my purse to grab my phone.

"Are you going to put me in one of your books?" she asks.

Put her in a book. Like she's a flower I'm going to crush between the pages.

"Do you want me to write about you, Mom?"

"Is this for school, dear?" She swivels to the mirror over her dresser and gently plucks at her hair, primping as if I'm about to take her picture. Before she turns back to me, she does a very subtle double take. I've heard my mother refer to her own reflection as "the old lady who watches me." Today is one of her good days.

But on a bad day, or even a not-so-bad day, over the course of a single visit, one moment she might remember what I do for a living, my career, and in the next, she'll think I'm still in college. Or in high school. Or in elementary school, and so the woman she's talking to is someone else, not me. "Parts of your mother's neural pathways are dying, and when those neurons have to leap across, it's not certain where they'll land," a nurse told me in the early days, back when my mother could still manage on her own.

"See you tomorrow," I say because it's much less complicated to just say "tomorrow" instead of "in two or three days, or a week, or two, depending on what else comes up."

I kiss her forehead, and she murmurs something.

"What's that, Mom?"

"You smell like cunt," she says.

Daisy, my wife, laughs when I repeat this, throwing her head back, pausing in her ministrations to the stir fry on the stove. "Takes one to know one," she says. Daisy is the kind of feminist for whom "cunt" can be an honorific, indicating strength, but still an insult.

"To be clear, she didn't call me a cunt." Aside from "dear," my mother doesn't call me anything, not even Titania, which is the name she used to insist I should have been given.

"Well, you are what you eat." Daisy practically shouts this, like Oprah announcing a guest.

"If Quentin hears you, he'll die," I say. My son isn't a prude, but no teenager wants his parent's sex life shoved in his face. "By the way, in German, it's a pun: *Man ist was man isst.*" I am always amassing and passing on funny factoids to Daisy, much in the way people impose collections of trinkets on others. *I saw this frog in a yoga pose and thought of you.*

"Who knew the Germans were so hilarious? Call the boy—I think this mess is ready. Shit, I forgot the rice. Does it matter?"

"I suppose not." I'm the only one who eats it anyway.

My mother is cuddling the doll, crooning to it and stroking its soft face. The scene is like a replay of when

Quentin was that small: she'd been a fool for him, besotted and patient in a way that seemed so unlike her and yet suddenly, mercifully, revelatory of who she truly was or could be, and I'd so wished I'd lived closer at the time since I could have used her help. I got the idea for the doll from a short news piece I'd come across about alternative therapies for Alzheimer's patients. At first I thought some department-store baby doll would do, and then I second-guessed being cheap: I had a vision of my mother rubbing one of my polyester-blend skirts between her fingers, and somehow, pairing her with a more plausible baby seemed more dignified. The "Real Baby," as it's called, has individually rooted hairs, silicon-molded features, realistically contoured limbs, and it costs as much as a designer watch. The eyes are permanently closed, which I think is the one feature that rescues it from the Uncanny Valley.

"I have the magic touch," my mother says—singsongs to me, really, with an edge of *nyah-nyah, nyah-nyah nyahhh.*

"How's that?"

"Finally asleep. Shhhhh." She waves me off, and I worry a little about her losing the doll—I actually hadn't thought much beyond presenting it to her—then I figure it's fine. I've already told the staff about it. The home has a policy against valuables on property, so I've said that the doll is of sentimental worth.

No one wants to visit my mother except me. My brother, Robert, usually pleads long distance; from the way he plays that card, you'd think he lived in another dimension irreconcilable with our own. Rob would argue that Marfa fits that description.

When I ask Quentin to come, he twirls both index fingers just above his earbuds, indicating the classic *cuckoo dans la tête* and also "I'm not listening." The surly teen thing is performative: I know Mom unnerves him. Lately, he can only be coaxed into coming along to play piano in the lobby for the zombies, as he calls them.

My second marriage coincided with my mother's cognitive decline, and so Daisy falls into the category of people my mother can't place. "Or won't place," Daisy has corrected. And I see her point, so most times I don't push it, even though I feel an acid burp of resentment whenever I head out the door to play dutiful daughter, solo, while she's snuggled up with a glass of wine and the lucid adult company of her Kindle.

From time to time my mother asks after Quentin or Robert or about Dad, who has been dead for half a decade, although in mom's mind he's just out on the longest grocery errand ever. More often than about any of them combined, she asks about my ex, Tom. She never had any time for the guy when she was *compos mentis*. Now her memory has revised him from a feckless, bearded bum into a sleek catch, to whom I am still married, lucky me. She asks after him again today while she's fussing about with the doll's swaddling. The pleats in the blanket are just so, like the folds of origami. Other than a faint pink smudge on the doll's forehead, it looks to be in good shape.

"Tom's fine," I say. "Quentin's going to be spending part of the summer with him in Oakland. He can't wait." Should I tell her? Why not? The slate will be wiped clean in a moment. "He's been working on a documentary about drag performers. Those are men who dress as women."

"Your brother was one of those."

"No, he wasn't. Isn't."

"Wasn't he? Oh yes, that's right. It was you. You were always dressing up. As a boy! How's Thomas? Will he be coming next visit? I know he's busy with work, so don't bother him about it. I'm knitting him a sweater." Margaret, she tells me, should really take better care of that man or someone else will.

I'm Margaret. Maggie to my friends; who knows who I am to my mother today. She has never knitted— not now, not for Tom, not ever. Maybe she's thinking of macramé? I seem to remember some knobbly owl tacked to our kitchen wall, which the house must have molted with the 80s. As for dress-up, for a stretch of time my mother used to dress me and Rob in identical outfits. Rob is just a year younger than I am, and as kids we could easily have passed for boy-girl fraternal twins; instead, with our matchy-matchy corduroys, striped shirts, and bowl cuts, I was often mistaken for Rob's twin brother. As I recall, it made me feel conspiratorial and close to Rob, as if we were both involved in some kind of grift. At the same time, I had a hunger for white sandals, pink dresses, and hair ribbons, and in later family photos, I can see that those eventually prevailed.

"Imagine," Rob says, during our regular debrief over the phone. "She could have been putting me in dresses."

"She didn't want two girls. She wanted two boys." I'm wondering if this might be true.

"She wanted attention," Rob says. Twins used to be a bigger deal, back in the 70s, hence the now-defunct *Lookit! Lookit!* fashion of dressing them alike. "Besides," he continues, "who wouldn't want two of me as opposed to two of you?" I won't rise to his mock sibling rivalry, which is actually a distant Xerox of the real thing.

"Give my love to Erica and the girls," I say.

Next visit, my mother resumes her sweater-knitting theme. Just because her memory is shot doesn't mean she isn't capable of sustaining ongoing obsessions.

"I keep having to redo it. The cleaning ladies keep taking it away to work on it, and they muck it all up every time. I'm sure they mean well, but they're not very educated. Stupid as gum. Some of them smell funny." By "cleaning ladies," she means nurses' aides. I checked her closet today and learned that she's been unravelling a few of her cardigans. I have no working theory on this. I wonder if I should bring her some wool and needles so she can actually get to work on something real, maybe on a blanket for her doll. I could watch some instructional videos on YouTube and then teach her. Maybe.

"Knitting a man a sweater is a surefire way to get him to break up with you," I say. "It's a well-documented fact."

She looks at me blankly, then says, "You think that's why he left you?" Then she leans in and taps my hand, like she's sending a telegraph. "Sounds like an excuse, dear. Dollars to dodos, it was another woman."

Dollars to dodos—I like how that sounds. Is it any more nonsensical than the original saying? Back at home, laptop warming my thighs, I look up the origins of the phrase and find that it dates back to the nineteenth century, when donuts cost significantly less than a dollar. I make a mental note to tell Daisy. When I'm working, I have to discipline myself not to justify every little detour as "research." I am, in fact, writing about the internet, so it's easy for the boundaries to get blurry. My working title is *Internet Memes and Other Online Executions.* I want to explore reputation and regret, shaming and schadenfreude— that's how I've pitched it. It's not the only book of its kind (do we ever get there first?), but it's all in the telling, the curating. I'm interviewing different people who've become reviled following a particular online incident, usually a involving a video they posted themselves or cellphone-captured footage someone else uploaded. I'm not so much interested in a gradual accumulation of notoriety as a pivot point and its aftermath. After the flash in the pan, there is the steady burn of shame and shaming, and this stretches on, as I explained to my agent, over the course of years. Unlike my mother, the internet never forgets.

I am going to visit my mother again at the home. I realize that term's a bit old-fashioned, and most people now say "retirement residence." Also, it is not a home, even though it's meant to evoke the home, with its beige carpeting and nonconfrontational, semi-genteel furnishings. Not quite the idiom of a hotel. Residents' rooms are staged with salvage from former lives, an ottoman here, a recreated arrangement of photographs there. Something to tell Daisy: the German term *heimlich,* meaning home-like, familiar, finds its opposite in *unheimlich,* which means not-home-like . . . that is, mirroring the home-like but off somehow. In other words, uncanny. No wonder everyone is perpetually disoriented—I mean, dementia aside. It's not so much like purgatory as being suspended in some dream. And from time to time, such as right now, I visit that dream. Sometimes, it all makes me think of some stupid experimental play with forced audience participation. I deposit my son at the lobby's piano, where he launches into the theme from *Cats* with virtuosity and unaffected gusto. I envy his generation's ability not to give a shit about what they like.

I find my mother trying to nurse the doll. Deflated boob resting on the baby's face, a look of bliss on her own, her head tilted back and rolling side to side against the armchair. The phrase "milking it" comes to mind, and I wonder what memory, exactly, is fueling this pantomime. And to think I'd almost persuaded Daisy to come along this time.

"Her name's Titania," my mother says. Her palm alights on the doll's forehead in the manner of a christening.

She'd so wanted to call me Titania, but thankfully Dad put the brakes on that idea. I can picture it: a period of innocence, where I believed myself queen of the fairies, followed by years of me being called "Tit" and "Titanic," followed by a battle-hardened phase where I insisted my name was Tania, followed by a faux-ironical reclaiming of the original Titania, with me pointing out the Shakespeare connection to everyone who didn't ask.

"She never had so sweet a changeling," I say.

"She needs changing?" My mother bends her head over the doll and sniffs.

"No. Never mind." I find that I don't have the patience today for some "Who's on First?" routine. Still, I thought the line might stir something, some embers, from all her days as an English teacher.

"My husband had a secretary named *Margaret*," she says. "Imagine saddling some pretty young girl with an old-lady name. Marrr-gret!"

Maybe she's my real mother, I almost say. I figure my mother wouldn't get the joke.

"Maybe she's your real mother," my mother says.

"Why did you say that? Mom?" But my mother is making eye contact with her reflection above the dresser, not me.

"Daisy," she says. "Now that's a pretty name. When is Thomas coming to visit? I'm knitting him a sweater."

You Should Have Known Better. That's another possible title for my book. Quentin suggested it. He'd been looking through the notes I'd left spread out on the dining room table as he crunched through an apple. I imagine he finds my use of paper and ink exotic and inefficient. He's no sooner made his suggestion than he retracts it.

"These people are idiots," he says.

"I can't entirely disagree. A lot of them have done idiotic things."

"Idiotic is boring."

"There I disagree."

One of my interview subjects, a high-profile vegan blogger, was caught on film gnawing on a piece of fried chicken. "I have a meat tooth," she told me over the phone, which almost made me like her before she reverted to her talking points. "I'm still a vegan," she said. "Sometimes I eat meat. But just for the protein. I was going to make a video about that. But I'm entitled to a private life, right?" She doesn't grasp her own contradictions, and what interests me most is not so much the *won't* of it but the *can't*. It brings to mind an article I wrote a few years back about adultery. "My husband wouldn't do that," a woman said, even after he'd fathered another woman's child.

Another of my interview subjects, a beauty blogger, did a video in what appeared to be blackface. "It was a charcoal mask. How many times do I have to explain that to people?" she asked, as if she expected me to come up with a number. She said the watermelon she ate was part of a fruit salad. "I always eat something. It's a combined *mukbang*-tutorial thing. That's my niche." I asked her if she'd intended to be satirical. "I'm making fun of myself, okay?" She sighed.

My most recent interview subject, my most notorious one, does claim that he was being satirical. He says that he was trying to bring awareness to bullying by *pretending* to be a bully. Years ago, in a video called "That's an L," he bragged about tormenting a kid from his high school. The previous week, the boy had committed suicide—but my guy was somehow unaware of that fact. "It's all been taken out of context," he began before stopping himself. "I don't know. . . . I don't know how to fix it," he said, ending the interview abruptly, I think to pass out: he sounded drunk and miserable. He has no other online presence besides this video, which has been reposted by others multiple times and has gathered several million views, and his apology video, which has likewise made the rounds. The police have verified that the guy has never had significant direct contact—virtual or otherwise—with the boy who killed himself, but it doesn't matter. People still hate him. I'm debating whether to circle back to this one.

Circling back. Quentin has sprayed my papers with flecks of juice from his apple, which I gently wipe away. I used to get angry about such things, messes, impositions, and the like, but from my very early days as a parent, I didn't so much watch my temper as keep a foot on its neck, and eventually, that red impulse just died off.

I try to impose some order on the pages that I let him mess up, but my mind is elsewhere. With my mother, I am always circling back, whether I want to or not. I've heard it said that with dementia sufferers, you need to appreciate *the moment*, stay in *the moment*. The thing is, you can get stuck answering the same question, hearing the same story on a loop, and being "in the moment" takes on a different meaning, with an emphasis on singularity—the same moment, again and again. A goldfish in its bowl, ever discovering and re-discovering the same treasure chest, *Groundhog Day* in miniature. So there's that. It's the long-term memory lapses that feel like the real whispers of decay. The first time my mother didn't recognize me, I thought we'd reached some ominous milestone. Then I realized we'd probably passed that marker earlier, without my even observing it. *Hello, dear.* When did that become nonspecific? I'd stopped paying full attention because it was hard to pay attention. There were things I didn't really want to observe, like how threadbare and sloppy she looked, despite the clean new clothes I dropped off regularly. Gone were her ironed blouses and jaunty pantsuits, her precisely executed lip liner and eyebrows.

For a while, my mother existed differently in my mind, and whenever I saw her, the rapid corrective left me taken aback. Imposter! Who is this shabby, muddled old lady, shucked of her polished shell? At first, the staff at the home let her carry around the last of her ladylike accessories, her purse, empty of cash or credit cards, of course. That didn't stop my mother from rummaging through her bag, looking for her wallet, wanting to give me a five-dollar bill because she wanted a pack of Dunhills and "God knows when your father will be back." She came to be so riled about her missing wallet, leveling accusations against "the cleaning ladies," that one day, the home's director handed me the purse and told me it would be better for it to disappear, for me to tell her that the bag was elsewhere, safely stowed. Thankfully, she's never asked after it.

"I have a solution," Daisy says. We've been flipping through the remainders of stuff we haven't watched on our various streaming accounts—really, it's too late in the evening for us to start watching anything—trying to make a selection. "You could bring along a sweater and tell her she knitted it."

"Who?"

"Your mother. I guess you'd have to bring it for every visit then sneak it home again so you'd be ready for the conversation each time. Hey, how about this one? It's about a British lady detective. Bet she takes zero bullshit."

"I'd prefer not to spin some lie if I don't have to."

Daisy puts down the remote and gives me the full glamor of her green eyes. "But what about the baby doll?"

"I'm not lying to her about the doll. I just let her believe what she wants. She's going to be demented with or without the doll. I'm just giving her something to do because it can't be all watching television and kindergarten crafts."

Daisy resumes clicking through the options. After a moment, she says, "I understand—I do. It's just that . . . maybe it's nice to see her a little vulnerable? But you know how quick that can turn, and you're the one I care about in this equation." Daisy puts her hand on my knee, and I put my hand over hers.

"Come with me next time," I say.

"You don't have to go, you know," Daisy says.

When I go to put some snacks away in my mother's mini fridge, I discover the doll stashed behind some half-eaten pudding cups. My mother is always stowing things in odd places, misfiling things, but also hiding them from imaginary thieves. Last visit I found her bottle of shampoo, uncapped, oozing into her underwear drawer.

"Hello, Titania! What are you doing here?" I say. The baby is grubby and damp, its once-curly hair, what's left of it, unwound and wilted.

"She wouldn't stop crying!" My mother has stood up and is pointing at the fridge with her fists.

I once heard about a woman who stuffed her newborn into the freezer—postpartum psychosis, that's what they'd call it now. I move the doll to the bed. Her cold rubber flesh is starting to bead with moisture in the warm room.

When Quentin was a baby, I would hear him crying even when he wasn't crying. It was like a ringing in my ears. In my brain! Set to a permanent channel of distress. "Colicky Critter" is what my mother called Quentin, but she'd been able to soothe him.

My mother looms over the doll. "Stop fucking crying, you little shit!"

"Mom, don't talk that way, please." I remind myself to speak to the staff about adjusting her meds.

After I settle my mother in her chair by the window, I bust open the package of gourmet cookies I brought along. It's not Diazepam, but chocolate does soothe the savage breast. My mother's chewing gradually slows to a contemplative, bovine pace. Like mine. We face each other and munch.

"Were Rob and I difficult, as babies?"

"All babies are difficult. That's why they're cute. So you don't kill them."

"Really."

"Margaret—your face! It's just a scroffly little doll. See?" She hoists herself out of the chair, scattering crumbs on the floor, and retrieves the doll from the bed. Like a cat, she gives its cheeks a lick and then scrubs at them.

It's true that cute babies are treated better. There have been studies. Of course, cuteness is no guarantee of good treatment. I watch my mother spit-clean the doll, and I think of all the Barbies I destroyed, all those sweetly smiling blondies, because I was bored with them. Or maybe I somehow thought their rubber limbs would heal, their hair would grow back.

Something to tell Daisy: one time I got a kill fee for an article I wrote about a fetish club that enacts BDSM on sex dolls. The scenes they played out included tableaux of capture and sexual assault. After reading my finished copy, the editor said it was too disturbing. Some of the men who were into it, and they were mostly men, were pretentious. ("Each man kills the thing he loves," said one, as he held a lighter to his dolly's breasts.) Most had been shy, barely able to look me in the face, never mind speak to me. In truth, it had made for an unbalanced article, and I never really grappled with the real questions. Such as: What sort of milquetoast would feel the need to subdue and silence a doll? What sort of bully?

On my way out the door, a staff member intercepts me. She says that my mother's doll has become a trigger for anxiety, that it's been making her agitated, and that really it might be best for it to disappear altogether, like the purse.

"I think she's a little more attached to this doll than her purse," I say, "but I'll see what I can do."

◆ ◆ ◆

"How's your book coming along?" Rob asks. I can hear my two little nieces, Rachel and Tilda, in the background, screaming with laughter. Their game seems to involve making the dog bark its fool head off.

"Great! I've got a whole ragtag crew of internet misfits."

"White ladies calling the cops on people of color? Karens?"

I tell Rob that I'm looking to turn up some lesser-known and more ambiguous villains, so I've advertised online in places like Craigslist and Reddit, encouraging people to contact me.

"Tell me about some of the ragtag-iest." I hear something crash on Rob's end. "Girls! Take it outside! Let me find somewhere quiet 'cause they'll be right back in here in five minutes."

Rob puffs into the phone as he climbs the stairs, and I describe a recent interviewee, a guy who shot a "sleeping" (dead?) piglet during a live video feed. He was making good on a threat that "Wilbur would get it" if he didn't make his Kickstarter goal. He'd been raising funds for a biopic of H.P. Lovecraft.

"I know that guy! Not personally. I read about him when he was just starting."

"Did you give him any money?"

"No. Maybe I should have."

"I thought I'd be finding that some of these people have been judged unfairly, but I think what I'm seeing is a representative slice of their personalities—"

"You make them sound like salami. How's the babe?"

"She's great. We finally got your wedding gift. Unless you weren't the one who sent the salad spinner."

"'The babe with the power!' I meant mom's baby doll."

I tell him that our mother is still very taken with the doll. Even so, she's been a bit rough on it. There are dent marks, head to foot, from where she's hit it with her hairbrush. I'd caught her in the act.

"Well, well. I guess old habits die hard," Rob says.

Oh, so we were going to have that conversation.

In which Rob would accuse *me* of having memory problems, and I would tell him to stop picking sores. My words tumble from me: "She spanked us when we were being little assholes. Was it ideal? No. She had too much on her plate, and Dad was never around, and sometimes she just snapped." It was a different era. People smoked in restaurants, didn't wear helmets, and hit their kids.

"Between you and Mom, I'm surprised I survived my childhood."

Rob's got that joking tone in his voice, stagey and slightly high-pitched, which is meant to let me off the hook. I picture my brother sitting in his "lair," that is, his pottery studio, surrounded by animals—mugs shaped like cats, bowls shaped like fish. And I picture him, a little boy, sprawled on the shag carpet of his bedroom, making tiny, elaborate Play-Doh figures. That I would later mash flat, one by one. We would have a fight about it, during which I would break his finger.

"I'm sorry I wasn't a nicer big sister."

"It's okay. We're still here, aren't we?"

Yes, yes we are. I tell him that I shouldn't have been such a bully. That I'd never meant to injure him on purpose. I'd gone too far that time, been too rough.

"I know."

"You were so afraid of me, you didn't tattle, even then—you told Mom some lie about getting your hand caught in a door."

There's a pause, then an intake of breath. "Maggie. I wasn't afraid of you. I was afraid *for* you. Mom would have killed you."

"This is a classic situation where you mistake the melodrama of a kid's perspective for something real. And I say that with kindness." Now I'm the one putting on a campy tone.

"You don't have to agree with me for it to be true," Rob says.

"Are you quoting your therapist at me?"

"No, I just read it off an inspirational poster I have hanging in my studio."

"You're only pretending that's a joke."

"Hang in there, kitty! Teamwork!"

A few of the people who answered the online ads so-
liciting interviews for my book were plain crazy. Seiz-
ing on my question, "Has the internet ruined your life?"
they claimed the internet was talking about them all the
time, giving them toxic, coded messages. Or not-so-cod-
ed messages. One woman was convinced a demon was
stalking her through all her YouTube selections. Her initial email was so articulate I thought she might be speaking metaphorically; during our phone conversation, she
seemed scattered, crow-voiced. She would be watching
something, she said, and then the demon would sneak in
somewhere in the background or reveal himself in some
brief flash in the speaker's face.

"Maybe you should stop watching," I said.

"The fuck the fuck! If I don't keep an eye on it, that's
when it'll get me! Don't you fucking understand?"

I'm tempted to meet up with her in person and
have her show me just what, exactly, I do not fucking
understand, but mostly my instincts tell me to stay away
because I might not be able to get away—she might
never leave me alone. And what if I started seeing what
she's seeing? I think if you stand next to a crazy person
long enough, you start going a little crazy yourself.

"Crazy," Quentin would likely tell me, if I used that
term in front of him and pressed him to explain his
eye roll, is not the correct term for such a person as my
internet demon lady. His objection would be that it's not
just unkind but uninformed. Something to tell Daisy: an
old Irish way of saying someone was crazy was to say that
they were *ar shiúl leis na sióga*, "away with the fairies."

I learned that from an Irish storyteller Tom was filming
in Cork. Fairies, the man said, could steal your wits away
with them, carry off your essence, leaving behind some
diminished version of you as a kind of decoy to all your
earthly cohort. Malicious, whimsical plunderers! In class
photos from rural schools, the man claimed, you see all

girls—not really all girls, but the boys were disguised as girls to confuse the fairies who preferred to take boy children. Now that's something to tell Rob.

In the lobby, Quentin pounds away at the poor old piano, striking out the chords of "Never Gonna Give You Up." My son, Rick-rolling the old ladies who have come to expect Andrew Lloyd Webber and Bach. For the first time in a long time, Daisy has also come along—no discussion, she just picked up her purse, touched up her lipstick, and followed me out the door.

Daisy and I have barely set foot in the suite when my mother rushes at us, her hair sticking out in spikes, gooey with something like hand cream.

"Where's the baby?" Her breath comes out sulfurous in my face.

"She's right there, Mom." I point to where Titania is lying facedown on the windowsill, her wounds bathed in sunlight.

"Not the doll, cunt-face! The . . . you know, the *baby*!" We've been through this before. She thinks that someone is playing a cruel trick on her and that I'm in on it. I've tried taking away the baby, just as the residence staff suggested, but it only makes things worse. When the doll's out of sight, my mother won't stop looking for her, tearing her room apart. And now the doll is in sight, and it's not helping: the room's in a shambles.

"Titania," Daisy says, sliding the chair cushion back into place, "is with her father."

Daisy has a way of slowing the pulse of a room. A way of bending attention subtly toward herself and activating some vibe of relaxed anticipation.

My mother, it seems, is not immune: "Oh, I see," she says. She straightens her shoulders, and it's only then that I notice she'd been holding herself in a crouch like some theater witch. "Yes, of course. Margaret mentioned that. People don't believe in playpens these days. The babies just wander off."

"I gather you used to tether Maggie to the garage door with a length of rope." Daisy has seated herself in the chair, legs crossed, hips slightly levered to the left. The effect is not so much ladylike as womanly. She's all but batting her eyes.

"Who told her that?"

Daisy just smiles and holds my mother's stare. I have busied myself with picking up clothes from the floor and putting them back in the dresser. For the time being, I leave Titania where she is. I may as well be invisible, and in this moment, I prefer it that way.

My mother takes a step toward Daisy. "Who are you?" She never asks this, never admits that she doesn't recognize someone—never assumes, never seems to realize, that she should recognize them. It's like she's breaking the fourth wall. And then—"I know who you are." My mother's lips compress, then smack open. "You're Margaret's *special friend*."

"Maggie's wife."

"I know what you are. I know a hawk from a handbag, so don't play sly with me."

"I wouldn't dream of it."

I continue tidying, mopping up a water slick from an overturned plastic carafe. Part of me is worried about what will happen next, and part of me is thrilled. When my mother—I was going to say, "when my mother was alive"—was still with it, I'd danced around what I assumed was her disapproval. I knew she thought outright bigotry was in bad taste; I also knew how she really felt, and although we'd telepathically dared each other to say something, neither of us ever did.

"My daughter already has a baby, so at least there's that. You're too pretty to be the man of the house, but I'll bet you wear the pants. Or maybe you take turns. How does that work anyway?"

"Beautifully. How's the sweater coming along?"

"It's finished!" My mother breaks into a smile so big, so open-mouthed, I can see her fillings, and just like that, the mood shifts. She goes to rummage in the depths of her closet, her rump toward us as she calls out, "The old lady taught me. I just watched her this time. I watched and copied. Just like when I was a little girl."

The sweater she produces is a lumpy patchwork, and I think she must have cannibalized other sweaters to make this one. What did she use for knitting needles—pencils? All that unravelling and sewing and purling, it would have taken some persistence, some ingenuity, both to make this thing and to keep it hidden. The phrase "Snitches get stitches" runs through my mind. That and "crafty," and it occurs to me that I, too, am always making my own sweaters from someone else's wool—a whole career based on magpie-d experiences, a crow by the roadside.

As we leave, I manage to tuck the sweater in my bag without my mother seeing me. I could mail the sweater to Tom. He might even wear it, with a minimum of snide showmanship, maybe even resisting an Instagram post. He'd leave it behind somewhere of course, on the back of a chair in some pub, like the bum that he is.

I want to take Titania, too, but my mother is holding her tight. Her grip is around her neck, and I notice that the doll has a piece of tape over her mouth. I know why it's there because I can remember—years ago—her pressing it to my own face, thumbs pushing into the sides of my cheeks. She told me it would cure my hiccups, which little girls get when they talk too much. This is something I don't need to tell Rob because he was there.

"I feel like I've gone through hell for it. . . ." My interview subject falters, then gives a rueful smile. "And so much time has passed, and I've lived with it, and I've finally moved on from it, and then I watch that video . . . and it's like it just happened." He's agreed to a Zoom conversation, although you'd think he'd be permanently leery of all potential audio/video capture of himself. He introduces me to his dog, who skitters into frame. "Rigsby is a retired greyhound," he says. They look a bit alike, true to the saying, both lean, handsome, with a bit of tragicomic hauntedness in the eyes. He says that he trusts me, that I seem like a nice lady, and even if I'm not, he trusts me anyway. "It's a choice I can make. Trusting someone. I used to flinch away from everyone, as a reflex. Or I'd get all desperate, trying to convince people. I'd be, like, 'I'm not that guy! I'm not that guy!' But I am that guy." The guy who: insert ignominious/ immoral/cruel/stupid/misguided act. Does it matter?

It matters: "The thing is," he adds, "I'm this guy too." Somewhere toward the end of the interview, the grey-hound whimpers then pees on the floor, cocking a leg near a bookshelf.

"Guess he needed a walk," I say.

"I just took him for a walk." Voice raised, hard on the heels of my words. "I walk him every day. He's just nervous." So he's also this guy—angry, his zen no more than a brittle pretense. And in that moment, I think, *My heart has gone out of this book.* I don't want to write about these broken people anymore. But I feel like in some other universe, the book already exists, so I have to make that true in this one. I remind myself that at some point or other, I always feel this way about everything I've ever worked on, and there's nothing for it except to shove down those feelings and push on through.

Our mother's needs have moved beyond the level of care this residence can offer: a nursing home is the next stop, with enhanced medical care but no bingo nights, no carpeting, no euphemizing mixed messages. When we clear out her stuff, Rob and I, we find the doll in pieces, hidden about the room. Serial-killer style. As I've said, I am used to finding my mother's possessions stashed in weird places—a shoe in the sink, her winter coat balled up in her laundry bag, pictures taken down from the wall and slotted behind the bookshelf. Even so, the doll's dismemberment represents a cohesive project, like her sweater. It would have taken some doing, wrenching all the limbs from the sockets with those arthritic hands, staying focused on the task with that misfiring brain, completing the systematic concealment.

"Bad baby!" I say, waving a leg. There are teeth marks on it. We find the head and see that all the hair has been pulled out, the face gouged. With what? She hasn't had access to scissors. A knife from the dining room, maybe. I hold the head up to the window like I'm showing it the view, and the light, the lovely white light, pours through the empty sockets. "Poor baby," I say. "What did you do to deserve this?" I feel Rob's hand on my shoulder.

"It wasn't you," is what he says.

Meaning, the doll wasn't a stand-in for me. Meaning, I've done my best or close enough. In the final stages, Alzheimer's can make people angry and aggressive; I understand that. They have delusions and act out in irrational ways. And also: It isn't happening to me. It's happening to our mother. Who is still our mother, no matter what she does.

The doll parts go into a bag, the bag goes into a dumpster, and we go into the back-row seats of the minivan, with my sister-in-law grinning behind the wheel, Daisy riding shotgun, and the two little girls in the seats in front of us, braiding Quentin's shoulder-length hair on either side, tugging his head back and forth as they work on him. "We're giving him a makeover! He's getting a makeover!" the girls shout. Several of the tiny braids they've formed are coated in silver glitter, which I can tell will be a bitch to wash out. Quentin is being martyred, he is being vandalized, and yet his face is serene. Like he's forgiven them already.

BIRDIE

She turned the pages, but she was not reading them. The book was a prop: she wanted to make it clear that she was not lonely. Without her book, she found it hard to maintain the correct, businesslike-yet-whimsical expression suitable for a woman sitting alone on a park bench, eating a sandwich.

As she chewed, out of the corner of her eye she kept seeing a little gray bird wandering around on the ground. The bird walked in slow spirals, with a kind of performative nonchalance that was hard to ignore.

"Hello," the woman said, at last. She could no longer stand the sustained pressure on her sense of propriety.

The bird made a slight shake of the head, as if startled, and said, "Oh! Hello."

The bird and the woman looked at each other, their pleasant expressions stiffening in the awkward, lengthening silence.

The woman suddenly noticed something peculiar and pathetic about the bird.

"It must be very difficult, being a bird without wings," she said.

"What are you talking about? I have wings. See?" The bird flexed what were either severely stunted wing buds or the remains of what had once been bigger wings but were now shorn to stubs. The gesture lasted less than a few seconds, after which the woman wasn't sure that she'd seen any wings at all.

"Ah, yes. Do you live around here?" the woman asked the bird.

"Right now, I don't live anywhere." The bird looked like she was trying not to cry. The little creature stared at the ground, and wind ruffled the soft feathers on her head. "I've got money. It's just that no one will—" Her voice faltered.

"Why don't you come live with me?" offered the woman. "You can live in my belly."

"Really? That's *ever* so kind of you," the bird said.

The truth was that the woman was eager to have another lodger. Years ago, she'd evicted a tenant whose presence seemed, at the time, inconvenient. The decision proved rash. It took her years to find a replacement. This subsequent tenant left hastily, in the night, after barely three months. The woman thought things had been uncharacteristically silent in the rental unit, and when she investigated, her suspicions were confirmed. The girl hadn't even settled in. Except for a ring around the bathtub and a bunch of blackened carrots in the vegetable crisper, you'd never have known she'd been there.

"Ever so kind," the bird repeated, the words coming out like song.

That must be a great advantage but also a great drawback to being a bird, the woman thought: you'd expect your life to be like a musical.

The bird was, at first, an ideal tenant. She was quiet and undemanding. She used almost no hot water or electricity. Prior to the bird's arrival, the woman had typed out a list of rules and taped them to the refrigerator ("No smoking on or within twenty feet of the premises. No modifications to the suite without written consent. No loud parties. Tenant must purchase and install drawer liners. . . .") but this sort of precaution seemed to have been unnecessary. The bird no more made her presence felt than a dust mote, a poppy seed, a bit of dandelion fluff.

Gradually, however, the woman began to notice small puckers in the placid fabric of their mutual space. She would hear faint noises; she would catch a whiff of an unfamiliar aroma, which would disappear upon her sniffing. These disturbances, she told herself, were to be expected. The impressions left on her senses were so minor she even convinced herself that she imagined them.

But she did *not* imagine them. The woman began to detect the shape and rhythm of the bird's day, based on all that she increasingly could not help but observe secondhand. Both she and the bird were homebodies, so the woman had ample opportunity to familiarize herself with the bird's habits and much to familiarize herself with. The woman began to take notes. Years ago, she'd bought herself a satin-covered journal but had never gotten around to writing in it; she thought she might as well get some use out of it now. Under the heading "Bird," she composed an ongoing list:

◆ *Bird uses rosewater atomizer, occasionally gardenia.*
◆ *Bird cannot cook hamburger without setting off fire alarm.*
◆ *Bird likes Bach, particularly cello suites.*
◆ *In afternoon, bird watches soap opera in Spanish but talks back to TV in English.*
◆ *Bird not satisfied with placement of bedroom furniture, has rearranged twice.*
◆ *Bird has slight dust allergy.*
◆ *Every Friday, bird bakes sourdough bread.*
◆ *Bird dabbles in oils, poss. also watercolors.*
◆ *Morning shower takes no more than twenty minutes, never fewer than ten.*
◆ *Sometimes bird cries herself to sleep.*
◆ *Bird is building something (bookshelves?).*

And of course, the bird often sang. The bird did not have a particularly beautiful voice, but she was conscientious in the way she carried a tune, which almost amounted to the same thing. She must be compensating, the woman thought, for those funny little wings—or whatever they were. Poor creature.

The woman added fewer and fewer notations to the list as the months passed by, until at last she stopped writing in the journal altogether. The novelty of the bird's presence had worn flat, like the plush on a velveteen seat cover. What had once been sounds became noises, scents became smells. A clatter of pans arising from the bird's kitchen would cause the woman to wince and then rub her arms to smooth down the goose bumps. The woman considered giving the bird a talking-to, but her complaints, when she rehearsed them in her head, sounded unjustified. Wasn't the bird just going about her business? Would it not have been the same with the other tenants, had they stayed long enough?

An invitation arrived in the mail. It was from the bird.

Please join me
7 p.m. tonight
I have something to show you!

Out of habit, the woman flexed the card between her fingers: good paper stock. She was charmed by the bird's gesture, although she had mixed feelings about being invited in such a formal fashion to a place where she, by way of ownership, was technically the hostess.

When the woman arrived at 7:15 p.m. (so as not to be gauche), she was surprised to see how the bird had claimed the space. She'd hung pictures on the walls, and she'd repainted. She'd laid down rugs, and she'd changed the ceiling fixtures. She'd made herself right at home. Was it a trick of the light, the woman wondered, or was the suite bigger than she remembered it? It was as if the bird had always lived there; it felt like a different place entirely. The décor's drastic alteration represented a violation of the lease, but the woman said nothing: it now seemed more the bird's space than hers.

The bird had set out bowls of various snacks, including pretzels, popcorn, chips, pistachio nuts, candy corn, and dried apricots, which crowded the coffee table in front of the television. The woman was the only guest.

"I have a project that I've been working on, but I have no one to share it with," the bird said. She pressed the remote control, and black-and-white images began to flicker on the TV screen. Great, thought the woman. An *art film*.

It was a dance. Onscreen, the bird spun and whirled through a blizzard—torn newsprint, milkweed, and tufts of cotton snow fell in a slow cascade. At first, the bird's movements were obscure, but the more the woman watched, the clearer the little creature became. The bird twirled alongside spreading puddles of black liquid, and her image danced with her, joined at her light-stepping feet, a ghost reappearing in a series of dark mirrors. The accompaniment was very like the sound of waves sped up and layered onto itself. The woman could almost feel her heart hitting the wet shore, again and again.

"That was beautiful," she said, when it was over.

"I'm so pleased," the bird said.

From that day on, the woman truly *felt* the presence of the bird. She felt her birdy feet tramping up and down the floorboards. Whatever songs the bird sang, the woman felt their notes filling her ears like water. If the woman was very quiet, she could feel when the bird was standing directly below her—which was often. At night, she could feel the bird breathing and would try to match her own inhalations to the bird's small sips of air. The woman no longer imagined the bird performing and improvising on her daily routines; she felt that she lived with her and that her mental motion pictures were more akin to footage. Hoping to influence the bird's choice of tunes, the woman found herself playing certain records on her old garage-sale stereo: she was thrilled later to hear the bird singing harmony, superimposing little riffs over the memory of the songs. The woman cooked foods that she thought the bird might find appealing and would wait for a replication of her own kitchen odors to waft up from below. It was exhausting, the woman felt, living this vicarious life. It was almost too much. At the same time, the woman was fearful that the bird would move out, like the others. She remembered, with tenderness, the bird's blizzard dance.

The woman began to notice things going missing from her apartment. She thought she may have misplaced the odd household item (her pink comb, the new booklet of stamps she'd just bought), but she couldn't explain the depletion of her pantry. Cans, jars, and boxes had been rearranged on the shelves, leaving untidy, telltale gaps. One afternoon, she came across a crumbled note that had fallen to the floor: "Making chilly (sp?) Needed garbanso beans. Thx!! Birdie." Other, similar notes had somehow found their way under the stove. They'd been written on the backs of fortune-cookie promises.

The woman did not remember ever having given the bird a key.

The noise level, which had risen sharply over the last two months, finally pushed the woman to pay Birdie a visit. The bird had obviously been undertaking some project, one that involved hammering and sawing, cracking and scraping, going on late into the night. The woman hadn't wanted to interfere with the bird's creative efforts, but enough, as they say, was enough.

Once the woman was standing on the bird's premises, she felt deeply confused. Such transformations the bird had brought about—it did not seem physically possible! The place was aglow with red, pink, and orange textured wall hangings, whose hues were reflected in a cylindrical crystal chandelier. The formerly poky series of rooms had been replaced with a sweeping, open area, featuring a sunken living room with a wood-burning stove. Long curtains of crimson silk hung on the far wall, through which the woman even thought she glimpsed ivy-strewn trellises lining a small patio.

"Who said you could build an extension on the unit? Who said you could raid my pantry? Who said you could take such OUTRAGEOUS LIBERTIES?" The woman held up her hands and spun around, gesturing at all she saw. She'd intended admonishment, but instead her words came out as congratulatory.

"I'm leaving," the bird said calmly. Sunlight, beaming through a newly installed plate-glass window, made her gray feathers golden. She looked lovely—stunted, strange little thing though she was.

"But—where will you go?" *Don't go, don't go, don't go.*

"Oh, I don't know. I thought I'd fly south."

"You? Fly? And how will you do that?" The woman made an ugly motion: she held her fists at her shoulders and levered her elbows up and down.

"I told you. I have wings."

"Let me guess. Are they wings that you've sewn oh-so-cleverly? Are they made of decorated cardboard? Are they made of wax? Did you order them off Etsy? Or maybe they're invisible?"

The bird closed her eyes.

"Don't cry," she said. And then: "The wings aren't invisible. Let me show you."

They lifted off the ground. Out of the blurriness that first surrounded her, the woman began to recognize the mounded landscape of clouds rolling beneath her as she soared, dissolving at the edges. And through the mists, so oddly still, like wafting smoke suspended in time, she saw tiny houses, streets, meadows, forests—a flash of a lake—and more forests with their masses of soft, green curves. In an instant, the woman felt herself falling, the cold wind having released its embrace. She screamed as she tumbled through the sky, flailing her limbs as if she could somehow gain purchase against the air, the details on the land beneath her rushing into focus. Such terror. Soon she would hit the ground: she forced herself to open her eyes. She saw birds in a tree, like so many notes of music, like a profusion of dark buds, ready to blossom, and she knew she was one of them. She stretched out her great, shining wings. And flew away.

ACKNOWLEDGMENTS

This is my first book, the culmination of many years' work, and I have many people to thank:

Kevin Watson, who has given me a home at Press 53, and Claire Foxx, whose keen editorial eye and cover-design prowess pulled my stories into fine form.

My agent, Amy Bishop-Wycisk, an early enthusiast of my book.

The Elizabeth George Foundation, the Canada Council for the Arts, and the Maryland Arts Council, who gave generous financial support. Also, the Sewanee Writers' Conference and Hedgebrook, both magical places: my visits were brief but their influence enduring.

All the literary journals that published my work over the years, who provided me with readership and encouragement.

My creative writing teachers: Jamey Genna at The Writing Salon in Berkley; Kathryn Davis, Kathleen Finneran, Marshall Klimasewiski, and Kellie Wells at Washington University in St. Louis; Holly Goddard Jones and Chinelo Okparanta at the Sewanee Writers' Conference. And of course, my fellow MFA students at WashU and my fellow workshop participants at Sewanee. Your careful attention to my writing, your insights, and your company have meant so much to me.

My dear siblings, Christopher and Leigh, who have provided me with lifelong models of sharp dialogue. I endeavor to keep up with you.

My mother, who impressed on me at an early age that books were as vital a supply in one's life as groceries, and my father, who is not here to see this book in print but who is, in many ways, here in this book.

My other parents, Jim and Penny Arthur, and my bonus sibling, David Arthur, who are always eager to read the next story.

My lovely friends, my former classmates, my coven: Katya Apekina, Emily Robbins, and Lia Silver, who have so kindly read different versions of these stories over the years and given invaluable feedback, who cheer me up and cheer me on.

My colleagues at the Johns Hopkins Writing Seminars, who inspire and support me and make me feel so happy to come to work every week.

Henry, my sweet boy, an excellent source of advice on all things D&D.

Aubrey and Kelly, who are indifferent to my work but not to me.

And finally, James, the poet I wasn't expecting, who has been there from the start. Without you, there would have been no start. You believed in me as a writer even before I was one; you were and are and shall remain my first reader. With you, there will be no end.

◆ ◆ ◆

The author also thanks the editors and literary magazines that first published these stories, sometimes in slightly different forms:

failbetter: "Origin Story."
The Gettysburg Review: "Zombies."
The Iowa Review: "Birdie."
Joyland: "Dirt" and "A Doom of Her Own."
New Ohio Review: "All Things Bright and Beautiful" (as "Intervention").
Nimrod: "Miscarriages."
Sycamore Review: "Secondhand."
Water~Stone Review: "The Rabbits."

Shannon Robinson's writing has appeared in *The Gettysburg Review*, *The Iowa Review*, *Joyland*, *Water-Stone Review*, *Nimrod*, *failbetter*, and *The Hopkins Review*. She holds an MFA in fiction from Washington University in St. Louis, and in 2011 she was the Writer-in-Residence at Interlochen Center for the Arts. Other honors include *Nimrod*'s Katherine Anne Porter Prize for Fiction, grants from the Elizabeth George Foundation and the Canada Council for the Arts, a Hedgebrook Fellowship, a Sewanee Scholarship, and an Independent Artist Award from the Maryland Arts Council. She teaches in the Writing Seminars at Johns Hopkins University and lives in Baltimore with her husband and son.